Fateful Night

Book One of the What She Knew Trilogy

K. R. Hughes
T.L. Burns

Master Koda Select Publishing

Disclaimer

Working on this trilogy was both fun and educational, though it is purely fictional. We scoured the local library for any and all resources from the time period and then camped out in our favorite restaurants that had both unlimited refills and free internet. You know, just basically making a general nuisance of ourselves. Together, we weaved our own theory about what could have happened on that fateful night in 1962 and the ensuing months. As with all good fictional stories, we leave it to you the reader to determine how much could be true, but more importantly, to enjoy the what if . . .

Preface

As we began to play with the idea of writing an entire book around a "What if?" question our excitement grew. Who do you know that doesn't get into the conversation of did Marilyn Monroe kill herself or was she murdered? No matter what side of that question you're on, the debate is always a good one. In that light, we decided to see if a book could be written about her and 'what she knew' about politics, the mafia, and Hollywood. What inner workings and connections did they have in common? The question was so intriguing that we decided to carry it to its logical conclusion. Even though it was well known that she'd had an affair with John Kennedy, no one really understood the depth of that relationship or where it could have eventually lead them both.

She knew too much and was far from being the "dumb blonde" she portrayed in her films. After all, in her own words she could hardly play an intelligent role and be taken seriously with her looks. So she did what any woman with a hundred and sixty IQ would do - she played a lifetime role and played it well. Until one fateful night when she revealed that she knew something she shouldn't to someone who needed that information kept secret.

It has lately been revealed that she was murdered and in that light we've written our own version of "What She Knew."

This book is dedicated to our dear friends who, like Marilyn, left us too early. May God hold you forever.

With Special Thanks To

We'd like to thank our biggest fan, Ken, for his undying support of this project. He has pushed us to finish this book from the moment he heard about the subject matter.

We'd also like to thank him for giving up countless hours of his time to help us edit and critique this book. He only lost faith for a few minutes one night while editing chapter 17. After getting to chapter 18 though, his faith was restored!

And

Anita for all of her input and support on our project!
Visit her at www.aghoward.com.

Connect with us on our website at
http://whatsheknew.wix.com/kandtproductions

Chapter 1

July 25, 1962

Joseph Kennedy tapped his finger on the desktop while he listened to the irate woman on the other end of the receiver. When she finally took a breath Joe snagged his chance.

"Now see here! I know it needs to be done, but we must have patience. Marilyn isn't an easy target."

"Well then," the woman insisted, "either you take care of her or I will."

Joe started to form a reply as the sound of the receiver slamming down and the buzzing of a dial tone droned in his ear. He replaced the instrument in its cradle, scratching his head as he rose from his desk.

"Bunny!"

His secretary poked her head through the doorway.

"Get Sam on the phone."

Frank stood in the casino holding a beautiful blonde on one arm and tossing dice onto a craps table with the other. Laughing at his roll the woman stepped out of his grasp just as Sam Giancana walked up.

"Beat it doll," Sam snapped. She stared at him and gave Frank a lingering kiss before she left.

"Looks like you're losing your touch there, Sam." Frank grinned as he threw the dice over the line on the table.

Sam snarled. "Never mind about her. We have business to attend to." As the dice rolled to a stop the crowd clapped, and Frank made a mock bow as the chips were pushed toward him.

"Not now, I'm winning." Frank gave the neatly folded orange handkerchief in the breast pocket of his tux a pat and winked at the mobster.

"Now." Sam grabbed Frank by the lapels.

Frank looked down, took hold of Sam's beefy hand and said, "Hands off the suit." Gathering up his chips one at a time, Frank said between clenched teeth, "This better be important." Glaring at Sam, Frank pocketed the chips and followed him out of the Sands.

July 28, 1962

Marilyn sauntered over to her lover, current president, John F. Kennedy and rubbed her leg invitingly against him. "Are you enjoying the party?" she whispered, giving his ear a caressing lick.

Marilyn smiled at Sam as he poured himself another highball and offered one to Frank.

"Mmm hmm, I am now," Jack mumbled as his lips pressed her ear. He encircled her waist with one arm and pulled her onto his lap.

"Let's go for a walk, lover, just you and me." She kissed him long and deep, leaving the heady flavor of her martini tingling on his lips.

"Yes let's." He ran his hand up the side of her thigh before he allowed her to stand up.

Frank exchanged a glance with Sam as the couple left the room with arms tucked around each other in a cozy half embrace.

As soon as they were outside, Marilyn straightened her dress as her mood became serious. She broke the silence as they strolled down the moonlit path. "Jack, I'm really serious this time."

"Don't do this now. We're here to have a good time. Relax this weekend. I think it'll be the last time for a while. You know Teddy is trying for the Senate run."

"But Jack, you must know that your life is in grave danger. I've heard things."

John stopped walking as he took her arm and turned her to face him. "Marilyn, I know. I'm always in 'grave danger.' It's part of being the president. Quit harping on me." He leaned in for a kiss, but she turned her back to him, allowing the tears to fall from her lower lashes.

"You always dismiss my fears. One of these days Jack, my fears will come true. Is that what you want?"

He reached for her, and then turning her back into his arms he held her close.

"No, but these are uncertain times, so one never really knows." Jack stroked her hair reassuringly.

"What are you saying?" Marilyn pushed back a little and leaned her face up to his in the lamplight.

"Things do happen. Besides, I have the whole of the government watching out for me." John felt the shivers wrack her body. He sighed, let loose and walked away from her.

"You heard from Hoffa lately?" Frank asked as he handed Sam a drink.

"Yea, he's working on the deal."

"So, what's the progress?" Frank lit a cigarette.

"He's not moving fast enough and needs the screws put to him soon. I'll give him more time, but there's a deadline to meet if we're gonna succeed."

"Sam, you know what to do to make this happen discreetly." Frank poured himself another slug and rubbed his forehead. "I need you to make this problem disappear so the president remains clean."

"Consider it done."

"Good, because you know what it means if you fail." Frank made a slicing motion across his throat with the tip of his index finger.

Sam shook his head. "You don't need to tell me how to do my business."

Bobby Kennedy encircled the slim waist of his wife and kissed her on the back of the neck. "Long day?"

Ethel leaned against him and sighed. "Yes, but I always have time for you, honey."

Bobby laughed, kissed her neck again and turned her around in his arms. He hugged her close and laid his cheek on the top of her head. "Do you have enough energy to talk about something serious for a minute?"

She looked up into his troubled face and patted his butt. "For you, anytime. How about we grab some cookies and milk to go with our talk?"

"Perfect." He held her hand as they moved into the homey kitchen, only letting go with a sigh as he settled down at the table. She poured two glasses of milk and brought over a platter filled with cookies.

"What's this all about?"

"John." Bobby sighed and wiped his forehead. "Isn't it always? Damn naïve John. He just can't understand that there is more to these death threats than just idle bull shit." Bobby munched on a chocolate chip cookie.

Ethel reached over and grasped his free hand. "What is it now, honey?"

"Hoover of course. That bastard is determined to have the entire White House bugged and John's personal phone lines in particular. John thinks that it's nothing to worry about, but I don't trust that Commie. He's trying to find some way to blackmail Jack and it's making me crazy." Bobby gulped his milk.

Ethel patted his hand as she got up to pour him more milk. "I thought Truman stopped that during his term in office."

"He tried, but he suspected Hoover was using the FBI as his own secret task force. Truman told us once that 'We want no Gestapo or secret police. The FBI is tending in that direction. They are dabbling in sex-life scandals and plain blackmail'. "

"I love your memory for the verbatim; of course, it is what makes you an excellent attorney general!" Ethel smiled at her husband as he vigorously rubbed his temples.

"That isn't all. He said, 'Edgar Hoover would give his right eye to take over'. Of course all congressmen and senators are afraid of him now. He's a queer fellow, you know, there's something not right in his determination to find fault with everyone. I hate the bastard. He'd sell his soul for power." Bobby finished his second cookie and swallowed the last of the milk.

"What can you do about it?" Clearing the table, she took the dishes to the sink. Turning back to her husband, she smiled as she recognized that old spark in his eyes.

"Nothing right now, but somehow someway I'll get that dirty son of a bitch."

Frank and Sam watched Jack walk back in and cross to the large polished teak bar alone. Frank started to say something, but closed his mouth. He left the room and went in search of Marilyn outside.

He found her leaning against a tree beside the pond, crying silent tears that dripped down her cheeks in little rivulets.

In silence he stopped in front of her and held out his arms. She walked into them without a word, and gave a wobbly smile before placing her head on his shoulder, sobbing for a long minute. When she sniffled he fished in his pocket for a hanky and handed it to her.

"Well, honey, this is not how my party was supposed to go." He waited until she blew her nose and wiped her eyes.

"Jack just doesn't understand. He knows I love him, but he doesn't seem to care. What is going to happen to him? Why doesn't he care about his own safety?"

"Don't you think you're over reacting?"

"What? Not you too!" Marilyn's questioning gaze met Frank's eyes.

"Honey, you know how you are. You must calm down and not worry so much. Besides, Bobby is there to help him see what's what." Frank placed his arm around her and led her back to the lodge. "Let's get a drink. That'll make you feel much better."

"Not when Jack's life is in danger and the man himself doesn't seem to care! I'm fairly certain who his worst enemy is. Oh, why won't anyone listen to me?"

July 29, 1962

Marita Lorenz hunkered down behind the dumpster in an alleyway watching the foot traffic in Harlem. The smell was really getting to her, and she had been waiting in this spot for over half an hour. Pulling her jacket collar over her nose to help block the smell, she checked her watch for what seemed the hundredth time. Just then, a man in a dark suit, sunglasses, and hat turned into the alley.

He stopped just shy of the dumpster and dropped a single cigarette butt into it. That was the signal. Marita walked out from behind the dumpster as he leaned against the brick wall.

Marita wasted no time. "What's the new order?"

"We need the file. Don't let him suspect you. Keep up the good work."

"How can I get that?" Marita lit a cigarette. "He has it under lock and key. It's guarded so fiercely no one could get to it."

6

"Use your feminine wiles." The man turned to leave the alley, stopped, and turned back to her. "You have extraordinary talents. After all why would a beauty like you want to be a lover to that pig?"

"It does take a supreme effort of acting. Those damn cigars are horrible." Marita grimaced as the man chuckled, disappearing back into the busy street. "Shit!"

Jack was busy consuming his breakfast while talking to Frank and Sam. Marilyn entered the large dining room, avoiding Jack's eyes. She found herself a piece of toast and some coffee then sat down beside Frank with a huge sigh.

"Morning," Frank patted her shoulder. "You look exhausted. Didn't you sleep well?"

"What a lovely compliment!" Marilyn struggled for a good natured grin. "I've got too much on my mind and this sinus infection won't let go."

"I'm sorry. Here, let me get you some orange juice." Frank stood up. "I'll add a little vodka to kick that sickness." Frank massaged her shoulders for a moment.

"No thanks. I want to stay sober and it's not even ten yet." She reached up and patted his hand, then nodded to John and Sam. "Good morning, boys."

"Morning," Sam mumbled, then stuffed a huge bite of pancakes into his mouth.

John smiled at her. "Good morning. Would you like to go for a bike ride after breakfast?"

"I guess we could. I'd rather sit by the pool, though."

"Either way is fine with me. I think we need to talk."

Jackie Kennedy sat on the fence waiting for her horse to be brought to her. Caroline was already mounted and waiting impatiently for her mother. The trainer came around the corner leading the horse and talking to a dark haired man.

As they came closer, Caroline squealed, "Uncle Bobby!" Her horse startled, jumped once as the trainer grabbed at the bit.

"Caroline! You know better than that," Jackie scolded as Bobby reached up to give the child a quick hug.

"I'm sorry."

Bobby winked at her. "I'm always happy to see you too! How are you?"

The two chatted for a moment before Bobby turned his attention to Jackie.

"I'll get right to the point. Be a little more discreet in your spending habits. I just got a report from Kenny that you spent another ten grand on clothes last month."

"But Bobby," Jackie batted her lashes and smiled seductively. "As the First Lady I must set an example. I'm always being photographed and you wouldn't want me seen in the same thing twice would you?"

"Actually that would be a refreshing change. Stop spending so much, Jackie. It just looks bad on the president."

The pool at the Cal-Nev Lodge was perfect for a hot day in July. The water was crystal clear and the scent of chlorine hung in the thick air. Jack was lounging beside Marilyn in his swim trunks as they soaked up the warm Nevada sun. "Now look Marilyn, you need to understand how things are with me."

"And how are things?" Marilyn eyed him curiously.

"Do you know the history about this lodge? My father and Al Capone used to use this place to run bootleg alcohol to Cali. You know, tunnels and everything. My family has been in a position of power here in the states pretty much since my dad arrived."

"Yes, and you hold the most powerful position of anyone in the entire nation. So why are we talking about your dad?" Marilyn sat up and applied tanning oil to her legs.

"Because, my innocent girl, it's all about family. Everything I do is because of them."

"That is complete nonsense." She had gotten so distracted that the suntan oil flowed from the bottle onto the concrete.

"You don't have much in the way of family loyalty, but we Kennedy's always have. We know that we'll protect each other regardless of personal cost. And now, it's Teddy's time. You and I have to accept that."

"But what about what you want?" She noticed the streaming oil and popped the lid back on the bottle.

Jack sat up, anger radiating from his pores. "I can see you don't understand at all."

Marilyn stood up. "And what exactly am I supposed to understand?"

Jack faced her and poked a finger into her chest to punctuate his words. "I'll always put the Kennedy political aspirations above that of my family or lovers."

Marilyn's face turned beet red. She reached up and slapped him hard across the face. "You son of a bitch!" She spun around and darted back towards the lodge. Stopping, she turned around and spat, "You're not the only one in danger here. I've risked my life as well!"

Jack closed the gap between them and took hold of her arms. "What are you saying? What have you done?"

She leaned against him for a moment. "I listen and ask ditzy blonde questions. I learn things and giggle like I don't get it. I've almost certain I've been found out though and I'm sure I'm on the 'list'."

"God, Marilyn, you know I can't protect you with Teddy making his bid for the senate. What do you expect me to do?" Jack tried to stroke her hair, but she pulled away with one rapid motion.

"Do what you usually do for me, Jack. Nothing. Just don't let my death be in vain. I've tapped my own house in case something does happen to me. Find the wires in the attic and catch whoever comes for me. You will be next, of that I'm sure."

Chapter 2

Later that morning, Frank still hadn't found Marilyn or Jack. Last he saw, she was heading for her room and Jack was walking toward the desert. As Frank made his way back to the living room the doorbell rang. He opened the door to find Joe DiMaggio standing there, madder than the devil if hell were freezing over.

DiMaggio stalked into the room. "Get Sam and let's all have a nice little talk. NOW."

Frank, who was several inches shorter and many pounds lighter, nodded and rushed out of the room.

He was only gone a few moments when he returned with Sam trailing behind him. "Why are you here?"

"I received a very distressing phone call from Marilyn and have come to make certain that she's all right." Joe glared at the two men.

"She's fine. Just had a little misunderstanding." Frank lit a cigarette.

"She'd better be fine. Where is she?" DiMaggio demanded scowling at Frank then over to Sam.

Sam responded, "She's with Jack at the moment."

"Really? I certainly hope so. Where are they - exactly?"

"They went out for a drive." Frank lied.

"I'll wait." DiMaggio perched himself on the back of the couch.

Sam asked, "Would you like a drink?"

"At this hour? No thanks." DiMaggio shook his head.

"If you'll excuse me," Frank stood up, "I've got things to attend to."

"Just as long as you're here when they return. I didn't drive all the way out here to have you disappear if something is wrong."

"What did she tell you?"

"She was pretty upset that you took Jack's side. She's sure someone wants them both dead." DiMaggio stood up, and walked around the couch, glaring at Frank.

"I'd never hurt her."

"Maybe not directly, but you do have a reputation." Joe pointed at Sam. "We all know who your friends are."

Frank opened his mouth, and then shut it again. He walked into the barroom and poured himself a large vodka while Sam seated himself on a bar stool.

"Well, this could be nasty." Frank took a swig of his drink and sighed.

"Yeah, especially if she told him the whole truth. How can we shut them up without drawing suspicion to ourselves?"

Frank thought for a moment. "Marilyn is high strung, but she's reasonable. I'll just have a talk with her."

"Car accident. It'll be tragic but. .. ." Sam mused out loud, and then shook his head. "No, let's see what DiMaggio knows first. He may just be the jilted lover coming to her rescue."

August 4, 1962

With an almighty kick the door crashed open and Peter ran into the bedroom. "Shit! Marilyn!"

Kneeling beside the bed the stench of vomit assailed his nostrils even before he saw it, staining the sheets and pillow around the woman.

"Marilyn, wake up." He shook her hard enough to force her to stir.

Sighing in relief, he scooped her up, carried her across the room, and out of the house unconscious in his arms. Pushing her into the backseat of his sedan, Peter jumped in and sped away.

"Hang in there, Marilyn. We're almost there. Don't die now."

Tossing the book he just finished reading on the floor, Dr. Ralph Greenson looked at the clock. "Coffee, that's what I need."

He filled the percolator with water and turned the stove on when the phone rang. Dr. Greenson smiled in anticipation as he answered. "Yes?"

"It's done." A deep male voice informed him.

"Good. I'll let the boss know."

Dr. Greenson hung up the phone feeling almost giddy and waited for the pot to finish brewing.

"Hey Dr. Bunner," an orderly greeted as he came down the hall. "Dead?" He nodded at the covered body as they wheeled it past him in the hallway.

"Yes. We're taking it to the morgue." Dr. Bunner answered as he kept walking. "See you later."

After the orderly was out of ear shot, Peter grabbed the doctor's arm. "We can't let what's happened get out. If they find out, they will try again."

Frank, dressed to the nines with his lucky orange handkerchief in his pocket, smiled as he walked into the restaurant with Lady Beatty. The sleek beauty glided across the floor in her floor length evening gown to their table.

The waiter helped her into her seat and turned expectantly to Frank. "Mr. Sinatra."

"We already know what we want." Frank ordered steak, green beans, and salad for both along with a vintage wine.

Several moments passed in silence between the couple before Lady Beatty placed her napkin on the table, and pouted her ruby lips just a little. "I didn't fly across the pond just to be ignored. What's wrong with you tonight?"

"I'm sorry Adele, I'm just jittery. I'll make it up to you later."

"Well, I hope so."

"Don't pout. I'm just a little concerned about a friend of mine." Frank took her hand and stroked it with his thumb. "You know how much I like you."

"Yes, because I'm not looking for a career and just want to be your trophy woman."

"Well, that too." Frank ran his fingers along her forearm. "Let's get out of here."

"Sounds great. I wasn't hungry for food anyway."

Peter helped Dr. Bunner get Marilyn's bed pushed into place in the deserted wing at the hospital.

"I'll be right back." Dr. Bunner left the room.

"Marilyn, wake up." Peter pleaded for the tenth time, but she didn't move. He turned at the sound of the door opening and saw a nurse enter holding a clipboard.

"I'm Nurse Hadley. We need you to answer a few questions for us." She strode into the room with efficiency oozing from every pore. "Patient's name?"

"Umm, Norma Jean."

"Age?" she questioned without looking up.

"36."

"Ailment?"

"Well, umm." Peter stuttered. "How should I, um, can't you just ask the doctor?" He turned from the inert form on the bed and asked, "Where is the doctor?" Peter paced the room. "I...." He ran his fingers through his hair. "I, um, found her like this."

Taking pity on the young man, she put her pen away. "All right. We'll fill this out later."

Dr. Greenson paced the room. The coffee pot was empty after two hours of endless waiting. "Where the hell are Kennedy and Lawford? What's going on? We need to get this over with. Damn!"

Dr. Greenson walked over to the window and stared out at the moonless night.

"Damn it Kennedy. Call me!"

J. Edgar Hoover sat at his desk staring at the Kennedy/Monroe file. As the head of the Federal Bureau of Investigation, he had unlimited access to acquiring secrets, which was his favorite past time. The ticking of the clock was the only sound in the office. When it began to chime the midnight hour, he closed the file with a faint grin and stood up. *Tomorrow, there's always tomorrow.*

"Is she going to be all right?" Peter's anguished question moved the doctor.

"I'll do everything I can, Mr. Lawford. They did a pretty good job of beating her up."

"She looks awful." Peter reached over to brush the hair away from her face.

"I'm more concerned about her kidneys and liver. I'll know what we're dealing with in a few hours. Try and rest." Dr. Bunner patted his patient's hand and moved towards the door.

Peter followed him. "I'm going to announce that she's dead. We'll see if the mystery can be unraveled once Marilyn has come around, if she comes around."

"Whatever you think is best. Discretion is my name." the doctor agreed. "Of course this will be billed privately. Not through hospital records, to keep it quiet."

"Yes. I do appreciate your help, Dr. Bunner."

Dr. Bunner looked intently at Peter, worrying to himself about the toll this evening's events were taking on the young man. Peter was still visibly shaking when the doctor left the room.

Peter walked down the deserted hall with purpose born of desperation. He knew all too well what was at stake. As he exited the hospital, the sweat that beaded on his temples and palms had little to do with the August heat.

Clint Hill stood watching Jacqueline Kennedy smile at the witty quip of yet another diplomat. He was tired and his wife wanted him to come back to DC, but as a secret service agent he had his duty to protect the wife of the president. He stood at attention and hoped Mrs. Kennedy would make it an early night. *How does she find the energy?*

Patricia Kennedy Lawford stood at the record player flipping through albums. She selected one and plopped it on the stack. Surveying the room she nodded as the maid passed by with a tray of glasses filled with champagne and fine wines. *I'm so glad that everyone has come. It would be a shame to miss this. Of course, who knows where my husband is right now. I'm going to kill him.*

Bobby stood chatting with Bing Crosby and Judy Garland.

"Bobby, do you agree?" Bing asked.

"What? Agree to what?"

"Really, haven't you been paying attention, dear?" Ethel moved a little closer to her husband. "Bing was asking if you liked his new album or if you thought it was too modern?"

"Oh. Um . . . well."

"Then Judy said she loved it and thought it was absolutely ring a ding ding." Ethel smiled at her husband.

"Of course. First rate. Please excuse me." Bobby walked down the hall. He turned into the guest bedroom and sat on the bed. "What's going on? Where's Peter?"

Getting into his car, Peter tried to shake the panic that was threatening to overtake him. *Where is it? How long do I have to find it?*

He arrived at the house in Brentwood, the newest in a long line of places that Marilyn never could settle down in, and went straight to her unkempt bedroom to start his search.

Ripping the drawers out of the night stand and dressers, he searched through her personal things without finding the object he sought.

Where? In this house? The Strasbery's?

Leaving the bedroom, he raced to the next one. Throwing open the door he saw emptiness. Where? Damn it, where is it?

He looked at his watch as he hurried to the living room. *In one of her books? She loves to read. In Tolstoy? Whitman?*

Throwing her beloved books from the shelves onto the floor as he searched them, he found nothing.

Where? Does Eunice know? Did she beat me to it? I wouldn't put it past Greenson to have his watchdog take it first. Damn housekeeper.

No, Marilyn would have hidden it where no one would think to look.

Only one place really. He hurried to her bathroom and stopped. *Where?* Unlike the other rooms in the house, this one was pristine. Nothing out of place, nothing dirty, no trace of face powder or eye shadow on the vanity. Spotless. Every jar of potion, lotion and youth claiming cream lined up like soldiers fighting a war on age.

17

He inspected each piece of furniture, even lifted the lid of the commode, but nothing. Frustrated, Peter stood for a moment thinking.   He crossed to the vanity table and dressing chair. The soft cushion on the chair came off easily when he pulled on it. There underneath the cushion lay the cherished item. He had found the incriminating little black diary.

Now, for the business of "killing her" I need Bobby's help. Will he handle this awful task?

Frank kissed Adele as she lay naked on his bed; she rubbed her body against his and moaned in pleasure."Take me Francis, please take me now." Adele writhed under him with insistence bucking her hips up to him.

"Yes, kitten. I'll take you." Frank kissed her with all the passion he could muster, but his body wouldn't comply.

"Hurry! I'm burning up with desire." Adele grabbed him. "What the hell is this?"

She sat up on the bed. "Don't I turn you on? I've never been so insulted."

Frank grabbed his robe as he jumped off the bed. "I'm sorry. This has never happened before."

"Well why is it happening with me?" Her lower lip came out. "Don't you find me attractive?"

"My God woman, you're very attractive." Frank nearly yelled at her.

"Then why are we fighting and not getting it on?"

Just then the phone rang. Frank sighed with relief as he went to answer it. "Yeah?"

"There's something I need to tell you."

"No change," the nurse informed Peter as he strode past her in the hall into Marilyn's room.

Peter tossed the diary onto the foot of the bed as he took Marilyn's hand. "I've found it. You've no need to worry."

Still unconscious, Marilyn didn't respond.

"It's odd, how you always keep the front door locked, triple locked, but you never even close the bedroom door. What happened? How did they get in?"

Picking up the phone, Peter listened for a dial tone, dialed his home number and prayed Bobby would be the one who answered.

With the party in full swing, he knew the phone would be hard to hear, but he hoped Bobby was paying attention. On the sixth ring he got his wish.

"We have a problem. I need help NOW." Peter, trying to whisper, still managed an authority that was so unlike him. "Marilyn was right. We need a body."

"I'm on it. Where are you?" Bobby took mental notes.

"I'm at the hospital with her. I found her locked inside her bedroom; try to find someone who could be a suicide." Peter insisted.

"Right. Did you get the diary?" Bobby asked.

"Yeah, I've got it right here."

"Ethel and I will take care of everything. You take care of Marilyn."

"Hurry." Peter's urgent plea hung between them as the dial tone began buzzing in his ear.

Hanging up the phone, Peter sat down to read the diary. The first several pages were of the usual womanly talk, but midway into it the inserts took on a menacing tone.

Chapter 3

Dr. Greenson watched the lone helicopter fly over as he twitched the shears nervously. "What in the world?"

As the chopper landed just out of sight, he turned toward the phone. "Ring! Why are you torturing me?"

He stepped into the living area and poured himself another drink. "I guess there's been a horrible accident. Why would there be a chopper at this time of night otherwise? It seems pretty close to Marilyn's side of town."

Bobby heard the whirl of the helicopter as it made its way to the clearing behind Marilyn's house. "Ethel, I'm going out to meet the chopper."

"Okay honey. I'll be ready with the hair dye."

As Bobby approached, he saw the van waiting to transport "Marilyn" to the house as soon as the chopper touched down.

Peter arrived soon after the helicopter landed. "Wow, you really know how to make things happen."

"I'm surprised that even the coroner managed to pull this together so quickly." Bobby shook his head.

"He must have some kind of connection to get us a double almost at the snap of our fingers." Peter chuckled.

The coroner approached them with a gurney. "Who'll miss one homeless drug addict?" the coroner asked.

"Hopefully, no one." Bobby handed him a wad of hundred dollar bills.

The coroner smiled, put the money in his vest pocket, and walked over to the chopper to remove the body.

Bobby smiled at Peter. "Having a name like Kennedy sure helps in a pinch. It's amazing what a couple of thousand dollars in hush money will do."

Peter nodded in agreement as he watched the coroner and pilot lift the dead woman onto the gurney.

"A few thousand more and he'll even fake the death certificate and autopsy results."

"Yes, it's good to be a Kennedy." Peter called over his shoulder as he went to help the two men.

Patricia stood next to Marilyn's bed. "How can you do this? Why didn't you just leave my brother alone? Don't you understand this is my father you are up against?"

Pat pulled the sheets tight around the unconscious woman, tucking them under Marilyn's comatose form. Moving around the bed, Pat found herself using unnecessary force, still talking to the unconscious woman.

"I can't believe I'm here. Really, this isn't the way tonight was supposed to end. What's going to happen if anyone finds out about this?"

Plumping up a pillow, Pat stuffed it under Marilyn's head. "You know that I care for you, but you've been blacklisted. You're out of our lives, see? We're not supposed to have anything to do with you anymore. You should've disappeared. Oh, honey, now look at you!"

Bobby, Ethel, and Peter looked at their handy work. Unless someone looked very close, no one would know the woman on the bed was not Marilyn. Bobby nodded with some slight satisfaction as he straightened her legs out and mussed up the dye job.

"All right, now I'll go clean up the mess in the bathroom." Ethel left the room with purposeful strides.

Bobby twisted the arm and hand into the correct position under the body, as rigor mortis began to set in.

As he slid the receiver of the phone into place, Bobby sighed. "Only ten minutes to spare, but we did it."

"I'll call the police now." Peter spoke breaking his long silence.

Bobby made a face and shook his head. "No, Greenson comes first."

As the helicopter flew back over the city, Dr. Greenson's phone rang. He dropped the curtains. "It's about damn time."

"Ethel needs to go home. Did you bring separate cars?" Peter asked while scanning the room one last time.

"Yes, I'll see to it right now. She shouldn't be here when Greenson or Mrs. Murray arrives." Bobby started out of the room.

"Where are the empty pill bottles?" Peter wondered aloud, looking around the bed and nightstand areas.

Bobby went into the bathroom at the question. He opened up the doors and found the prescription barbiturates and sleeping pills. "Here, in the medicine cabinet, but they're full."

"Let's flush them and set the empties beside the bed."

Less than thirty minutes after Peter called, Dr. Greenson arrived, took a quick look at the corpse, nodded with satisfaction, and sat down on the end of the bed. "Here's the story men. . ." he began.

Bobby and Peter nodded at the doctor; sighing their collective relief at having pulled it off. They'd fooled Dr. Greenson with the phony corpse.

Before Dr. Greenson could finish his sentence, they heard the rear entrance door open. All three men knew who it was, Eunice Murray, Marilyn's housekeeper. They sat waiting in silence for her to make her way into the room. Her purse and keys clanged on the kitchen counter as she continued into the house in search of Marilyn, talking all the while.

"There are certainly a lot of cars outside," Mrs. Murray called out in a slightly raised voice. "Did you have a party?"

Coming into Marilyn's room, Mrs. Murray flew into hysterics at the sight of her "mistress" lying dead on the bed. "Oh dear Lord, what happened? How could this be?"

"She overdosed on sleeping pills," Dr. Greenson explained. "She was distraught when I saw her yesterday, but I didn't think she was suicidal."

"But she was okay when I spoke to her on the telephone last night. I told her that my husband was feeling ill and I wouldn't be able to come to stay the night with her. She said that was fine, she was tired from moving the furniture around and wanted to make an early night of it."

Mrs. Murray did not try to get close to "Marilyn" lying sprawled on the bed. She stood rooted to the door frame looking spooked.

"We've contacted the police. They should be arriving anytime." Peter stood up and went over to the maid. "Why don't you go fix us a nice pot of coffee? It's been a long night and we could all use a cup."

Turning her around, he nudged her into the hall. "You can't do anything for her now. The authorities will take care of everything. It'll be all right, don't you worry about a thing, Mrs. Murray."

Eunice left them, sobbing, but she agreed to make them coffee and some toast.

While Peter was handling the maid, Dr. Greenson stood and checked the night stand. The empty pill bottles were there, and he turned one on its side to make it look more convincing. He looked at the top of the blond head. Thankfully, Bobby had turned her face away from the edge of the bed. Dr. Greenson picked up the sheet, peering under it for the first time, and then gently pulled it over the dead woman's head. Both Bobby and Peter stood motionless, neither one daring to even breathe.

"Well, this should be simple enough. The obvious cause of death is overdose. Just look at all of those pills." He shook his head, "Tsk, tsk. What a shame."

Peter looked over at Bobby who was staring very intently at Greenson. Peter then turned his attention back to the doctor and in a surprisingly strong voice he asked, "We loved her very much. Don't you care?"

"Certainly, but she had to be removed. We all knew it. Don't get squeamish on me." Dr. Greenson glared first at Peter then at Bobby.

Bobby straightened up to his full height. "She was a very close friend of the family. We'll miss her even if she did need to be out of the way."

"Okay, okay." Dr. Greenson threw up his hands, "You win. She'll be missed. Don't let sentiment get in the way of our job here."

Peter watched as Bobby began pacing the room, but neither man commented on the doctor's statement.

"We won't have to do anything to convince the cops that she took her own life. Nor why you two are here. Any friend would've stepped in to help someone who is unresponsive." Dr. Greenson walked around the messy room, kicking a few stray articles of clothing into a corner.

The doorbell rang and the men heard Mrs. Murray let in the police. "Right this way, officers. It's just terrible and her naked as the day she was born."

25

"Thank you, ma'am." Sergeant Clemson followed her to the bedroom.

Taking in the scene, the sergeant approached the bed noting that the victim's foot stuck out of the sheet. He walked to the other side and lifted the shroud to look under it. He dropped it and took out his pad and pen.

The other men in the room waited until he was finished writing on his notepad. He looked up to officially assess who was present.

"Mr. Kennedy, what connection do you have with the deceased?" Sergeant Clemson asked.

"Well, Sarg, if you don't know then I can't help you."

Sergeant Clemson snorted his amusement. "Point taken."

Pat found the diary Peter left for her to read. He wanted to make certain that it remained as guarded as the woman who had written it. His instructions were clear. Hide the book, hide the girl. Where would be the safest place for her once she was able to leave the hospital?

Perhaps the cabin in the mountains? No, somewhere warmer. What about the beach house in the Bahamas?

"Marilyn?" Patricia whispered. "Honey, can you hear me?"

No response.

Patricia waited a minute and then left her friend's side to tell the nurse in the hallway.

"She opened her eyes twice, but seems to be asleep again."

"Be right with you, Mrs. Lawford." The nurse put some papers together in a neat pile and picked up her clipboard.

Nurse Hadley came into the room and stuck a thermometer in the patient's mouth. She picked up the right wrist and felt for the pulse, which she timed, then wrote the numbers on the clipboard. Next she lifted one eyelid and shone a flashlight in at the pupil. She let the lid close and wrote some more.

"Well, what do you think?" Patricia asked.

"I think she should be fully awake in an hour or less." Nurse Hadley took the thermometer out of Marilyn's mouth.

Pat watched as the nurse wrote the temp on her clipboard and took out her stethoscope.

Nurse Hadley listened to Marilyn's breathing and put her instrument away. "Her vitals are getting stronger and she should make a full recovery. The doctor left instructions that he will set the arm as soon as she's awake."

"Why not do it when she won't feel it?" Patricia asked.

"Because he didn't want to waste the casting material if she didn't pull through. It's much easier to bury someone without all that plaster attached to them," Nurse Hadley told her. "It's harder to shut the lid on the casket with the extra volume and he would have to cut it back off."

"I see." Patricia answered, barely able to conceal her shock at the bluntness of the nurse.

The nurse left the room, leaving Patricia to stand guard over the defenseless woman.

"That's one heartless nurse."

Dr. Greenson had just shifted his glass to the table at his elbow as Bobby returned from the bar.

Peter nearly jumped out of his skin when the phone next to him rang. "Hullo?"

He jolted to an alert position and listened.

"Yes, it is done."

A short pause. "No, we didn't find it, sir."

Now, yelling could be heard from the other end of the receiver, though the words were indistinguishable.

"Yes, Mr. Vice President, we'll find it. No, the senator need not worry." Peter hung up the phone with a shaky hand.

Dr. Greenson spoke. "Well, no need to ask who that was. I suppose he wanted the letter?"

"Yes, and the diary as well," Peter replied.   He began pacing the living room with quick strides.

"Have either of you fellows looked for them?"   Dr. Greenson picked up his glass and hesitated before lifting it to his lips.

Bobby answered before Peter could respond. "A little, but you arrived only a few minutes after we did.   Perhaps we should all search now."

"Where is Mrs. Murray?   She may be able to tell us where it was kept."   Dr. Greenson stood and headed toward the kitchen.

"Keep calm, Peter."   Bobby patted him on the back. "Don't blow it now."

"I need a cigarette."

"Here you are."   Bobby handed him one, then held out a lighter.   "You go act like you're searching the bedroom and I'll look around in here."

"Thanks."   Peter's hand shook as he lit the cigarette.

"We'll get through this and then we won't be around Greenson as much."

"You're right.   It'll be okay."   Peter started down the hall as he heard Greenson returning from the kitchen.

Pat stood close to Marilyn's face. "Don't try to talk just yet. I'll get you a few ice chips to wet your mouth first."

Marilyn nodded once as a paper cup was held to her mouth.   She opened it like an eager baby bird and Pat dumped a few chips onto her parched tongue.   Swallowing, she opened her mouth again.

Nurse Hadley came into the room, "Not too much now. We don't need her retching as well."

"Too late for that."   Pat answered and nodded her head toward the little bowl.

Marilyn made a face and closed her eyes.

Nurse Hadley turned to leave. "I'll go get the doctor now. He wanted to see her when she woke." The nurse picked up the bowl, checked its contents, made a note on her clipboard and left.

"Bully for him," Patricia whispered to Marilyn, patting her hand for reassurance.

Dr. Bunner entered the room a few moments later pushing a cart with plaster and water on it. He had some gauze and netting materials as well. He smiled at the patient as he came up to the bed.

Pat moved over to the sink to rinse the wash cloth out and give him room to work on the patient.

"It's good to see you awake, Norma. I hope that you won't feel much pain when I set this arm."

He pushed the controls on the bed to get an upright position for the patient. He took hold of the arm and pulled until he heard a popping noise.

"Yeowwwwwuch. What the hell are you doing?" Marilyn cried out in agony.

Dr. Bunner continued with his work. He felt the wrist in question to make certain the bones were aligned again.

Then he wrapped the gauze tightly and proceeded to put netting dipped in plaster around the broken wrist, onto her hand and a little ways up her arm. Satisfied at last, he set her arm back against her body and smiled curtly.

"Now, how are you feeling?"

"Like someone tried to kill me, bring me back from the dead, and kill me again, you bastard." Marilyn croaked as she wiped the sweat beading on her brow with her good hand.

"I would offer you a pain killer, but I'm afraid that your liver just won't handle one more pill. No aspirin, no morphine, no drugs of any kind."

"Bull shit. I am absolutely going to have morphine. Where is my agent? Where's Joe? He'll make you give me drugs."

Dr. Bunner merely smiled. "Sorry Norma, but no can do."

Marilyn sat straight up in the bed, screeching. "What do you mean 'no can do'? You absolutely can do. I want my lawyer. Where is Dr. Engleberg? Why are you even in here?"

The doctor smiled again while he gathered up his materials. Pushing the cart out of the door, he turned before closing it. "Good luck, ma'am." He eyed his unhappy patient then glanced back at Patricia. "I'm sure you'll need it."

"Great." Patricia turned to Marilyn who had lain back against the pillows. "Don't worry, honey. We'll get through this."

Tears ran down Marilyn's face. "What happened?"

Patricia came over to her and wiped her face with the cold wash cloth. "Let's not think about anything right now. Try to get some rest and we'll talk about it later."

With the pain still surging through her arm, Marilyn was too exhausted to argue and closed her eyes. Patricia lowered the bed so that Marilyn could rest easier. Sighing, she sat down beside the bed and picked up the diary, opened to where she had left off and started to read; growing more and more uneasy the further she got into it.

Bobby pushed the door closed to the liquor cabinet, having refreshed his glass once more. "Nothing in here, gents."

Dr. Greenson looked at the clock on the living room wall. It was nearly noon. They'd been searching for hours to no avail. "Apparently the letter must be at the studio in her dressing room. We can't very well go barging in there until things are calmer."

Peter came into the room, walked over to the bar and poured out a glass of whiskey. He gulped it in one swallow, then poured himself another and handed a glass to Greenson.

"This is unsettling, but we should leave now to avoid talk," Dr. Greenson told them. "I'll be in touch."

Chapter 4

August 5, 1962

As she approached the bed, Pat smiled at what looked like a ghost of the Marilyn she once knew. "Hi. You don't look so good," she stated as she wiped her face with a damp rag.

Marilyn nodded and let the tears run down her cheeks.

Nurse Hadley came in the room. "How's she doing? Has she been awake long?"

Pat turned to the nurse. "No."

"You're both in for a rough time of it." Sticking the thermometer under Marilyn's tongue, Nurse Hadley picked up her ever present clipboard to jot down her patient's progress.

Sergeant Clemson sat at his desk finishing the report on the Monroe death. One of the detectives knocked on his open door and came in.

"So Sarg, was Robert Kennedy really there? That's the buzz word all around."

"Close the door, Binford." Clemson waited for the door to latch before continuing. "Okay, yes, Kennedy was there." Sergeant Clemson chewed on the end of his pencil as Binford sat down.

"Well, aren't you going to tell me the whole story?" Binford tapped his finger on his knee.

Sighing, Clemson began tapping his pencil on the desk. "Kennedy, Lawford and Greenson were all there. They found the body about 3:30 this morning. The story goes that the Lawford's had a party, but Ms. Monroe didn't want to go. After a while, Lawford and Kennedy got worried and went to check on her."

"Is that when they found her dead?" Detective Binford leaned closer to the sergeant.

"Yes. So they called Dr. Ralph Greenson and us. Apparently, Greenson thinks it was a suicide."

"What do you think?"

"I'm not so sure." Clemson tapped the eraser against his front teeth.

Patricia accepted the coffee gratefully. "Thank you. This has been trying."

The nurse pulled a chair in close to the one Pat sat in. "It's only begun. You should get some sleep. I've prepared the room next door for you. Go lie down for a few hours; I'll tend to our patient."

"As wonderful as that sounds, I simply can't leave her. Mr. Lawford should be returning soon and then I can sleep for a little while."

Nurse Hadley leaned a little closer to Pat. "I was a nurse in the Army and I've seen things that are much worse than this. I'll try to keep her suffering to a minimum."

"Thank you." Patricia smiled at the nurse, really looking at her for the first time. After a few moments of staring into the nurse's eyes, Pat said, "I think I will go lie down for just a few minutes. Please let me know the moment she stirs again. I want to be here when she wakes." Nurse Hadley nodded and noticed the furrow between Patricia's brows. *Something is really bothering her, and it's not Ms. Jean's*

*health. I bet it has to do with that little book she keeps close
at hand.*

"Yes, I will."

Dr. Greenson's knuckles were turning white as he clutched
the receiver, the voice on the other end of the phone still
yelling at him.

"I'm sorry sir; it wasn't my fault that it's so late."
Greenson cowed down in the chair warding off the verbal
blows.

"You idiot, can't you do anything right?"

"Look, I've been there. She's dead.   That's all you
wanted, right?"

The receiver clicked and a loud buzzing sound indicated
the other's unhappy answer.

"How long?" Marilyn croaked out.

"For what?" Nurse Hadley asked as she rinsed the bowl
in the sink across from the bed. She watched Marilyn in the
mirror.

"Until this is over."

"It depends on how long you've been a user and what
you've been using." The nurse brought a fresh wash cloth
over and placed it on Marilyn's forehead.

"I'm not a user." Marilyn's words punctuated the dry
retching coming from deep inside her while she shivered in a
cold sweat. Nurse Hadley bundled the blankets around
Marilyn then sat down beside the bed.

"I'll distract you by reading to you. How'd you like
current events?"

Marilyn's teeth chattered as she nodded her head in the
affirmative.

"Let's see." Nurse Hadley opened the day old newspaper
at random, and read the first article she came too:

"Mary Mullen was killed on June 28th while, Nina Nichols and Helen Blake were both strangled on June 30th in Boston. After five weeks, the police are still at a loss. The newest evidence is that these three women were all killed by the same man who uses the victim's own clothing to strangle them with and then ties the item into his signature bow tie."

Marilyn shuddered and shook her head.

Nurse Hadley saw the reaction to her reading. "Sorry, maybe we should read about something else instead."

Marilyn nodded her agreement.

Turning the page, Nurse Hadley quickly summarized the current news. "It says that there will be a twenty five mile space center near Cape Canaveral, Fl. and it will be ready soon.

Also President Kennedy said that he could not understand why city officials in Albany, Ga., would not sit down with Negro citizens to work out racial problems there."

As Nurse Hadley was perusing the paper for some other tidbit to help distract her patient, Marilyn fell asleep. Nurse Hadley smiled to herself and in a rare show of fondness placed the blanket more firmly under Marilyn's chin.

Frank turned on the TV a little after noon and went into the kitchen to start the coffee. He walked back into the living area just as the set flickered on.

Dr. Ralph Greenson stood at the front of Marilyn's Brentwood house giving a press conference.

"It is with great sadness we mourn the passing of our dearest friend and favorite actress, Marilyn Monroe." Greenson continued, but Frank didn't hear another word.

He sat in a numbed stupor on the edge of the couch, like a man sucker punched in the gut. Placing his head in his hands, the reality began to sink in. "What the hell?"

Peter entered Marilyn's room and motioned to the nurse. "Go take a break for an hour or so. I'll stay with her."

"Are you sure, Mr. Lawford?"

"Absolutely. We're all exhausted, but you haven't had a break. It's time you did. Hey, see if you can bring a cot in here so we can all rest when the patient is asleep."

"That should be easy to arrange. I'll be back in a minute." Nurse Hadley, stifling a yawn, gave in to a good stretch before she left the room.

Settling into the chair next to the bed, Peter watched Marilyn sleep for a moment before his own eyes closed.

Patricia entered the room some minutes later to find him sound asleep while Marilyn lay awake with silent tears escaping her eyes.

Pat leaned in close to Marilyn.

"You have to protect Jack." Marilyn whispered, grabbing at Patricia's hand.

"You mean my brother, John?"

"Yes." Her voice struggled with the single word.

"Okay."

"You *have* to protect Jack. You don't understand what's happening." Marilyn struggled to sit up.

"Why? What's happening?" Patricia helped her to sit up. The pain showed on her face, but her words appeared urgent. "There is a plot to kill Jack." Marilyn began to shake as the retching started again.

Pat grabbed the bowl and placed it under Marilyn's chin. When the episode had passed, Marilyn lay back against the pillows exhausted.

"Take care of Jack." She insisted, falling back into a restless sleep.

Bobby sighed as he dialed his brother's private residence. "Great, this is not going to be easy."

John picked up the bedside receiver. "Hello?"

"Are you sitting down?"

John sat on the edge of the bed. "I am now. What's up, Bobby?"

Patricia stood for a moment watching Marilyn. With care she made her way around the bed and thumped Peter on the head. He jumped slightly, waved his hand over his head to shoo an imaginary fly away and settled back into sleep.

She gave him a little shove and he came fully awake. "What are you doing?" Peter asked as he rubbed at his blood shot eyes.

"We need to talk."

"So, talk." Peter closed his eyes and folded his arms across his chest, wiggling into a more comfortable position in the chair.

"Outside. I need you awake and listening." She jerked on his coat sleeve to get her point across.

Sighing, Peter forced himself out of the chair and stretched before following his wife out into the abandoned hallway.

"So, talk." he repeated, his exhaustion evident as he continued to yawn.

"I don't know what you have gotten yourself into, and I don't really want to." Patricia held a hand up in front of his face to keep him from interrupting her. "Whatever is going on between Marilyn and my brother isn't my concern. We don't need to be involved any more than we must. I think that we should just go home and let her be."

"Are you crazy?" Peter asked no longer sleepy.

"No, I am merely protecting myself, and you. Dad said that she should be excluded from the clan and I for one don't wish to continue to help her."

"Have you no sense of truth, Patricia? Are you so caught up in being a Kennedy that you've lost your basic human compassion?"

"I have compassion. Haven't I been here for hours cleaning up her vomit and wiping her face? Haven't I been kind to her? Dad will have a fit if he finds out how much I've helped her." Patricia stood tapping her foot in agitation.

"I'll have a fit if you don't. It's more than just about us, this is really big." Peter answered angrily, trying to keep his voice down.

"Well, I'm finished. You and the nurse can figure it out from here. I don't want anything else to do with it." Pat started to walk away, but Peter grabbed her by the arm and twirled her around to face him.

"What of your brother? You remember him, the president of the United States. Aren't you even concerned that the conspiracy plot is true and he is the target of some mobster or worse?" Peter asked, intently searching her face.

He watched her for a few moments and then sighed. "I guess not."

As she slowly walked away, Peter spoke bitingly to her retreating back. "Apparently Daddy's little girl will always do what Daddy says. Regardless of the threat to her brother and her friend, we must make Daddy happy."

Stopping short, Pat turned and glared at Peter. "Still, after all this time, you don't understand the family, Pete. I must go, but I will keep silent, for all our sakes."

Chapter 5

Bobby stepped into the private limo that would take him home to Ethel and the children. As the limo rounded the corner of the circular drive, Ethel came to the front door to greet him. Eagerly he stepped out of the vehicle, bounded up the steps and then into her open arms.

Home, at last. He kissed her soft lips, and sighed into her hair. Still holding her around the waist, they walked into the house together as he pushed the front door closed.

The vice president of the United States answered the summons on the first ring. "Hello?"

"What's the verdict, Johnson?"

"She's dead."

"Excellent, most excellent."

The next morning dawned bright and beautiful. Bobby stepped onto the porch in his jogging shorts and tennis shoes. Stooping to tighten the laces first, he then stretched and began the daily ritual he had established years before.

Odd that the day isn't overcast and overburdened with rain, as is my soul. Why have I gotten involved in this mess? Easy enough to answer. I love Jack and he loves her.

The dirt road loomed up ahead and he made the corner without even looking where he was going. He'd taken this route so many times that it no longer required his attention. Complete freedom was given to his thoughts as he whizzed down the path he usually followed.

Do I tell Jack what Marilyn suspected or do I investigate first? What can be gained if Jack has that knowledge? There are so many reasons to want him dead. The opposition to the Cold War in Russia for one, the ongoing conflict with the Vietnamese governments for another, then there's the civil rights movement here at home.

Strife is all his presidency is about, so how can I find just one person amid many who pose as a real threat? Is he being targeted from within the political parties here at home, or has our soil been infiltrated by an outside enemy?

Bobby turned and headed toward the lake, kicking up dust as he jogged along, completely unaware of the beautiful August morning.

If I tell Jack, will it keep him on his guard? Will he flip out? Certainly there've been threats before, but we've seen the enemy and known how to foil the plan. This, this is much more difficult without any real proof or evidence to show him.

I guess the attempt on Marilyn's life would be some concrete evidence, if we could prove she's not crazy. The good Dr. Greenson would argue differently.

By now Bobby had made his usual loop and was returning to the main house. *Who should I talk to about this? How can I get information without it seeming that I am asking too many suspicious questions?*

The likely sources aren't where I really want to look. They'll suspect something if I ask for details. Who then? Who's in the know, but not involved in politics directly?

Mother. Of course. I need to go visit the dear old girl anyway. It's been many weeks since I've had her lasagna. Perhaps I can talk her into making one while we visit. That'll keep her busy while we talk.

Bobby returned to the house, sat down on the front porch, took off his shoes and sat back a moment, smiling.

The front door opened and Ethel came to join him, bringing a tall glass of ice water. Handing it to him, she sat down one step below and leaned against his leg.

"Thanks, hon." He smiled down on her when she turned her face to his for a brief kiss.

"Of course. What are good wives supposed to do for an attractive man?"

"I'm surprised that you still find me so." Bobby moved his leg around her and scooted her between his thighs. They sat for a few moments, not speaking.

"Bobby?"

"Yep."

"Do you think we did the right thing?" Ethel leaned her head into his stomach in order to look up at his face.

"Yep."

"What about that poor girl's family? Do you even know her name?" Ethel asked.

"You're adorable when you worry. I don't think she had any family to worry about. She was a druggie on the streets. Don't concern yourself too much about it, honey."

He tightened his arm around her waist and pulled her closer to him. She snuggled against him savoring the close moment.

"How is 'she'?"

"It's rough going, but she'll recover. I heard from Peter and he said they're going to move her this evening once it's dark. She'll be able to tell us more once the withdrawals are over." Bobby tugged at a lock of his wife's hair. "I think that her doctor's been drugging her to make people think she's crazy or a drug addict.

"What I don't understand is why he'd go to so much trouble?"

Ethel stretched her legs out in front of her, allowing them to drift down the steps to the sidewalk. "There's a good reason if he knows about John."

"True, although as much as the good doctor scares me, I'm much more concerned about Peter. He's as skittish as an abused kitten and likely to break with too much pressure." Bobby ran his fingers through his wife's hair.

She turned her upper body to face him. "I appreciate your concern, since he's never been the most stable brother-in-law. He certainly has the sensitivity of an actor."

"And drinks away his sorrows." Bobby agreed.

"What about John? Should you tell him?"

"I really don't know yet. I've thought about it, but can't decide if he'd gain anything from knowing. Maybe it's better to let her rest in peace." Bobby stared over his wife's head and watched a bird flit into a tree across the lawn.

"Maybe," Ethel agreed. "Jackie's never cared too much if he strayed, but she certainly got her hackles up where Marilyn was concerned."

"She's afraid that it would cause the first Kennedy divorce in history. You can't blame her since he's hardly discreet in his affair and very nearly flaunted it in her face." Bobby sighed. "This is such a mess. I hope we can untangle it all soon. I'm so worried about Jack. If the information we have is right, there'll be an attempt on his life made soon and we only know part of it."

"What do you know?" Ethel asked. "Did you get to read any of her diary or see the letter?"

"No. I only know what Peter told us both, but that's enough proof for me. He may be a bit prone to the dramatic, but he's not a liar. I think that's why he's so jumpy and nervous. It'll be really hard for him to keep silent."

"Maybe you could arrange for him to go away on a film shoot for a few weeks so that he won't be running back and forth checking on her."

"Great idea, honey. I'll call the LA Times editor and have him announce that Peter's going to be in London on a film shoot for several days. That should keep the press at bay and off of Pat. It'll also allow Peter to get Marilyn away for a while and take care of her."

"I'll certainly feel much better once we've discovered who's behind this and we're sure Jack's safe." Ethel stood up, dusted the dirt from her skirt and smiled at her husband.

"You and me both, honey." Bobby stood up and pulled his wife into his arms. "I'm going to visit Mother later tonight. Maybe she'll be able to tell me how Dad is really doing and we can have a chat. I'll call you from New York."

Bobby exited the taxi in front of the two story brownstone house that his parents purchased after the kids grew up.

He was looking forward to spending a few hours with his mother. He walked up the steps, opened the front door and stepped in to see his mother parading around in a new dress, tags still intact and a new hat with the molding paper trailing down her back.

"Hello, Mother. What a beautiful new outfit you're wearing. Did you buy that just for my visit?"

"Robert. How nice to see you. How're the children?" Rose walked over to her son and hugged him tightly.

"Everyone is great, Mother. You remember we're having a family birthday party in a couple of days."

"Whose party is it? Little Rose's?"

"No, it's little Joe's birthday. Don't you remember?"

"Joe? Oh, he's doing much better. He did get upset with me the other day, but it was so silly."

"Who did? Dad?" Bobby, temporarily confused, asked. Smiling to himself, he had to readjust his mind to follow the many rabbit trails his mother would take.

"Of course your father. Don't know who else you would be calling 'Joe'." Rose twirled around again and smiled at her son.

"I was hoping we could make lasagna, Mother. You haven't done that in a while." Bobby moved toward the kitchen, "Do you have the ingredients?"

"No. We'll need to go to the market to get a few things." Rose chirped with glee. "You know how I love to shop. Why just the other day your father got so angry at me for purchasing this vase."

"Why would that be a problem?" Bobby eyed the vase and noted nothing appealing about it, but if his mother liked it, then she should have it.

"Well, he was positively irate about the price. He said that seventeen thousand dollars was too much for such a small vase and I should return it.

"I told him that it was from the Ming Dynasty and was priceless. You don't get priceless pieces every day and at such a price as seventeen thousand. How could I turn it down?" Rose pouted and held the vase up for Bobby to inspect.

"You couldn't now, could you?" Bobby agreed.

"No, and you know how I love a good bargain. If you can purchase a priceless item for a price then you have actually gotten a pretty decent deal." Rose replaced the vase on its stand with great care and picked up her purse.

"Well, Ma, I can't argue with that." Bobby grinned and took her arm.

"Your father certainly could. He went on about how frivolous I've become and that good money should not be wasted on such trifles.

"Of course, I explained that Jimmy Hoffa's wife would not possibly own one and so I should be allowed to show off unique treasures when they came to the house." Rose chattered on while they walked down the sidewalk to the corner market.

46

"The Hoffa's?" Bobby was struggling to keep up with his mothers' random musings.

"Oh yes, they've been over a few times, but usually Mr. Hoffa comes alone. Your father is very agitated when he leaves, and then he nearly bit my head off over a little statuette of a purple elephant on a circus ring. I only paid two hundred dollars for it. So I don't understand why he was fussing about money. We all know we've more money than King Midas and God together."

"Perhaps he's still unwell after the stroke and feeling a bit isolated. Don't take him too seriously. He's just frustrated that he's not in the middle of everything right now. He'll be better once he can go back to work." Bobby hoped his words would sooth his mother.

They entered the small corner market and Rose was checking the cheeses to find just the right one. She picked out a couple of blocks, sniffing each one. She made a choice after some moments and then headed for the vegetables.

"How is Nellie?" Rose asked. "Such a nice young girl. I hope you marry her."

"Mother, I've been married for 15 years now. You were at my wedding." Bobby stood watching his mother squeeze the lettuce heads.

"Well, I always liked Nellie and I'm certainly glad she's been a good wife to you. How many children do you have?"

Shocked, Bobby could only stare at her for a moment before answering. "Seven. We have seven children, Ethel and I."

"Ethel? Did Nellie change her name? What a shame. I like 'Nellie' much better than 'Ethel'.   That sounds like a poor Jewish name."

"Mother, I love Ethel very much. I dated Nellie for one week in junior high school."

"Well, you boys always did the exact opposite of what I wanted you to do." Rose picked up some tomatoes and tossed them into the basket, bruising them when she did so.

"I'm sorry to be such a disappointment to you." Bobby scratched his head and followed his mother to the register.

Without any further revelations from his mother's ceaseless flow of chatter, they arrived back at the house and started the lasagna. Bobby left his mother for a moment to check on his father. He found Joseph Kennedy asleep in his chair and Bobby didn't wish to wake him.

He returned to the kitchen to find his mother chattering on about hanging drapes and making slip covers for the living room furniture.

As she chattered on, Bobby's mind was free to process what he had already learned from her. What did she mean about the Hoffa's? *Does she mean the leader of the teamsters? Why would Dad be upset about a two hundred dollar purchase? I wonder who can tell me what is going on here?*

You would think there is enough drama in this family without Dad acting crazy. I bet his office gals know something that'll be helpful. I may just stop in and pay them a little visit tomorrow before I head back home.

"Don't you agree, dear?" Rose was asking.

"I'm sorry, Mother. What did you say?"

"I just thought it would be a nice treat to put some chocolate chips in with the lasagna." Rose had the bag in her hand ready to drop them into the casserole.

"Gee, umm, I really can't have them in mine. I'm on a diet."

"All right, fine." She put the bag down and slipped the meal into the oven.

"Thanks for sparing me those extra calories." Bobby kissed his mother on the head and turned on the oven.

I really need a vacation.

Chapter 6

Peter looked over at Marilyn as he drove along toward Topanga Beach. "How are you doing?"

"Better." She managed a wobbly smile.

"You look green."

"Thanks. I feel at least green, maybe a bit aqua."

Peter slowed the car and turned into the driveway of an ocean side bungalow.

"Are you sure you know where the key is kept?" he asked as they pulled up to the carport.

"It's always behind that apron hanging on the hook right beside the door." Marilyn answered. *Suzie's so predictable.*

"How long will Ms. Strasberg be in London?" Peter asked as he got out of the car and came around to open the door for Marilyn.

"At least another month. She was trying to wrap up the shoot quickly so that she could return to make another film here in the states."

"I sure hope we have this mess sorted out by then. Let me get the door open and lights on then I'll come back to help you."

Marilyn tried to stand, but couldn't manage on her own. "Good idea."

Peter searched for the key, found it and unlocked the door. He flipped on a couple of lights and returned within a few seconds to help Marilyn.

Firmly ensconced on the sofa, Marilyn lay back, exhausted. "I think we should talk about what's happened. Did you find the letter?"

"Yes. I couldn't believe that they're really planning on escalating the war."

Sitting down on the coffee table in front of her, he handed her a cracker. "When did you find this out?"

"It was at the last gala at the White House. I got there late because of the film shoot and Jack greeted me with a glass of champagne. We toasted, but I hadn't eaten since lunch. It went to my head making me dizzy. So, I went to rest on the sofa in the library and that's when Mr. Kennedy came in with Mr. Johnson."

"Did they see you, Joe and the vice president?" Peter asked as he held out a glass of cream soda.

"Thanks. No. The sofa faces the fireplace and they went over toward the desk to sit in those two chairs."

"What happened?"

"Well, Mr. Kennedy was telling Mr. Johnson that he wanted the conflict to become a full blown war." Marilyn swallowed hard, and started to tremble.

"Take it easy. We'll sort this out a little at a time." Peter pushed a clean cool cloth onto her neck to help soothe her.

"Thanks. I'm okay. The reason he needed it to be a war was to provide arms to the other side. Then he mentioned something about the teamsters. My head was hurting so I only caught snatches of the conversation."

Marilyn paused and took a deep, cleansing breath. Letting out an audible sigh, she continued. "Mr. Johnson left and Mr. Kennedy remained in the library. He made a couple of phone calls. I could hear him talking about a letter and he read part of it over the phone. When he finished with the second call, he left the room."

Marilyn sighed again, struggling to finish her tale. "After a few minutes, I stood up, went to the desk, found the letter folded in half under the blotter and took it." Smiling more to herself than to Peter she smirked, "You know the rest."

"Do you know who he made the calls to?" Peter mopped her forehead, which was sweating profusely.

The retching began anew and Peter grabbed a nearby trash can for her to throw up in. When her body had settled down, her eyes closed and she fell instantly asleep.

Joe DiMaggio stood in front of Frank at the Sands in Las Vegas. With his fists clenched he shouted, "What the hell happened? You said she was all right and now she's dead. What did you do to her, Sinatra?"

Frank's hand trembled as he tried to light a cigarette. "Nothing. I didn't do anything to her. I thought she would be fine. No one told me she was on the list."

"I don't believe you. You'd do anything to cover your own ass. Watch your back, Chairman, or you'll wish you had."

DiMaggio stalked off while Frank slumped against the nearest wall.

"I see you have found us without too much trouble." Peter opened the door for the nurse. "Can I help you bring in your things?"

"Yes. There is another case in the backseat along with my nursing bag. Where's our patient?"

"She's in the living room. She just fell asleep."

"Where am I staying?"

"Pick any of the guest rooms. I'm sure that Norma will take the master." Peter called to her through the screen door as he went to gather her things.

Coming back into the house, he had a newspaper tucked under his arm and her bags balanced in his hands. "Where did you go, Nurse Hadley?"

51

"I'm in the bedroom next to the master suite. That should keep me close enough to hear her during the night."

"Here's your stuff. Thanks for bringing the paper." Peter tried to act casual as he put her luggage in the room. "Are you finished reading it? I haven't had time to pick one up."

"Yes, help yourself. Such a shame about that actress." The nurse gave him a sly look then turned to open her nurses' bag.

"It is." Peter turned quickly and changed the subject. "I'll be in the kitchen if you need me. I'm going to make a pot of coffee. Do you want some?" Peter asked as he was leaving the room.

"That'd be great. I'll be done here in a few minutes."

"No hurry." Peter rushed off to read the headlines.

'Actress commits suicide'. It read, 'Millions shocked by the loss of the sex goddess, Marilyn Monroe. Private services to be held later in the week. Mr. Joe DiMaggio is heading up the funeral arrangements until family members arrive to handle her affairs.'" Peter read the article with interest. Sighing as he put the ground coffee into the percolator, he added the water and continued to read.

'Apparently, Miss Monroe overdosed on sleeping pills in her home late Saturday, August 4, and was found by her physician, Dr. Greenson. Close friends of Miss Monroe say that she had been ill with an infection. Dr. Greenson said that his session with her on Friday proved she was distraught and possibly suicidal, which prompted his visit to her home'.

"That Norma Jean looks an awful lot like Miss Monroe, don't you think?" She took a sip of her coffee, made a face and added another spoonful of sugar.

"I guess so. . .hadn't really thought about it." Peter turned the page of the *Los Angeles Times* pretending disinterest.

"She sure does. I was thinking that she could be her twin if you dolled her up. Even in her condition she sounds like Marilyn Monroe."

"Well, maybe when she feels better she can go to one of the studios and see if they will hire her. I know that Marilyn was still working on a picture and they may let her be the stand in." Peter continued to stare at the paper without seeing it.

"They might at that. You should get some rest. Let's take two hour watches during the night. I'll take the first shift." Nurse Hadley picked up the mugs and took them to the kitchen.

The office building the Kennedys owned was on Madison Avenue in the heart of downtown. The structure was imposing with its huge glass windows and revolving doors.

Bobby nodded as the door man opened the VIP door for him. "Thanks, Krandell."

"You're welcome, Mr. Kennedy."

Bobby continued to the private elevator that allowed access to the top. He punched the button to the 53rd floor. The elevator whizzed straight up and opened into a well-appointed waiting room.

The secretary sat behind a huge mahogany desk typing legal documents.

Bunny looked up as he stepped off the elevator. "Good morning, Mr. Kennedy. How is your father?"

"You know Dad. He's chomping to get back to work. The doctor says he should make a full recovery. I think he'll be back to work in the next few days. He's supposed to take it easy so he won't be here but a couple of hours a day to start with."

"That's good news. What can I help you with?"

"Dad asked me to come get a few things from his office."

"Let me know if you need anything. Can I bring you some coffee, sir?"

"No thanks, Bunny. I doubt if I'll be that long."

He opened the door to his dad's office and flipped on the switch. The fluorescent lights flickered on.

Stepping into the room, he walked to the overstuffed chair and sat down behind the massive oak desk. He pulled the side drawer open and thumbed through the files. He found one marked "Hoffa". Intrigued, he lifted it out and laid it on the desk.

Once opened, he scanned the file page by page. The last thing in the file folder was a small receipt, folded in quarters and tucked up in the staple between two pieces of paper.

Odd. I wonder why this is in here like this? Bobby opened the little scrap of paper and noted the amount. *Whew! $200,000.00. What in the world? Why would Dad pay Hoffa so much money?*

He stuffed the receipt in his pocket and replaced the file in its slot. He continued to search the office, but found nothing else of interest. Gathering the check book and other items his dad might actually want, he hurried from the room, turned off the light and shut the door behind him.

"Tell your dad that we're looking forward to having him back." Bunny looked up from her typing as he passed by her desk.

"I will. Try not to work so hard." He continued to the main hall still wondering about the little slip of paper and punched the elevator button.

When Peter awoke, it was morning. He rushed out of the bedroom down the hall to find the living room empty. He tip toed to the master suite, pushed open the door and found Marilyn tossing slightly, but sleeping. He looked around the room and saw the nurse asleep in an arm chair near the window.

Walking over to her, he softly touched her arm. "Nurse."

"Wh...what?" she managed thickly.

"You didn't wake me. How did it go?" Peter looked over to the bed, noting that the bandages were gone from Marilyn's upper arm, just above her cast. The purple and yellow bruises showed an outline of fingerprints.

"She was fitful, but I think the worst is almost over." The nurse pulled herself into a proper upright position. "She slept most of the night once we got in here."

"That's wonderful news." He smiled at the nurse for the first time. "Why don't you go get some real rest? I'll take over now."

"Let me check her vitals and then I will." Yawning, Nurse Hadley performed her duties, wrote the stats on her clipboard and left the room.

Peter sat in the chair that the nurse just vacated and stared at Marilyn. Her coloring looked more pale than green and her lips were pink not grayish blue. He noted that her breathing was not as ragged as it had been and took comfort in her progress.

I wonder what she will be able to tell me that can help finish putting the pieces together. Why would Joe and LBJ be together on anything? Doesn't Joe know the president's stance on the conflict? Does Pat know what's going on and that's why she is refusing to help me anymore? I miss you, honey. Why don't you answer my calls?

He shook his head to clear it, and peeked out the window at a beautiful new day. The sun rose about an hour before and its rays were still bouncing on the ocean.

Maybe we can take a walk along the beach this afternoon or tomorrow. It would be good to get some fresh air.

He turned around in his chair. Bored, he picked up the magazine that the nurse had been reading the night before. *Vanity Fair.* Thumbing through the pages he saw pictures and articles about his friends. The one about "The Rat Pack" was entertaining, if not entirely true.

He left the room and tried to call his wife again. The maid answered and said that Mrs. Lawford was not at home. *Not at home? It's 7:30 in the morning. Of course she is home; she doesn't want to talk to me. Fine.*

Chapter 7

August 6, 1962

Peter watched Marilyn stretch and open her eyes. She smiled when she saw him sitting near the window.

"You're looking better." He brought her the freshly squeezed orange juice from the night stand beside the bed.

"I am feeling better." She wiggled to sit up against the headboard, careful not to bump her broken wrist. Though there was a cast on, the whole arm was still very sensitive.

"Good. I was hoping we could talk, but not here. Do you think you could manage a short walk?"

After sipping her juice, she nodded. "I think I can manage."

"I'll be back in a few minutes with some breakfast. Do you want toast and eggs or cereal?"

"Toast with strawberry jelly sounds wonderful."

"You got it, kid." He left the room humming "These Foolish Things," a catchy little tune Frank had recorded earlier in the year.

Good, this is progress, Marilyn thought as she walked over to the chair that Peter had been occupying. She sat there a moment, smiling to herself, just watching the ocean peacefully ebb and flow.

"You surprised me. I didn't expect that you would make it out of bed without help." Peter had come in carrying a small tray with the toast, a glass of milk and a bunch of grapes.

"I surprised myself." Marilyn dug into the grapes with gusto. Then she nibbled on the toast.

"Will you be able to get your clothes on without help or should I go get Nurse Hadley?"

"I'll try to do it myself. Just pick me out something from the closet please."

"Sure thing." Rummaging in Susan's closet was simple. Everything was neatly organized. Luckily the women were nearly the same size. He took out some lounge pants and a button up shirt and placed them on the bed with a pair of socks. "Just holler out if you need anything," Peter called out as he left the room and closed the door behind him.

Marilyn stood beside the bed balancing on one foot trying to force her leg through while holding the pants with only her right hand. "This is not working. Maybe I should sit."

She sat down on the bed, leaning forward trying to get her foot in. Once that was accomplished, she struggled to get the other foot into the velour leg while it seemed to dance away from her with a life of its own. "Damn! This is harder than I thought it'd be."

At last she managed to get both legs into the pair of pants and wiggled to pull them up around her waist. "Great. I guess I'm not as coordinated as I used to be."

Sighing, she picked up the shirt and pulled the sleeve through the left arm to the cast. It went on easily since the buttons were undone. The right side was much more difficult because she couldn't hold the shirt up to get her arm through it. "Well, crap."

"Peter." She finally called out while she stood up.

He opened the door and came into the room. Silently, he stood behind her holding the shirt for her to slip her arm into and turned her to face him. He buttoned the shirt in record time.

She sat back down on the bed while he grabbed the pair of socks. He placed them on her feet and then found a pair of shoes in the closet.

"Thanks."

"No problem."

He took hold of her good arm and escorted her to the back door and down the wooden steps to the deck. They crossed the beautiful wooden deck and descended the next set of steps leading down to the beach. Continuing on, they got a little closer to the ocean. With a heavy sigh, Marilyn stopped suddenly and dropped into the sand. He sat down beside her.

"You okay, kid?"

"Yeah."

"What a beautiful day it is. I'm so glad you're feeling better."

"Me too. It's been rough."

"Well, it may get rougher. I have to talk to you about some things we had to do in order to save you." Peter picked up a handful of sand and allowed it to sift through his fingers.

"It's bad isn't it?" She could tell that whatever he had to say, it wasn't going to be easy for her to hear.

"Yes." He picked up some more wet sand and molded it into a round shape. He put it on the beach and packed more sand around it.

"Tell me, Peter. I won't be able to stay out here all day." She had begun playing with the wet sand adding it to his creation.

"Here goes." He took a deep breath and let it out. "I don't really know how to begin so I'll just tell you."

He stopped patting the sand and looked over at her. She was watching him intently and waiting. "Okay."

"Marilyn, when I found you nearly dead on that bed, I panicked. I rushed you to the hospital. After they had gotten you taken care of I went back to your house and found the diary." Peter turned his head to face her.

"I'm sorry that I didn't listen to you about Jack."

"Where is the diary?" Marilyn ignored his apology.

"I have it in my suitcase in the house. I wanted to keep you and the diary safe. No one knows where you are, but I think we need to let Bobby in on your whereabouts."

"Why?"

"He helped me. He knew that you were trying to tell us something after your weekend at Frank's house, but we wouldn't allow you to finish what you were trying to say. Bobby and I talked later that week and more during the party that you missed. Something just wasn't adding up and we were both really worried about you. Besides that, Dr. Greenson had been acting peculiar, even for him."

"Go on." The wind brushed the hair back from her face and she tilted her head up toward the sun.

"When you called to say that you had a letter, I believed that you were telling us the truth... that the president was in danger, but I couldn't leave to discuss it. I called you back a few hours later, but there was no answer. I rushed to your house and you know the rest about that.

"What you don't know is that we had to fake your death."

"You . . . did . . .what?"

Bobby turned back from the elevator and approached Bunny's desk. "I was wondering if I could get the mail for my dad."

"Sure, Mr. Kennedy. It's piled right here." Bunny turned to retrieve the mail from a slot on the side of her desk. "Here is everything including today's."

"Thank you." He turned to walk back to the elevator, flipping through the letters as he walked. He stopped walking as he came to a letter from Dr. Greenson.

"We had no choice," Peter stammered. "We had to let whoever did this to you, think that they succeeded. We had a body flown in, paid off the coroner and let everyone, including Greenson, believe that you were dead."

He paused to let this news sink in. She was looking a little pale and a bead of sweat formed on her forehead. She wiped at it with the back of her sleeve and waited.

"I . . . see."

"Do you? I mean do you really understand it all?" Peter studied her for a long moment, allowing it to sink in for a minute.

"I'm dead. Okay, I get it. This'll be over soon and I can go back to being me."

"No. For your safety, you'll need to move far away and never return. I just don't see any other way around it."

"What about my career? My friends? Jack?"

"I'm afraid it's over. We may be able to figure something out later on, but for now everyone must believe you're dead. In fact, you're already being mourned."

"Yes. I can see that would be true." Tears slipped down her cheeks unheeded.

"For what it's worth, I'm sorry it has to be this way." Peter pulled her closer and held her for another moment until she calmed down.

"Why did no one believe me? Why did I nearly get killed before you believed it, Peter?" She sniffled, rubbing her sleeve over her eyes.

"Because Dr. Greenson wanted us all to believe that you were crazy. He is in on this. I know it."

"How can you be so sure?"

He remained silent and she waited, brushing again at the tears that continued to run down her cheeks.

"Peter?"

"At the party at Frank's house, Joe called. When you came back, Frank told you to leave. When you went to see Dr. Greenson on Friday, he phoned me to tell me that you were most distraught over the argument with Frank and not being with Jack. He told me you were suicidal. There is only one reason he would call me; to make sure I knew you were on the edge."

"I don't get it."

"Because he wanted to cover his tracks. He went on and on about your fight with Frank."

"Yes, I remember." Her tears came quicker, as the memory upset her again. "It was over Jack. I couldn't see him ever again. I was upsetting his wife with my displays of affection. So, Joe Kennedy demanded that I be cast out of the circle."

"Greenson knew about the command. No one could argue that he was in charge of your mental care. No one would charge him with murder if he overdosed you." Peter allowed a handful of sand to sift through his fingers.

Marilyn caught his hand and he looked into her eyes. "Dr. Greenson and I got into an argument that day because I no longer wanted his help and he insisted I really needed him. For weeks I had been flushing his pills down the toilet to avoid confrontation.

"That old bat, Mrs. Murray, took careful notes of my every move. I caught her counting the pills in my prescription on the day right after we moved into the house."

"There is little doubt that he had a desire to make you appear crazy, but the big question is why?" Peter smashed the sand down level with the beach, smoothed it out and began to draw a moat with his index finger.

"Maybe it was because of Jack and the things I knew. Maybe it was easier for Jackie to deal with our affair if I seemed mentally unstable, or maybe it was easier to pass my 'death' off as a suicide if I'd been depressed and nutty."

"All true, but there's more to it than just jealousy. Let's get you back to the house. I don't want you to over tire yourself." Peter stood up, dusted the sand off of his trousers and held out a hand to Marilyn.

Together they walked back to the deck.

"Oh, Marilyn, there is one more thing that you should know," he told her as he helped her up the last few steps onto the deck.

"What?"

"Your family and Joe DiMaggio are planning your funeral."

A soft moan escaped her lips as she slid to the floor in a dead faint.

Ethel picked up the phone, "Hello?"

"Hi Ethel, it's Peter. I've been trying to get in touch with Bobby, but I can't reach him at his office."

"Yes, he's been with his mother in New York. He was checking around the office as well. How are things?"

"Well, Norma is feeling a little better. We've had a talk about what happened and how she broke her wrist. She's not vomiting anymore and has started eating again."

"That's good news. How can we reach you?"

"My car phone is on. I'll try to keep the window down in it and the screen door open."

"Great. I'll tell Bobby that you're fine. He'll be home tomorrow evening and you may be able to reach him after the birthday party. I'm not sure when it will be over. Perhaps the next evening will be better."

"I'll try again in a few days. Tell little Joe happy birthday for me."

Vice President Johnson's secretary buzzed him. "Sir, Senator Smith on line two for you."

"Senator," LBJ picked up the line. "Did you hear the news?"

"Yes. It's terrible." Senator Smith sighed.

"Job well done is more like it. Yes, there are those of us who are well pleased."

"Hi, Pat. How're you doing?" Ethel asked.

"I'm doing all right. I miss Pete terribly, but there was no other choice in the matter. You know how Dad can be when he is on a rampage."

"Yes, I do know. I just wanted to fill you in. Pete just called and he's doing well. He wouldn't tell me where he was, which is probably really good. I might say something to someone and not realize it was the wrong person."

"That's why I won't answer his calls. He's going to be so upset with me, but he just doesn't understand how all of this works."

"Try not to get too upset, Pat. This should be over soon and we'll know what's going on. I hope that it's an outsider and not someone in the White House that's behind all of this."

Pat paused for several seconds before she asked, "Perhaps we could get together and have lunch next week? I could really use a friend right now. I bet you'd have more information by then to tell me."

"I'd love it. Are you coming to the birthday party tomorrow?"

"How could I miss it?"

"Good. We'll have a chance to compare schedules and set a lunch date then."

"Thanks for calling, Ethel. I appreciate you letting me know."

"Anything for the family."

Chapter 8

August 8, 1962

Bobby entered the master bedroom of the home he shared with Ethel. She was asleep, buried under a pile of blankets and a quilt. Only the top of her head was visible from the moonlight coming in through the curtain.

He smiled at his wife, walked over to the bed and shook her gently. "Honey, I'm home."

Ethel lifted her head from the pillow with a sleepy half smile. "How was your trip, dear?"

"You won't believe what I've found. Get up and come with me to the kitchen."

"Must I?" Ethel pushed herself a little further under the covers.

"Only if you want to hear what I've found." Bobby flipped on the light and went back downstairs.

Sighing, Ethel got up, found her robe and followed him.

As she descended the stairs, the smell of fresh coffee filled her senses. Heading straight to the kitchen, Ethel smiled at her husband and grabbed the tin of cookies from their secret hiding place. *I hate to hide them, but the kids would eat them all in one sitting if I didn't.*

"What's so exciting that you must wake me at midnight?" Ethel asked when he hadn't volunteered any information.

"My father has received an interesting envelope from Dr. Greenson, but I'm not sure how to open it without it looking like it's been opened."

"Oh, Bobby. That's Crime 101. Don't you know anything? As the attorney general for the United States you should have studied this in your first semester of law school."

"Don't be silly. They don't teach you crime in law school. Anyway, I never wanted to be in this position, but Dad insisted that Jack appoint me." Bobby turned around with a hand on his hip, looking hurt.

"I know, honey. I was just teasing. Put some water in the tea pot and we will steam the letter open."

They drank coffee and ate a few cookies while they waited on the kettle to whistle.

"What else happened?" Ethel asked after she had finished her cookie.

"There is also a receipt to Jimmy Hoffa in the amount of $200,000.00." He took another swallow of his coffee and refilled his mug. He held the pot out to Ethel, who shook her head and he replaced it.

"Are you sure? What's it for?"

"I don't know, but I intend to find out. There was nothing more in his office in New York so I'll have to check out his stuff at the White House. I'm fairly certain it has to do with the teamsters and may even have something to do with Dad's anger that Mom spent money on frivolous trinkets.

"He's always been happy when she goes on her shopping sprees since it means he gets time alone. She seemed hurt when he barked at her over it."

The kettle whistled and they tiptoed over to it like naughty school kids. Looking around the room, Bobby checked the door before he handed the letter to Ethel. "You do it. I'm too nervous."

"All right." She held the letter a couple of inches away from the steaming kettle. In a few moments the seal began to weaken.

Carefully she pulled at the flap of the envelope until it slowly parted. Bobby bumped into her in his nervousness.

"Watch out, honey." Ethel scolded.

"I'm sorry. I just can't see that well." Bobby moved closer to her again.

"Come over on this side. You're going to make me tear it."

She'd moved the envelope away from the steam so that it wouldn't get saturated with water. He finally got settled next to her near the stove and she replaced the envelope over the steam.

The flap came loose and she pulled it completely open. They stepped back from the stove in unison. Bobby turned off the burner and moved the kettle to the back.

Ethel laid the envelope flat on the counter so that the flap would dry without a wrinkle. He came up beside her and watched as she skillfully pulled the letter from the envelope while it still lay on the counter.

"I had no idea I had married such a good detective." Bobby kissed the nape of her neck. "Perhaps there are some further secrets we can discover."

"Well, I want to see what this secret is before I go looking for any others." Ethel took up the letter and opened it with great care.

They read it together, then looked at each other and read it again.

"I don't understand." Ethel stood re-reading the contents one more time. "It doesn't make sense."

"This is a bill for a mental hospital." Bobby stared at the letter.

"Yes, I see. Has your mother been away?" Ethel tried her best to stifle the laugh that threatened to escape.

"No." Bobby looked into her laughing eyes and laughed in spite of himself. "She's been too busy taking care of Dad. When is the admittance date?"

"There isn't one. It only says for a six week stay. But there aren't any dates on it that I can see."

"Me neither. This just doesn't make sense."

"What's he been doing? We have a bill for this and a receipt for $200,000.00 to pay Jimmy Hoffa. Are the two connected?" Ethel continued to stare at the bill as Bobby opened the little yellow receipt.

"Jimmy Hoffa is just the head of the teamsters. What in the world does he deserve so much money for?"

"The teamsters?" Ethel studied the receipt, "Did you read the Detroit papers after the election? It said that the election was won by the votes of the teamsters."

"Yes, I vaguely remember that now. Do you think...? Nah, Dad wouldn't do such a thing." He looked at Ethel with doubt. "Would he?"

Peter stood irresolute with his hands full of trash bags. His car phone was ringing, but the garbage was stinking. He put the trash down by the curb and ran to his car. Picking up the receiver and depressing the talk button he answered. "Hello."

"This is the operator. Please hold while I connect you." A series of clicks could be heard, then a familiar voice.

Peter quickly pressed the talk button. "Hold on. I need to get out of here."

Peter put the receiver down on his seat and opened the screen door. "I'm going into the village to get a few things; I'll be back in less than an hour."

He climbed in the driver's seat and backed out of the carport. "Okay, I can talk now. What's the problem?"

He listened to Dr. Greenson rant. "Where've you been? I was told you had gone to London, but I thought that couldn't be right since you were so upset over Marilyn's death."

Peter could feel the sweat begin to form on his forehead and the back of his neck. He had to think fast. "I told that to my publicist so that I could have a few days of peace and quiet."

"That would've been fine except that I wanted to talk to you." Dr. Greenson growled.

"Well, Pat and I needed some time. This has been very stressful." Peter answered truthfully.

"There is no time for that now." Dr. Greenson told him. "I need to know where that diary is. Did you find it?"

"No. I thought that you'd have it by now." Peter smiled at his own cleverness.

"Why would I have found it? Do I have access to the house? Studio? Her friends?"

"Probably not."

"I need that diary. You must get busy and find it. You're the only one who can search her dressing room or the studio. You know where she hung out and what she did with her friends."

"Dr. Greenson I really don't think. . ."

"Lawford," the doctor interrupted. "Find that diary!"

The phone went dead as the doctor hung up his end. Peter drove into the village and parked in front of the drugstore. As he turned off the engine, he laid his head on the steering wheel for a moment.

I haven't juggled this many roles since I directed the star studded review for Jack's campaign.

John sat at his desk with newspapers from around the world spread out in front of him. He was just picking one up when his wife opened the door.

"John, I received a letter from my sister asking me to join her next week in Italy. I'd like to go." Jackie moved slowly into the chair by his desk.

"It's not a good idea for you to leave right now. You've got a schedule to get back to."

"Don't you think I know what my duties and obligations are? I'm just so tired and so . . . well sad. I can't seem to get myself back together." She wiped a tear from her eye with a handkerchief.

"The timing is just bad. I don't want you half way around the world with the nation in such turmoil."

"We'll be staying in Ravello, in a secluded villa. There's nothing menacing going on there. It'd be for a few weeks with Lee and the kids. Don't you want me to get well?" Jackie caught and held his gaze.

"Of course I want you to get well, but being apart doesn't seem the way to do it." John insisted.

"I won't be in Russia and I think it'd do me good." Jackie stood up. "I'm going. I'll have my secretary clear my schedule. I want to spend time with my sister. I need her and I need to heal."

"If you're going to insist then there will be stipulations, Jackie. I can't just let you go off without being able to contact you. I'm going to have the secret service install a phone where I can reach you anytime.

"I also want to know where you are and how you're doing on a daily basis. We need to make sure that you're safe and well protected." John stood up, rounded his desk coming face to face with his wife. He slowly reached out and placed his hand on her shoulder.

"Don't touch me, John." Jackie backed away enough so that his hand fell to his side. "I need this trip and I'll die if I don't take it. I haven't the will to continue with this hectic life, in this hectic pace, and our crumbling marriage. Let me go, John."

"If you agree to my conditions and if you'll come home when or if you're needed, then we can work out an agreement."

"All right. I'm too tired to fight."

"Who owns the villa?" John returned to his desk as Jackie headed toward the door.

"I don't know; my sister's made all the arrangements."

Chapter 9

<u>*August 9, 1962*</u>

Bobby spread the charcoal out evenly across the big grill; he then took the lighter fluid and doused the briquettes in it. He looked over at Ethel, carrying presents to the large family picnic table set up just beside the pool.

She sensed him looking at her and smiled.   When she placed the gifts on the table, she turned around to talk to Rose.

"We're certainly glad that you and Dad were able to make it to the party." Ethel told her.

"Where is Nellie?" Rose asked looking around. "You can't be her. You are too frumpy."

Ethel stared at her for a moment, "I'm afraid that she couldn't be here today. I'm going to be the hostess instead."

Turning around, Ethel glared in the direction of her husband. He had told her about his conversation with Rose, but still – *Frumpy? I have a great figure, especially for a woman who's had seven children.*

Bobby smiled back with a "What?" look.

Ethel turned toward his mother and then back to him.

He smiled again. "Oh," he mouthed and lit the grill.

Little Joe came to sit next to his mother on the picnic bench. He was counting his gifts repeatedly.

"Happy Birthday, Joe," Pat told him as she placed her gift on the table.

"Thanks, Aunt Pat." He clapped with joy at the size of the present she just put down.

She tousled his hair and kissed him on the top of the head. "You're welcome. Uncle Peter wishes he could be here, but he is making a movie right now."

"That's okay." He grinned at her, got up from the table and went to find his cousins.

Pat sat down beside Ethel. "Hi. Thanks for inviting me. Hello Mother. How are you feeling today?"

"I'd be fine if I could only go shopping. I need a new bathing suit."

"Mother, I can go with you this week. Why do you need one?"

"Well, I heard your father telling someone on the telephone that he wanted me to go swimming with the fishies. I told him that I needed a new suit."

"Why would he say such a thing Mother?" Pat asked.

"He said that I'm always in his business and I would be better off to leave him alone."

"What kind of business did you get into?"

"There was a foul and I overheard him saying something mean about the Hoffa's. I really like her so I stepped into the room and told him so. That's when he got mad."

"Do you mean a strike?" Ethel joined the conversation.

"Maybe, anyway he said I should go do something else or he would help me find something to do." Rose sighed and got up, leaving the sisters-in-law to wonder what she'd really been saying.

Bobby started to toss the hamburger patties onto the grill. Jack joined him while Jackie clung to his arm. Joe Sr. sat a little distance away watching his family.

Jack had been sipping a beer and sent Jackie in the house for a new one.

"How ya been?" Bobby asked as soon as she was out of ear shot.

"Okay."

"I'm so sorry about Marilyn."

"Me too. Jackie has been hanging on me ever since we got the news. I don't think I can take much more."

"Did you know that Marilyn told Peter a secret before she died? She told him you were in danger."

"Yes, she tried to tell me, too. It's no use. I am always on someone's list." Jack replied, watching the charcoal turn from red to grey as it burned down.

"This seemed different somehow; more menacing."

"Well, the secret service is always watching me."

"Just be extra careful. I don't fully trust them." Bobby flipped the burgers over and added the hot dogs to the top rack.

Jack sighed, shaking his head. "You know that Jackie told Dad to get rid of her. He called us at Frank's the weekend before her death, and I never saw her again. All the political bull shit that I'm dealing with hasn't given me a moment to grieve."

"Maybe it's just as well. We don't want your wife to think you cared that much, do we?"

"No, but I did. And to top it off, she's going to Italy for a few weeks to join her sister."

"What? You better have that talk with Clint Hill before they leave." Bobby turned back to the grill, flipping the hamburgers over and placing a few buns on the top rack in place of the hot dogs he took off. When he turned back around, it was to find Jack walking toward their father.

Ethel and Jackie were bringing out the trimmings for lunch. Rose stood next to the large banquet table dipping potato salad out of the bowl with her finger.

"You're looking so gaunt, Jackie. Are you still feeling guilty about Marilyn?" Rose asked, licking mustard from her knuckle.

Jackie blushed before turning back to the kitchen. Ethel coughed to cover up the snort of laughter that threatened to escape.

After everything had been placed on the table, the women called the children to go wash up.

Bobby scooped the last patty onto the serving tray and joined the ladies. He served all of the kids first and then took his seat as they scrambled off to the deck chairs and loungers by the pool.

Joe took his place at the head of the table with Jack on his right side. He smiled all around. "It's great to be with the whole family again."

"Here, here." Rose shouted and held up her mustard stained finger. "A toast to Joe. May he have the strength of Samson."

Everyone stared at her for a moment. "Do you mean before his haircut or after, Mom?" Bobby asked.

"Well, I don't know. I just thought he was always strong."

"To Dad then," Jack said and held up his beer bottle.

"To Dad." They all agreed in unison.

Joe smiled at his family, looking at each one in turn.

Rose lifted up her plastic tumbler. "To Jack. May his heart finish grieving for his lost love and may he find true happiness once again."

There was a slight gasp from Jackie as the entire family turned to stare at her. Jack put a protective arm around her as he addressed his mother. "I don't know what you're talking about, Mother. I'm sitting beside my beautiful wife."

An expectant hush silenced the usually noisy family. Everyone watched Rose and Jack.

For a moment Rose looked confused, and then she brightened. "But you loved Marilyn. We all knew it, even Jackie knew."

"Mother . . ." Jack began.

Joe cut him off, with surprising strength in his voice, "It is forbidden from this moment forward that anyone in this family ever mention that name again."

All faces turned to the patriarch of the family, no one moving. He continued once he had made certain that everyone was paying attention. "Further, if I ever hear 'that name' even whispered, I will cut off all family funding for those involved."

Murmurs went around the table until all eyes were turned to John. Jackie was waiting for his agreement as were the others. But instead of doing what was expected of him, he stood up, put his napkin on his plate, pushed in his chair and walked into the house.

Peter propped the screen door open with his foot while he elbowed his way in the door. His hands were full of bags from the drug store in town.

Nurse Hadley was just coming into the kitchen with the dirty lunch dishes. "Hey! Where've you been?"

"I had to go to town. I yelled in the door to let you know, but I guess you didn't hear me."

"Did you get some new magazines? The ones I have are old." She poked her nose in the bag he placed on the counter.

"Of course. I got *Vogue* and *McCall's* to help you ladies pass the time. I also got a floppy hat for our patient and a pair of large sunglasses."

Nurse Hadley pulled out a few bottles of soda and a box of chocolates. "I suppose these are for Ms. Jean?"

"Those are for you. A sort of thank you for all that you're doing." Peter handed them to her with a flourish and his most charming smile.

She returned his smile. "Thanks."

Peter picked up some licorice and the other bag. "I'm going to go see how our patient is doing."

"She's had her lunch and is resting on a lounger on the deck. The fresh air is good for her."

"Yes, I think she's making great progress." Peter left the kitchen and headed out the door.

"Now Clint, on this trip to Greece it is imperative that you keep my wife away from Onassis." John sat behind the desk in the Oval office. He leaned back and stared hard at the agent in charge of his wife's safety.

"Yes, Mr. President." Clint Hill stood at attention in typical secret service stance facing the commander-in-chief. "Anything else?"

"No. Just make sure that under no circumstances are those two even in the same room together." John leaned forward in his chair and placed his elbows on the desk. "Barring that, have a good trip."

"Thank you." Clint turned and left the room.

John leaned back in his chair, ran his fingers through his hair and sighed. He picked up his pen, twirling it in his fingers and stared blankly in front of him.

Marilyn was lying on a deck chair with her face tilted up toward the sun, eyes closed, her body relaxed.

"Hi, kid."

She opened her eyes, shading them with her good hand. "Hi yourself."

He sat down at the end of her lounger. "It looks like the worst is over. How're you feeling?"

"Almost human. It's wonderful to sit out here and relax. Well, relaxing isn't exactly right. I feel helpless about Jack. I fear for him every moment."

"Well, there's something you can do to help him." Peter handed her the bag.

Digging through the contents, she frowned when she came upon the diary at the bottom. "Why did you buy this? I don't ever want to see another one again as long as I live."

"Precisely the point. They don't know you're alive or that we have the diary. I need you to make another one. Same dates, same words with a slightly different ending. Let's work on it together."

"We could just forget about it. I don't want to do this; it brings up too many awful feelings."

"Marilyn, you must if you want to save Jack. He needs your help." Peter pulled a pen from his shirt pocket and then took the original diary from his back pocket.

Marilyn stared a Peter for a long second, and set her jaw firmly. "To save Jack, I'll do it." Marilyn took the diary and opened it on her lap. She began to write in the new one.

"I'll be back in a few minutes. I need something to drink; do you?"

"Sure, a cola would be good."

"Be right back." Peter left the deck and returned to the house. He could see her writing from the service bar in the living room. Pouring her a cola and adding a few ice cubes, he made himself a highball and took them both to the deck.

"When you get to the middle, we need to talk about what you are going to say." Peter handed her the cola.

"Thanks." She took it, frowned at his drink, but didn't comment.

He sat back down and watched her while they enjoyed the early afternoon sun.

"How's Pat?" she asked, after she had finished her cola.

"I don't know. She won't answer my damn calls. The housemaid tells me she's out every time I call." Peter ran a hand through his hair.

"Is she?"

"Probably not; she doesn't want to talk to me."

"What did you do that was so upsetting to her? Did she find out about one of your girlfriends?" Marilyn turned to him.

"Much worse – she doesn't want to help me with you. Since Joe said that you couldn't see Jack anymore when you

79

both were at Sinatra's place, Pat has decided not to go against his wishes. That puts us in conflict, but I think that you and Jack are worth trying to save."

"I'm sorry to have caused you so much trouble. I doubt that I've thanked you yet." Marilyn took a deep breath. "Thank you for saving my life; thank you for helping me with Jack, and thank you for bringing me here."

"You're welcome. Now, let's just find out who wants to kill Jack so badly."

"This is going to sound crazy, but I think it has something to do with the conflict in Vietnam. The letter indicated that it was about an arms agreement. We need to find out who authorized the funds to supply the Vietnamese with guns."

"Yes, you said the letter doesn't have a signature so that makes it difficult. Can you remember what Joe was saying on the phone that night?"

"I'll try. Just let me think for a minute." Marilyn stared out at the ocean.

Peter stood up and paced the deck. He was watching her closely, waiting for any sign that she remembered more.

"Sit down; I can't think with all that thumping. You sound like an elephant."

"Thanks. I need a cigarette all right, but I was afraid you would start talking before I could get one and come back."

"By all means, go get one. I really can't think with all the noise you're making. Bring me one too."

He left and came back a few minutes later. "I'm sorry, but Nurse Hadley says you can't have one. She thinks the nicotine will throw your body into shock and possibly kill you."

"Shit. I can't smoke or drink or have any fun. Who am I now, stinking Sandra Dee?"

"Not forever. For now though, I won't let you do anything foolish because I risked my own neck to save yours."

Peter went through the French door to the coffee table in the living room, he returned within seconds with a cigarette and lighter. He turned to Marilyn as he lit it.

"Thanks Pete. You're a true friend." She wrinkled her nose as the smell assaulted her nostrils. "Now, LBJ was upset with Joe. They were having an argument. Joe said something about LBJ not minding his hands being bloody. What does that mean, do you think?"

"I don't know. Do you remember anything else?" Peter tapped the ash from his cigarette over the deck railing.

"Joe told him that if he valued his position he would take care of 'it' quickly and quietly." Marilyn rubbed her forehead with her fingertips. "I don't remember anything else right now."

"You did fine. Hopefully, Bobby will know what's going on. I'll try to call him again tomorrow night. I think there's some big birthday party at the ranch today."

"Pete, help me inside, please. I'm suddenly rather deflated."

"What a cad I've been. Of course any reference would make you sad. I'm sorry." He helped her stand up and walked her to her bedroom. "Do you need anything?"

"Just a nap. I'll be fine after some sleep."

"All right. I'll tell Nurse Hadley not to disturb you." Peter watched her walk over to the bed and then closed the door softly.

Jackie stood with John just outside the White House waiting for the pilot of the private chopper to motion her aboard.

John shifted from one foot to the other. "Now be sure and let me know if you have any trouble. I want to be certain that you girls are safe."

"I'll be fine. Mr. Hill will be with me the whole time. This trip is just what I need to make me whole again." Jackie attempted a smile.

"I hope you're right. You look tired. Have a good time." John hugged her briefly before she turned to the waiting craft.

"I will. See you in a month." Jackie tied her headscarf tighter around her chin and walked to the chopper.

As she started to board she turned around. "Oh, by the way, some of the Onassis family will join us in a week for a few days. Just thought I'd let you know." She waved as she climbed up the flight stairs.

"Who?" John yelled, but she had already ducked into the chopper.

Clint Hill tossed his suitcase onto the chopper and started to hop in. John grabbed his suit jacket and pulled him back. "You make sure and keep her away from Onassis. I just learned he'll be visiting. Do what you have too. Sleep on the floor outside her door if you must."

Clint nodded. "Yes sir, Mr. President. As he ducked under the rotors he mumbled, "God, we all know she'll do what she wants to."

Peter went back out to the lounger and sat down. He gathered the diaries and opened the original. He flipped to the middle of the book and began re-reading it.

Several pages later he ran across some information that could help.

June 3, 1962 – Today Jack told me that he had an argument with his dad. They had been talking about the election results; he wasn't sure how this subject had come up, but it got nasty. Joe told him that he had bought the election from the teamsters and Jack had to pass a bill to help the union. Jack was furious at his dad's interference and refused to pass it. Joe insisted that if he didn't, there could be trouble with the teamsters. He had promised to help them if they elected Jack.

I soothed him in the usual way and he left me with a smile. I wish that I could be his wife and then he would never be alone again.

That's interesting. Now we know there is a connection with Jimmy Hoffa and his teamsters. Peter closed the diary.

He picked up both diaries, stood up and went to the nearest telephone. He dialed, heard it ring a couple of times and then the maid answered.

"Peter here. Is Mr. Sinatra there?"

"One moment, sir. I'll see if I can find him."

"Hey, Peter. I thought you were in London."

"I'm heading out in the morning. Could I come and see you?"

"Sure. I'll be here for a few more hours. My show doesn't start until nine tonight."

"Great. Be there in an hour." Peter hung up and went in search of Nurse Hadley.

"Keep an eye on her, will ya? I need to go to town for a while."

Frank answered the door. "Come in. Want a drink?"

"Sure. Highball."

"At this hour? Well, I don't mind if you do." Frank walked over to the bar and dug out a bottle of scotch, soda and two glasses. Peter sat on a black vinyl bar stool and watched him as he prepared the two drinks.

"What brings you?" Frank asked as he handed Peter his drink.

"A week ago, there was a to-do about Marilyn being here and I just wondered what happened exactly." Peter stared into his glass without looking at his friend.

"An awkward business, that." Frank took a decanter out of its place and poured himself bourbon, his hand shaking a little as he lifted the snifter to his lips, the lie trembling them. "I went into the other room to answer the phone. It

83

was Joe Kennedy ordering me to break up his son and Marilyn. Since they were walking along the beach, I went in search of Sam and told him about this new development.

"Sam looked real uneasy like and sat on the deck waiting for them to come back. The rest of us went on with our drinking and games, but I noticed that Sam kept glancing along the beach waiting for them to return.

"Let me tell you, I was livid with Joe. I couldn't believe I was being told who could be in my house. But when I calmed down I could hardly refuse. I mean, I had fronted a bundle for Jack to be elected president and I even helped him out with bits like 'That old Jack magic...' and corny stuff like that."

Peter looked up at Frank. "Yes, I remember. I'd been doing all of the fundraising shit. I know how much you gave and that you put your name behind him. Why?"

"Politically speaking Pete, it was a good business move. He has a liberal way that will help me with what I want."

"What do you want, Frank?"

"Hell, you know what I want. Why even ask? Anyway, back to Sam. I agreed to throw her out and help keep them apart. So when they came back, all moon faced and holding hands I let her have it.

"Now, I regret ever doing it. She's dead and I can never apologize or make her understand why it happened. I tried to call her all that week, but she wouldn't answer my calls. Worse, I know that she hated me for it. She wasn't such a bad kid. She just wanted to be loved." Frank drank down his bourbon in one gulp and poured another.

"Just to be clear, I believe that she was loved and adored by many." Peter nursed his drink, twisting the glass between his hands.

"Yea. So Sam did his job, I did mine and Jack did his. He left the party a few minutes after she did early Saturday morning. I don't know if he followed her or went back to Bobby's, but he hasn't spoken to me since then."

"What about Joe? Has he called you?"

Frank nodded. "He called late that night to thank me for my help with the matter."

"Some help; but you did what you had to do. Jackie had been furious that he was flaunting Marilyn in front of her. This was no casual affair and she knew it."

Frank came around the bar and sat down on a stool next to Peter. "Joe told me that Jackie is the one who demanded that it be stopped. 'What's a father-in-law to do?' he asked. I agreed that he had to respect her wishes. That was the end of it."

"There was no choice. You did the right thing." Peter sipped the highball. "Can I ask you one more thing?"

"Shoot."

"What do you know about the teamsters and Joe? Is there a connection there?"

"Why would you think that?" Frank finished his second bourbon and sat the glass on the bar.

"No real reason. It just seems that he has upset a lot of people lately, and I was thinking since you were friends with Jimmy, that he may have said something."

"Like what?" Frank raised an eyebrow and steepled his fingers, drumming them together.

"Pat seemed to think her father was upset over something the teamsters said or did, but then he fell ill and she couldn't ask him. No big deal," Peter hedged.

"I see. Joe owes the teamsters a great deal. I hope that he'll come through with his promises or Jimmy is liable to get irate." Frank had visibly relaxed, his hands dropped into his lap and he smiled at his guest. "We don't want that now do we?"

Chapter 10

August 10, 1962

Marilyn sat in what was becoming her favorite spot. She was out on the deck, relaxing in a chair with her face to the sun, eyes closed and a slight smile on her full lips.

Nurse Hadley came through the sliding glass door with a tray of lemonade. "Ms. Jean, I brought you some refreshment."

"Thanks." Marilyn opened her eyes and held up her good hand to receive the glass. "I'd love a walk on the beach. It'd be so refreshing."

"Well, that may be true, but orders are orders." Nurse Hadley left her with a magazine and returned to the living room.

A few minutes later Peter came out with a newspaper and a couple of candy bars. He handed one of the candy bars to Nurse Hadley, opened the other and gave it to Marilyn. "You're looking much better."

"I'm getting bored just laying around all day." Marilyn accepted the offered candy and bit into it with a wrinkled brow.

"Uh oh, that look always means trouble. What're you thinking?"

"Let's go for a ride, or a walk or something. I really feel a little activity will do me a world of good." She stuck out her bottom lip and batted her eyes at him.

Laughing, Peter took her good arm and helped her to her feet. "I'll see what can be done, but we must be cautious that you're not seen."

"I know. What I need is a disguise. You could run to the drug store in the village and pick up black hair dye and some lip gloss. That should keep people from noticing me with those great sunglasses you picked up."

"Maybe," Peter hesitated, "but you have to promise to behave when I'm not around. No funny stuff."

Marilyn held up her good hand. "I promise to be good."

"All right then. I'll get what you need if you'll give me a list. I'll see if your nurse needs anything while I'm out."

"Oh thank you, Peter." Marilyn threw her right arm around him and placed a smacking kiss on his cheek.

"Don't overdo the act, kiddo or I won't buy it." Peter winked at her and led her back inside the house.

Hoover called the attorney general's office and waited to be connected.

"Kennedy?" Hoover barked into the receiver. "I've been trying to reach you for a week. "

Bobby sighed and picked up a cigarette. "What do you want now?"

"You know your friend Frank Sinatra, is hanging out with known communists. He's been seen with Sam Giancana in public of late."

"Yes, Hoover, and it's pretty certain that you've had all of the phones tapped to listen in on their conversations. You know that is a direct violation to Truman's orders."

"I know no such thing. What are you going to do about Sinatra?"

Bobby blew a smoke ring and tapped the ashes into the tray, taking a moment to reply. "Look Hoover, I'm not going to do anything about it.   You're outside your boundaries. You need to knock it off or I'll form a committee to investigate you and your sterling reputation."

"Oh, Bob, there is no need for you to investigate my reputation; it is that of your brother and our president you should be more concerned about.   I know things."   Hoover hung up the receiver and grinned at his own cunning.

An hour later, Marilyn sat in a kitchen chair while the nurse combed the jet black dye into her locks.

"I just wanted to apologize to you for thinking you were a drug addict, Ms. Jean."

"Why would you want to apologize to me?   I'd have thought the same in your shoes."   Marilyn held the hand mirror up to watch the application of the color.

"Most of the time when patients are in that shape, they're strung out on speed or worse and naturally I thought the same of you.   I'm sorry and hope we can be friendlier." Nurse Hadley had finished applying the color and placed a clear plastic cap on top of Marilyn's head.   "Now we wait for twenty minutes and check it."

The nurse went to the sink, took off her plastic gloves and washed her hands.   Then she set out a couple of plates and got the makings for tuna sandwiches out of the fridge.

"I could use a friend about now."   Marilyn finally conceded.   She turned in her chair and watched the preparations.

"Good.   I'm glad that's settled."   Nurse Hadley placed a large bowl of lettuce on the bar along with an open bag of potato chips.   "Do you want to tell me what happened to you?"

"I don't think that's such a good idea."   Marilyn hedged, picking up a chip and popping it into her mouth.

"Can't say I blame you for not trusting me, but I won't tell a soul and it might make you feel better to get it out."   She placed the bread in front of Marilyn and sat down on the stool after she handed her a glass of lemonade.

Marilyn made herself a sandwich and watched the nurse for a minute. "I doubt that you'd believe the story if I told you."

"Try me. I've been to Korea with a M.A.S.H. unit. There's not a lot that I haven't seen or heard in my life."

Taking a bite and chewing it slowly, Marilyn took a few moments to think it over. "I'd like to tell you what happened that night, but not deep details or anything."

"It's up to you." Nurse Hadley shrugged her shoulders. "I'm here if you want to unload a little or the whole sorry mess of your life."

"What you're telling me is Hoover is trying to blackmail us?" Jack strolled around the park with Bobby looking carefree, but scowling inwardly.

"Yes. He practically laughed at me. He's been tapping the phone lines of the mafia and any suspected communists. I've no doubt he's been monitoring you as well. Arrogant bastard!"

"It's all over a man."

"Isn't it always?" They laughed and toasted their lemonade glasses.

"Of course. This is a bit more complicated because this man is married and he's in a position of power." Marilyn took a long drink, watching the nurse's reaction over the rim of the glass.

"Usually they think they're more powerful than they really are. So besides the fact that he's married, you were involved with him?"

"Yes, but he wasn't happy with his wife."

"Honey, that don't make it right. But get on with the story. I'll try to reserve judgment."

"Thanks. So, I was in the wrong place at the wrong time at this big event and overheard some things that were being set in motion to hurt or even kill my man. I foolishly told a close confidant and my friend told me that I was crazy. From that comment, I kept the news to myself in fear of my life as well as his. But apparently the person I told wasn't so quiet about it.

"I'd been sick with a sinus infection and went to bed early. I felt something creepy was going on so I called another friend and told him that if I didn't make it he needed to find the letters. So I'd just hung up the phone with him when it rang again. As I answered it someone grabbed the cord from behind me and pulled it toward my neck.

"I rolled over off the bed and jumped up, but there was someone else coming out of my bathroom toward me. I was trapped by these two masked men that were determined to give me a shot of something, the needle was pointed at me and I guess I wanted to survive pretty bad.

"My heart was thumping hard as I fought back and threw my bedding at them. I actually managed to get past them into the hall. I thought I was free, but I was grabbed from behind, my arm twisted up against my back and then the other guy came rushing up next to me.

"The first guy pushed him with his free hand and he hit the wall, bounced off and hit me hard on the rebound. I heard my wrist snap and screamed in agony. I guess the one guy made the other one mad or something.

"The second guy started yelling at the one who was holding me. When he waved his fists in the air, the guy let me go to fight with the other one. They forgot about me for a moment while the other guy kept yelling, 'Stop it Sam, you clumsy oaf.' I took off again and headed for the front door. I was nearly there when I was grabbed around my upper arm and jerked backwards so hard I hit the floor.

"I kicked and struggled, but they were too much for me. After a few seconds I felt a needle going into my arm. When I woke up I was in the hospital." Marilyn wiped her mouth with a napkin and sighed.

"Wow! That's some story. You've had quite an ordeal. Explains why you were presenting like a drug addict. Tell me, what were you taking for your illness?"

"I was on a pain killer and antibiotic regimen." Marilyn watched the nurse begin to pick up the lunch mess.

"I'm sorry I didn't want to listen to you and I'm sorrier still that you were nearly killed. You seem like a nice lady." Nurse Hadley looked her watch, "Well, it's time to check your hair."

"Wow, this is so normal - telling stories, coloring my hair and having a sandwich in the kitchen. This is what real people do on a daily basis and I've missed being just a person. I'm so tired of feeling hunted. I just want to be free of it all." Marilyn wiped stubbornly at a tear that threatened to escape.

"It'll be all right now. You're safe and hopefully the healing process has begun." Nurse Hadley lifted the plastic cap and checked the hair. "Looks good. Let's rinse it and I'll dry it for you. That'll make you feel like a new woman."

After Marilyn's hair was all dried and brushed out, Nurse Hadley helped her into a clean shirt. Marilyn stood in front of a large cheval mirror and studied her reflection. She turned to the paper sack on her bed and pulled out the large round white sunglasses that Peter brought her.

Slipping them on, she smiled at the resemblance she bore to her arch rival, Jackie Kennedy. "Miss Prim and Proper would die if she could see me now."

Standing with her shoulders straight she pushed her hair behind one ear and tried to mimic her nemesis. She was laughing at her own antics when Nurse Hadley came in to check her vital statistics.

"Ms. Jean? What's so funny?"

Sobering abruptly Marilyn turned with a shy smile. "I'm just laughing at my new look. Entirely too Mrs. First Lady don't you think?" She pushed the sunglasses on top of her head and gave the nurse a wispy smile.

"Indeed. You could be her sister." The nurse sat her bag on the bed. "Now, be a good little patient and let me check your progress."

John sat across the table from Bobby while Ethel served them coffee. After she'd poured, she set the china pot on the table and left them.

"It's nice of you to invite me to dinner. I'm glad I got to see the kids again."

"They miss John Jr. and Caroline. They don't get to see each other as much as Ethel would like them to. She's so into family."

"She's a good one, your wife." John sipped his coffee.

"How's Jackie?" Bobby placed two cubes of sugar in his cup and added cream.

"Okay. She's safely ensconced with her sister Lee, for a few weeks to Ravello, Italy."

"You know, Aristotle Onassis owns a couple of villas off that coast. You did have that talk with Clint Hill before they left, didn't you?" Bobby sipped his coffee.

"Yes. I made it clear to him how we felt. I do know they'll be alone all this week with the kids."

"That's reassuring. However, I don't trust that Greek bastard any further than I can throw him." Bobby stirred his coffee with forced movements.

"I know. Jackie told me that he and Lee have been seeing quite a bit of each other."

"That's disturbing."

"Why?"

"I bet there's more to his seeing Lee than meets the eye."

"Oh, they'll be all right. We've known the family they are staying with for years, so no need to worry."

"Yes, we do. Don't you see? I think Aristotle likes your wife." Bobby stared at his brother.

"Isn't that a good thing?" John took another sip.

"Not when you consider that even the devil can be charming."

"Ms. Jean," Nurse Hadley called out. "Mr. Lawford just called and said he would be gone for a few days. He asked about your hair and I told him you were unrecognizable, so he agreed that you could take short walks along the beach if you kept the house in sight and the sunglasses on."

"Oh, how nice. Would you join me on a walk?" Marilyn asked as she pulled herself up off the couch.

"I'd love to, but only if you call me Barbara."

"Of course, but you'll call me Norma, won't you?" Marilyn was now standing beside the sliding glass door waiting for her companion to join her.

"Norma? It's hard to call a patient by their first name, but since we're friends, I guess I'll get used to it." Barbara smiled, grabbed the sunglasses for Marilyn and they started off toward the beach.

They walked in silence for a little bit before Barbara spoke up. "It's so sad about Ms. Monroe. I just loved her work. They're going to have her memorial service tonight – you know the one for the family and a public one at the gardens tomorrow afternoon. I bet that everyone will be there for that."

Marilyn kicked at the waves as they walked. "I doubt that. She was either madly loved or madly hated. Most women hated her and the men who loved her were told by angry wives to stay away."

"You sound like you knew her." Barbara sent her a puzzled look.

"I knew of her. We were in some of the same circles. She wasn't well liked by women of any kind so it was rather lonely for her if I were to guess."

"But she was so popular and the movie producers loved to have her star in their pictures. She had a lovely home and cars and went to all the best parties. Why I'd have been thrilled to be in her shoes." Barbara sounded envious.

"You wouldn't want to be in her shoes now though, would you?"

Chapter 11

August 11, 1962

Barbara placed the breakfast tray over Marilyn's knees as she sat on the couch in the living room. The nurse straightened the room while she ate.

Removing the tray, Barbara returned to the kitchen with it. Marilyn followed her. "Would you like some orange juice? I'm going to pour me some more."

"Thanks, Norma. That would be nice." Barbara started running dishwater in the sink.

Marilyn poured two glasses and tipped a sleeping capsule into one of them. She swirled it until the powder dissolved and handed it to the nurse with a smile. "Here you are. Do you want to sit and talk for a while?"

"Sure." Barbara pulled out the bar stool and perched on it. "What do you want to talk about?"

"Oh, I don't know. Tell me about you. Are you married?"

Laughing, Barbara shook her head. "No. I've never had time. Not even a steady beau."

"That's too bad," Marilyn observed as the nurse finished her juice.

"I guess." Barbara sat for a moment. "How about you? Ever married?"

97

"Yea. No big deal. It didn't work out."

"What did he do?" Barbara asked as she got up and returned to the sink to wash the breakfast dishes.

"He was into sports." Marilyn answered with forced casualness.

"Most men are. Is that why you didn't stay with him?" Barbara placed a hand over her mouth as she yawned.

"Sort of. What're we gonna do today?" Marilyn asked.

"Maybe we could go for a walk on the beach. I could really use a break. Or, how about a drive to the village later?"

"That would be great. I could use a change of scenery too. I'll go get ready while you finish the dishes."

"Yes," yawned Barbara. "Some fresh air is definitely needed."

Marilyn left the nurse and went to her bedroom. Marilyn listened as the nurse finished putting the dishes in the rack to dry and then made her way to the room down the hall.

Listening at the door, Marilyn heard the nurse kick off her shoes and the metal springs creak with her weight as she sat down on the bed. A loud moan, the rustling of the bedcovers and silence descended upon the house.

Tiptoeing out of her room, Marilyn peeked in on the nurse. She lay with mouth open sound asleep.

Smiling like a Cheshire cat, Marilyn turned back into her own room and began the tedious job of dressing herself. After forty five minutes, the hose were finally in place and she slipped on the pumps.

Satisfied that the nurse was still sleeping, she put a few finishing touches to her hair, donned a wide black hat with a veil and went in search of the car keys.

At precisely two o'clock the minister stood in front of the podium and waited for the mourners to gather round. A framed picture of a serious Marilyn set just off to the left with mounds of flowers underneath the tripod.

Marilyn stood away from the group behind a large oak tree. She watched as several people she had worked with made their way toward her memorial.

There was Frank Sinatra with Juliet Prowse, her friend and ex-husband Joe DiMaggio, Peter and Patricia Lawford, Dr. Greenson, all the movie producers she had ever worked with as well as the directors and crews. Several news media were on the scene taking stills and footage of the events.

All of the Rat Pack were present: Dean Martin with his wife Jeanne Biegger, Joey Bishop, Tony Curtis and Janet Leigh. A little way from this crowd were Bobby Darin and Sandra Dee.

"I'm sorry, Sandra. I didn't mean any harm. How'd I know you'd show up at my funeral?" Marilyn whispered to the birds chirping in the trees.

The minister began, but his words couldn't be understood from her position so she looked over the crowd with thoroughness.

"Men, mostly men. Not one presidential aide, not one Kennedy brother. I suppose Joe would never allow that. Who am I kidding, neither would Jackie."

She stood with silent tears running down her cheeks. She snuck closer to the podium behind a large bush in the garden.

As Joe DiMaggio was getting up to speak, he stroked her picture for a moment before standing in front of the podium.

"I loved Marilyn. I could never live with her. It's no fun being married to an electric light."

A slight snort of laughter was heard as he continued. "What you may not have known is I've never gotten over her. I never will."

Joe left with his head bowed.

"I loved you too, Joe, but not like you loved me." Marilyn dabbed at the tears flowing freely now.

Frank stood up to say his part, looking at the ground as Joe walked by.

Clearing his throat, Frank began. "Everyone knows how sexy Marilyn was. We all adored her and she has left a gaping hole in our hearts. Marilyn was a very generous woman and that is what made her beautiful."

Marilyn came even closer as the minister said the final prayer, covering her face with her good hand to keep from being seen.

The service was over and the mourners began to disperse. Peter and Pat stood nearest the podium as the others made their way back to the Rolls, Mercedes and Caddies parked along the street.

Frank and Juliet approached the Lawfords as the minister shook hands with them. As Frank turned to Peter, two men stepped from behind the awning that had shielded the service from the blinding Hollywood sun.

Marilyn shivered despite the heat of the August afternoon. The booming voice of one of the men sounded oddly familiar as he greeted Frank.

"Tragic, just tragic," Sam smirked as he shook Frank's hand.

Now that the service was at an end, the lowered voices were raised to a normal level and Marilyn could hear Frank's enthusiastic greeting. "Sam my man, we need to talk."

Marilyn's knees buckled and she pressed heavily against the shrub. Leaning her head into her knees, she listened to the normal conversation about her death.

"It's a shame. She was so talented." Frank was saying.

"Yea, she was, but everyone has to go sometime." Sam replied calmly.

How can he stand there talking to Frank like he had nothing to do with my murder? How can he be so calm and calculating? Marilyn slowly sank further into herself on the ground, weak and trembling.

Patricia caught the movement out of the corner of her eye and whispered to Peter, "Who's that over there by the shrub?"

"I don't know. Let's go check it out. Excuse us, fellas. We're going to take a short walk around."

"We'll catch up to you later." Frank shook Peter's hand and smiled to Pat.

As they approached her, Peter shook his head. "It can't be. Surely she wouldn't do such a thing."

Pat watched as the young woman lifted her arm up to grab hold of a branch, the other hand hung uselessly in a sling around her neck. "She wouldn't be that bold, would she?"

"Looks like it. Hurry up before someone else sees her."

As they reached Marilyn and lifted her to her feet a photographer snapped the trio and took off.

Marilyn was shaking as Peter shielded her from any more cameras. "What do you think you're about?" he grated in her ear.

"I thought I could find out who had attacked me and I was right." Marilyn forced herself to stand rigid in an effort to stop the shaking.

"What?"

"Those men that Frank's talking with are the two goons that tried to kill me. One of them is Sam Giancana. I'm sure he was one of them." Marilyn swooned in his embrace.

"Pat, she's fainted. Help me get her to the trees over there. We've got to hide her until everyone's gone."

They lifted her around the waist and half dragged, half carried her to the safety of the trees. Pat placed her skirt down around her knees as Peter laid her on the ground.

Moaning, Marilyn opened her eyes. "What happened?"

"Nothing much. You fainted." Pete held her shoulder to the ground to keep her from rising.

"Oh my God," Pat placed a hand over her mouth, "you're the spitting image of Jacqueline. Were you looking at the camera when he took our picture?"

"I don't think so. My head was down."

"But it'll still say you're Mrs. Kennedy in the tabloids. Oh Lord. We're in for it now." Pat began to pace around the small area. "Dad's been acting really weird and paranoid. He's been staying in his study all the time and won't talk to Mom without yelling at her."

"If they print the picture, what will we tell everyone?" Peter ran his hand through his hair.

"Why did you have to come here?" Pat wagged a finger in front of Marilyn's nose.

"Don't you realize how foolish this was? If someone recognizes you we could all be in serious danger." Peter pulled Marilyn to a sitting position.

"Don't either of you care that I've identified who tried to kill me? Isn't that worth something?" Marilyn asked, pushing the hat back into place and straightening the veil with her good hand.

"Of course we care, but this is hardly the place to go accusing your attackers and exposing the fact that you're still alive." Peter pulled her up to a standing position and then placed a steadying hand under her elbow.

"I wouldn't do such a thing, Peter. I only wanted a little fun." She shook her head. "I mean, how many people get the chance to see who came to their funeral?" Marilyn pouted.

"Not many." Peter smiled, but Pat still grimaced at them.

"You've risked all that we've tried to hide just for a silly whim. Really, Marilyn, I thought you had more sense than that." Pat shook with emotion.

Pat stormed off before Marilyn could answer.

"You've done it now. I'd just gotten her to agree that we would ask Rose some questions and now you've scared her out of it." Peter shook his head. "Can you walk?"

"Yea, I think so." Marilyn tried a step and succeeded without any trouble.

"Everyone is walking away now so we should be safe. Where's Nurse Hadley?"

"She decided to have a nice long nap this afternoon." Marilyn walked a little quicker, leaving Peter to catch up.

"Oh really? That doesn't seem like something the steadfast rules and regulations Army nurse would do - sleeping on duty."

"She's been really tired. I'm wearing her out. What can I say?" she shrugged.

"We'll see about this." Peter stared at her and then led her away without another word. Helping her into Nurse Hadley's car, he closed the door after she had situated herself behind the wheel.

"Good thing this is an automatic," he observed.

"Yes. It would've been hell if it was a stick shift." Marilyn agreed.

"Get yourself back into hiding. I'll check out Sam Giancana, but I don't know the other one."

"When they were fighting over me I heard one of them call the other 'Sam'. I'm certain he's the one who gave me the shot. He was also at Frank's lodge the weekend before I was 'killed'."

"Go back home and don't leave again until I call you." Peter turned back toward Pat, starting to walk away. After a few steps he looked back over his shoulder. "And that's an order, kiddo."

Dr. Greenson pulled Sam to the side. "Did you find that diary?"

"No. I've followed Lawford, but he just goes to a bungalow to entertain his women friends."

"Is he even looking for the damned thing?"

"Not so far as I can tell. He seems mighty engrossed with this woman at the beach."

Chapter 12

Peter pulled the Rolls Royce to a stop in front of their ranch house style mansion in Beverly Hills. He got out of the car and opened the door for Pat.

"Thank you." she nodded to him as she gracefully stepped out.

Peter swept her into his arms before she could retreat. "Darling, thank you for coming with me. I know it'll be hell if your father finds out."

"You know that's not the half of it, Peter."

Peter chuckled. "He would be hard pressed to deny the publicity we can generate for the Kennedys with our appearance at the memorial service."

"He can deny anything he likes and he probably will be furious. See if you can get the negatives to that picture. I don't like to think it will show up in the tabloids in the next few days, but it might." Pat smiled at her husband with the security of a woman who knows he'll succeed in his mission. "I have to go in now."

She hugged him closer and kissed his cheek before gently untangling his arms from around her waist. "Cheer up, darling. Once those negatives have been placed in our safety deposit box, we can both rest better."

"I'll see what can be done. I saw the rag's name on the press tag so it shouldn't be too difficult to pay them off."

"That's a good darling." She patted his cheek.

"I'm going to the studio. I shan't be late for dinner." Peter whistled as he got back behind the wheel of the car.

Peter drove through the wide gates of Fox Studios without slowing at the check point. The guard smiled and waved at him as he passed.

He pulled into his parking slot, turned off the ignition and reached in the glove compartment for the bogus black diary. He stuffed it into the breast pocket of his suit, got out of the car, and walked with determined purpose into the dressing areas.

Peter went down the long hallway and up the stairs to the women's dressing rooms. He knew where Marilyn's was located and hoped the ever efficient cleaning crew hadn't taken her things and hidden them in some attic already.

Reaching the door that still had her name and a star under it, he placed his hand on the knob just as the door to Jane Russell's dressing room opened.

He dropped his hand and stood with head bowed.

"Ah, Pete. Don't mourn her so." Jane soothed him, placing her hand on his shoulder. "I know you were pals. I'm sorry. We're all gonna' miss her, dahlin'."

Peter lifted his head until his eyes were level with hers. "Thanks. I really appreciate your concern."

"I respected her work. We had a great time on our last picture." Jane patted his shoulder once more and made her way down the stairs.

Once her head disappeared, he turned the knob and rushed into the little room. It was dark and he bumped into something, sending it crashing to the floor.

Flipping on the light switch, he realized he had knocked over a giant vase with no less than four dozen white roses.

He pulled it upright and searched for a card. "Condolences, The Wainwrights."

The entire room was covered with flowers while the make-up table had cards that overflowed onto the chair. "What in the world?" Peter looked at the cards, all of it fan mail from people crying with grief for their lost star.

Shaking his head, he looked for a likely place to say he found the diary. After a moment he decided that the bottom of the small closet where her shoes were all in boxes would be the best bet.

Leaving the room exactly as he'd found it, Peter went back to his car. As he pulled off the lot he phoned Greenson's office.

Jackie and Lee sat on the beach in Italy watching the children build sandcastles. The waves broke over the sand closer to the children with every incoming tide. A diver popped his head out of the water and swam to shore.

"Uh oh. What do you think he's up to?" Lee asked Jackie as the diver came out of the ocean and approached them.

"No good." Jackie watched him through her sunglasses.

He was within a few feet when he dropped his tank and pulled off his hood to reveal a good looking Greek Adonis.

"Hey, Ari." Lee jumped up to embrace her friend. "What brings you here?"

"I wanted to visit two of the most beautiful women anywhere in the world, but I couldn't bring the media circus with me, so I chose to dive from my yacht and swim to you." He unzipped his wetsuit to the waist.

"Fit as always." Lee winked at him.

"I try to impress the ladies." Ari sat down between them.

"You do a great job." Lee batted her eyes at him.

"Why thank you. How are you enjoying the villa?"

"It's wonderful. Everything is first class." Lee smiled at him, but his attention was focused on Jackie.

"Aren't you going to greet me Jacqueline?" Ari took her hand and gave it a quick kiss.

"Hello, Aristotle. How have you been?" She smiled in return while pulling her hand back gently from his grasp.

"Excellent. Now, how are you holding up as the First Lady of the United States? Must be quite a job for such a delicate woman."

"It is rather exhausting. Thank you for allowing us this time here. I really needed the break, but everywhere we go around the village, we are bombarded with photographers. It's keeping me firmly planted on this beach. Otherwise there would be no peace for me or the children." She put her hand up to her eyes, shading them from the sun to get a better view of Caroline holding John Jr.'s hand as they waded in the surf.

"They're adorable, just like the Mother, yes?" Ari moved a little closer to her.

"Well, how long are you staying? Would you like a drink?" Lee broke in.

Ari turned his attention to the older sister. "I won't be staying long enough for a drink, but thanks. I must get back before someone spies me here."

He stood up, just managing to zip the front of his suit when a small boat approached and a bright light blinked with a sudden pop of the flash bulb.

The trio stared at each other until Ari broke the silence. "Well at least my back was turned away. Now they'll only speculate about my identity."

Jackie crossed her arms, glaring at the retreating boat. "Great. If this gets back home, I'm certain John will be furious."

"I'm sorry, Mrs. Kennedy; I certainly didn't want to bring any unpleasantness into your life. I hope you'll forgive me for my impetuous visit."

He zipped the hood back into place, donned his air tank, saluted the women and walked back into the waves.

"Gee, Jacks. You didn't have to be so rude to him. He's an absolute hunk and I want him to marry me." Lee poked out her bottom lip in a pout.

"My comments won't keep you from getting him if that's what he wants." She stood up and motioned for her children to come to her. They walked back up the slope to the house.

Bobby knew this meeting with his father was going to be difficult. He summoned all of his diplomatic charm and opened the door to his father's study.

"Hello, Dad." Bobby announced his presence as he came to stand in front of his father's desk.

"Robert." Joe Kennedy looked up for a second, and then returned to the papers on his desk.

"I've come to talk to you, Dad. I need a minute," Bobby insisted as he sat down in the deep leather chair in front of his father's desk.

"Well, that's all you're getting, I'm catching up on paperwork and there seems to be mountains of it." Joe continued working.

"This is real important or I wouldn't be here. You see, I know about Hoffa." Bobby crossed his legs at the ankles as he waited for his dad's reaction.

Joe slowly put his pen down and shifted the papers to a corner of his desk. He looked up to find Bobby staring back at him. "I see."

"I'm glad you do. Now I'd like to understand what you've been about. Why are you paying Jimmy Hoffa?"

"That's my business and none of yours. What're you doing getting into my affairs?" Joe slammed his fist down on the desk.

Looking as sheepish as a kid caught in his mother's wallet, Bobby shrugged, "You know how it is, Pop. Everybody knows everything in this arena. I'm the attorney general. It was bound to come to me sometime."

"That's not how you know. Why not tell me the truth?" Joe leaned back in his chair and sat tapping his index fingers together.

"I don't care to argue with you, Father, but you're the one who needs to do the explaining, not I." Bobby leaned forward. "I've enough evidence to cause you real harm, so come clean."

"You're hard son, real hard. It's a shame that we've ended up on opposite sides of the political fence. When did you grow a conscious? You and John used to believe me without question and do as good sons will. Follow in their father's wake." Joe shook his head. "Where did I go wrong?"

"I think it was when you paid to have John elected and then put me in as attorney general. Once we were sworn in we had to do what was right for the American public, and organized crime is just plain wrong."

"Lots of men better than you have toadied to the mob and prospered because of it. That's where I accumulated much of our wealth and you didn't have any problems with that in the past."

"I didn't know then, but I know now and you must understand it is my sworn duty to bring a halt to such crime rings." Bobby placed his elbows on the desk, leaning closer to Joe. "Tell me Dad, why are you paying Jimmy Hoffa?"

"I'm not really paying Hoffa; it's the teamsters that are getting the money. Hoffa just collects it for them."

"Why?"

"They're the real reason John was elected to the presidency. Frank ordered them to vote for John, telling them they'd be well paid with favors once he was in office."

"Oh, good Lord." Bobby sat forward.

"Now you've turned against me by going after the mobsters. Sam Giancana has ordered more and more money from me to keep it hush hush." Joe leaned his head in his hands and ran shaky fingers in his receding hair.

"Give me a few days to work this out, Dad. You know that whatever you are or who you've become, I'll always be a true Kennedy and protect my kin."

Joe Kennedy looked at his son. "I hope you can do something about it, but I won't hold out much hope."

Peter arrived at Dr. Greenson's office with the diary in hand. Tossing it on the psychiatrist's desk, Peter smiled. "Here it is, Greenson."

"Well, this is good news. Now I can deliver it." Dr. Greenson snatched it up and turned the pages. "Where's the letters? I need them."

"There weren't any letters with it." Peter told him in all honesty.

"You must go back and search. Where did you find this?" Dr. Greenson held up the black book.

"Her dressing room closet in a box of shoes." Peter stood facing Dr. Greenson, clenching his hands together to keep them from visibly shaking.

"Did you search thoroughly?" Dr. Greenson threw the book onto the desk.

"Yes, well as much as I could with all the flowers and fan mail cluttering every available space." Peter walked to the window and stood staring out.

"Go back – look again. I must have the letters." Dr. Greenson looked a bit green. "Don't you understand? It means everything."

"I'll go look again."

"Thank you. You're not such a bad sort, Lawford. I'm glad we're in this thing together."

"Yes. . .together." Peter left the office and shut the door behind him.

As Peter got into the car his phone began to ring. Taking the handset and pressing the talk button Peter answered, somewhat out of breath. "Hello."

"Hang on, I can't talk here. Give me a second to get out of the parking lot." Releasing the button, he switched the receiver to his other ear, placed the key in the ignition and started the car.

He backed out of the spot and moved quickly to the gated exit. He nodded to the parking attendant as he turned onto Rodeo Drive.

Peter pressed the talk button. "Hey Bobby, I'm finally on the road. What's up?" Peter listened as he drove. "Let's meet tomorrow. I've lots to tell you, too."

He stopped at a traffic light. "Yes, I'll come to DC. That'll make it easier for you. I'll book a flight tonight and we can meet for an early lunch at our favorite Italian restaurant. Say eleven?"

Bobby returned to the oval office and walked in on his brother's press conference. He waited in the back of the room until everyone had left, then he opened the door that led into the private chambers of the presidential office.

"Hey, Jack," he called out as he came into the room.

"Bobby, what brings you here?"

"I needed to talk to you. Is there somewhere that we can talk privately?"

"We can talk in here." John sat down on a sofa near the fireplace in his office.

"Are you sure? I've heard rumors that the entire White House has been bugged." Bobby still stood waiting for an answer.

"Of course I'm sure. I'm the one who had the place bugged. Something isn't quite right and I intend to find out what." John motioned for Bobby to have a seat in the chair across from the couch.

"You're looking awfully worried. Is it this organized crime ring you're after?" John leaned back with deliberate slowness.

"I see your back is still killing you. Didn't the last procedure offer any relief?" Bobby leaned toward his brother, a rare showing of sympathy between them.

"Not much," John shrugged, "but what did you want to talk about?"

"Dad. He's in real trouble with the teamsters. He's been paying them off since they helped you get elected."

"What? I knew Jackie's tea parties were a big help in getting me elected. But Dad bribing the teamsters?" John raised his eyebrows in question.

"Don't sound so shocked. Frank offered the votes of the teamsters to put you over the top and Dad accepted. Now he's paying off Sam Giancana and Jimmy Hoffa to keep the matter under wraps." Bobby now leaned back against the soft cushions of the chair.

"But, why should he pay them?"

"You really are naïve aren't you? They figure with Dad paying to keep them hushed up that we won't go after them to incriminate our own father."

"Good Lord! What should we do about it?"

"I don't know. I may see if Dad's old connection with the FBI will gain us some insight. I'll let you know as I find out." Bobby stood to leave.

"I wonder if that's why Dad had a stroke." John slowly rose from the couch and faced Bobby.

"It could be. I'd imagine he's been under a great deal of stress with us turning away from him and LBJ. I'm glad you're with me against the crime rings. They need to be stopped even with Dad firmly enmeshed in them." Bobby shook his brother's hand and then suddenly embraced him in a bear hug. "I'm sorry about Marilyn. Now that her funeral is over maybe you can get on with your life."

"I don't have much choice do I? Jackie's been spending more than usual while pretending to be the devoted and attentive wife. Did she have something to do with it, do you think?"

"Surely not Jackie. She's got her reasons for wanting Marilyn out of the way, but I don't think she's capable of going that far." Bobby let go of John's hand and moved back a step.

"I certainly hope not or there will still be a divorce. The first ever in the Kennedy family." John moved over to his desk and sat down. "Now don't worry about me and get busy saving Dad's ass. He's going to need it."

Chapter 13

<u>*August 12, 1962*</u>

Ethel rushed into the Brown Derby restaurant tugging off her hat and gloves. She waved to Pat in a corner booth and forced her way through the crowd to the table.

"Hi ya, Pat. I'm so sorry that I'm a little late." Ethel slid into the seat opposite her sister-in-law.

"No problem. I just got here myself."

"What'll ya have?" The waitress appeared from nowhere.

"Two iced teas, with the specials, Velma. Thanks."

"I'm dying to ask so I'll just dive right in. Have you gotten the negative of that picture yet?" Ethel asked.

"Not yet, but Peter is going to take care of it this afternoon. He managed to buy the paper off and they agreed not to print it. He's going to stop by and pick up the film later."

"That's a relief. I can't imagine how Jackie or Joe would have taken that bit of publicity." Ethel picked up her flatware, unwound the napkin from around the utensils, and demurely placed the napkin on her lap.

The waitress placed the tea in front of the ladies and plunked down a bowl with lemon wedges in it.

"Thanks." Pat smiled, picked up a lemon wedge and squeezed it into her glass.

"Well, since we got that little matter out of the way, have you heard from the third person in that photograph?" Ethel poured two teaspoons of sugar into her tea and stirred it with her spoon.

"Peter was pretty rough on her after everyone had left. I doubt if she'll call for a few days, yet knowing her temper...."

"Speaking of tempers, I overheard your favorite sister-in-law yelling at your dad a few weeks before the 'death'." Ethel took a sip of her tea.

"Do tell; it's not nice of you to bait me." Pat chided.

"It wasn't too long after Joe came home from the hospital. He was still confined to his bed with doctor ordered peace and quiet. John and Jackie arrived just after Bobby and I did.

"We had already visited with him so we stepped outside and let them go in. A few minutes went by and John left to go see Rose in the kitchen.

"Bobby and I looked at each other when Jackie didn't come out after a minute or two. Suddenly, Jackie was screaming. 'Well Joseph Fitzgerald Kennedy, if you don't do something with that . . . that actress, I'll have something done with her'." Ethel paused to take another sip of her tea.

"You can't just leave me here. What did Dad say?" Pat leaned closer to Ethel, nearly knocking over the bowl of lemon wedges.

"He didn't have an opportunity to say anything that we heard because out comes Jackie, storming and stomping like an enraged bull running down the streets of Madrid.

"Rose and John rushed in from the kitchen to see what the commotion was all about. Poor Rose still had a half pealed potato in her hand." Ethel smiled, "Your mother is such a sweet person. She went over to Jackie and tried to calm her down. Of course, Jackie pulled herself together and put on her 'I'm a sympathetic person' face and everything settled down."

Pat snorted. "You know that wasn't the first time that has happened, her demanding Dad do something." Ethel and Pat sat in silence as the weight of the situation hung in the air.

Velma placed two lunch plates on the table in front of the women and refilled their tea glasses.

Pat took a bite of her tuna salad sandwich and chewed over the situation. "It's nice that she can try to be sweet to Mom at least. I'm glad to hear that she's been better to Jack lately. Maybe it's guilt over Marilyn."

"Possibly, but she's still spending a ton of money. She's having the clothiers come into the White House with thousands of dollars' worth of goods for her to choose from. I didn't think even her family could afford that." Ethel munched a potato chip.

"Well, let me tell you she would absolutely die if she could see Marilyn with her hair dyed black and those wide sunglasses. I swear from a distance at the memorial service I thought it was Jackie, come to gloat that her arch enemy was gone." Pat wiped at her mouth with a napkin.

"I can't wait to get a glimpse of that. I'm sure it's much better than that photo she took pretending to be the First Lady. Imagine looking like Mrs. Kennedy all the time. That must be a shock to her whenever she looks in the mirror. Talk about irony." Ethel chuckled as she nibbled her sandwich.

"Yes. She can't have Jack as 'that...that actress' or his real wife's double. It's not a good position to be in."

"Not at all - poor girl. Speaking of poor girls, are you going to go see your mom this weekend?" Ethel sipped her tea.

"Yeah. What about you? Do you want to come with me?" Pat finished her sandwich and methodically began on her chips.

"Sure. We could ask her more about Jackie and see if she has heard anything else from Joe."

"Sounds like an excellent plan. We can take her to get a new bathing suit and treat her to lunch." Pat grinned. "I'm glad you'll be there. You know how Mom can be."

"Jackie? What is this nonsense in the tabloid? Who is that man?" John demanded.

"John, calm down. You'll only aggravate your back if you continue to yell."

Taking a couple of deep breaths he tried again. "All right, Jackie. Who is that in the photo with you and Lee on the beach?"

"Don't be so childish. It was Aristotle come to pay a visit to Lee. She wants to marry him, you know. He only stayed a few minutes, but the press keeps following me so we're not getting any rest."

"Agree to a press photo shoot if they'll leave you alone. I'll have your secretary set it up."

"That's a wonderful idea."

"So, Lee is the one he's courting?"

"Don't fret so much, John. We're fine. I'd put the kids on, but they're already asleep. We've mailed you post cards."

"Take care of yourself, Jackie, and for God's sake no more pictures with unidentified men."

Bobby entered the Italian restaurant to find that Peter reserved a secluded back booth. He'd already ordered wine, lasagna and bread with a large salad.

"How did Greenson accept the new diary?" Bobby nodded a greeting as he sat down.

"Fine. He never suspected anything, but he threw a hissy over the letters. I thought there was only one letter and some memos. Any ideas?" Peter speared a piece of lettuce and stuffed it into his mouth.

"No, but I can find out a lot easier than you can. I'm close to discovering who sent that first letter for certain. We know that LBJ is suspect, but who else might be involved?"

"I think that maybe Sam Giancana is a major player as well as Hoffa. Did you get any information from Joe?" Peter shifted in the booth.

"Yea. He said that it was the teamsters who wanted the money as payoff for giving their vote to Jack."

"I should visit with Frank again and see what he knows about this. Jack hasn't spoken to him since the weekend before her 'death' so I don't know if I'll make any head way in that direction or not. I could always talk to Ava Gardner. She generally knows what Frank is up to."

"Don't do that. We don't need anyone else involved in this. It's pretty complicated as it is." Bobby sat shaking his head. "I'm just about up to my neck in sorting out this mess. I think the best thing for you to do is disappear for a day or two and keep your head low. I'll talk to Johnson's secretary and see if I can sweet talk anything out of her."

"Do you think I should go visit our patient?"

"Yea, you can probably ask her some questions that maybe she can answer now." Bobby sipped his water.

"Good luck with LBJ's secretary and if you need help with the teamsters let me know." Peter continued to down the lasagna while Bobby sat playing with a bread stick.

"I'm really concerned about Dad. He doesn't seem to think he's in danger, but he's already paid out hundreds of thousands of dollars. If he refuses to pay them anymore money, I'm sure he'll be targeted. I'm going to the FBI on this one."

Late that evening Bobby arrived at the house in Malibu. "Hi honey, I'm home." He flipped on the bedroom light and stepped over to the bed to kiss his sleepy wife.

"Hey yourself.   You didn't tell me you were coming in tonight or I'd have waited up for you." Ethel pushed a stray lock of hair out of her face and smiled at him.

"I like to see you sleeping. You're so cute with your arm and foot thrown out of the covers." Sitting on the bed, Bobby swept her into his arms and hugged her close.

"How'd the meetings go today?" Ethel drew back a little to look at her husband.

"Peter's good, but Dad's in trouble. He needs protection."

"From Hoffa?" Ethel kissed Bobby lightly on the cheek, "Do you want some milk and cookies?"

"Nah, I just want to come to bed. It's been a rough day and I can't think anymore."

"All right. I'll scoot over. You didn't answer my question. Does your dad need protection from Hoffa?" Ethel repeated as she smoothed the covers on her side.

"Yea, and more likely the entire mafia. I think he's in it big, but he's lost his edginess."

"I've every faith that you'll take care of him. Now come here and let me take care of you, tiger." Ethel pulled him into her arms and smothered him with kisses.

Ethel and Pat stood outside the dressing room door listening to Rose while she tried on bathing suits. "I really hate red. Why did you give me a red one, Nellie?"

"I didn't, Mother. The sales clerk added that one." Ethel glared at Pat who stood with her hand over her mouth chuckling softly.

"Well take it back. It'll make me look like a fire truck. All that's needed is a siren on my bathing cap and I'll look a complete fool." Rose tossed the offending garment over the door to the dressing area.

"Yes, Mother." Pat giggled as she handed it to the shocked sales girl who'd been standing at the ready near the stall. Pat made a circular motion with an index finger in the air around her ear for the clerk's benefit.

Smiling her understanding, the sales girl took the suit and went to return it to the rack.

"Now it's gone.   Have you found anything you like?" Ethel asked with forced patience edging her voice.

"I do so wish I had Mrs. Hoffa's figure.   Thinner than sliced bread she is and I'm like an entire pumpernickel loaf. I don't even like pumpernickel.   Don't order any at lunch, okay Nellie?"   Rose tossed a white suit with huge flowers over the door.   "This looks like a garden exploded on it.   It seems like something that...that little chicken would wear. No, that's not quite right."

"Do you mean, Lady Bird, the vice president's wife?" Pat asked, puzzled.

"Yes. That's it. I told Joe I never wanted her in my house again," Rose hollered from the inside of the dressing room. "Who picked this thing anyway?"

"Ethel." Ethel replied with a straight face.

Pat laughed out loud for one brief moment before covering it with a coughing fit.

"Well, we never should have invited her," Rose's muffled voice came through the door. "She's never been part of the family.   Nellie here is much prettier and considerably curvier.   Are you sure you don't need a new bathing suit, dear?"

Ethel shook her head at Pat. "No, Mother. I just got one when we arrived in California. Bob. . .Robert really likes me in it."

Pat left the dressing area and could be heard laughing hysterically just outside.

Rose emerged from the dressing room wearing a black bathing suit with a wrap around her waist. She held out her arms and twisted left then right for Ethel's approval.

"Very nice, Mother. I think you should get that one."

Pat reappeared. "Oh bravo. That's it!"

"Well, it's not like Mrs. Hoffa's, but she's really young. She can get away with the kind that has two pieces. Such a lovely girl. If Teddy weren't married I'd set those two up."

"But Mother, isn't 'Mrs. Hoffa' married too?"

Rose shook her head. "I don't think so, dear."

"Most women with the title 'Mrs.' have a 'Mr'. Are you certain there's not a Mr. Hoffa?" Pat tried to cover her exasperation with a limp smile.

"I suppose there might be, but I don't think I've ever seen him." Rose returned to the dressing room to put on her day clothes.

Pat and Ethel looked at each other for a moment, and then shrugged simultaneously.

An hour later the three women were sipping hot tea at the Tea Room on Fifth Avenue.

"Isn't this nice, Mother?" Patricia wiped her mouth with a lacy linen napkin.

"Yes, so nice to be able to leave Joe for a while and be with the girls." Rose sighed with contentment.

"Indeed it is. How is Joe feeling?" Ethel asked politely after her father-in-law.

"He's a bit tetchy. I got the cutest little tea pot with little matching cups. They're shaped like the faces of monkeys and the tea pot's spout is the mama monkey's tail and the handle made up her arms – it was a whole family."

"That's great, Mother."

"He came in and smashed little Georgie and threatened to smash Banana, but I took him away before he could dash it on the floor. I had to have a little funeral for the broken remains of poor Georgie." Rose wiped a tear from her eye with her napkin.

"Oh Mother, I'm so sorry." Pat came around to Rose and gave her a big hug. "Maybe we can find another cup to match the set."

"It's no use. The mama monkey would never accept it. I'll be all right. I just worry about Mona grieving herself to death over the loss of Georgie."

"Well, I'm sure that she will be okay once some time passes." Ethel patted Rose's hand gently.

"I hope Joe thinks this new suit is good for swimming in the river. He keeps telling me he's going to take me to swim with the fishies and I certainly hope we go soon. It's so hot."

"Yes, Mother, it is." Pat exchanged a worried look with Ethel.

Chapter 14

August 14, 1962

Bobby sat in the cluttered office of Agent Rex Stansel, waiting with concealed impatience for the dratted man to get off the phone with his wife.

"Ahem." He cleared his throat.

The agent held up a finger and rolled back in his chair. "Okay darling, I'll get two filet mignons on my way home. Yes, I did write it down. I must go now. . .really I won't."

The FBI agent replaced the receiver in its cradle. "Now what can I do for you, Mr. Kennedy?"

"Under normal circumstances I would have requested that you come to my office, but this is a private matter. It involves someone you'd dearly love to pin something on . . . and my father."

"I'm listening." Agent Stansel leaned his elbows on the desk and intertwined his fingers. "I respected your dad when he was with the agency. He's in some sort of trouble?"

"Let's just say that if my father has earned your respect, you might be able to help us out with removing a certain member of the teamsters from the streets temporarily."

"Would this person be of any consequence to the teamster's movement?"

"Yes, he would indeed. I think we both know who we're talking about here." Bobby uncrossed his legs and looked for a place to straighten them out.

"Do you have a plan, sir?" Agent Stansel asked, leaning in closer to hear the answer.

Frank sat on a bench in Central Park feeding the pigeons. After a few minutes Sam perched himself on the other end of the bench.

"Hey Sammy. Whatcha been up to?" Frank greeted his old friend.

"Just working on the next big thing." Sam answered with a shrug.

"I don't want to hear the details pertaining to your latest little project. We need to talk about something potentially big."

"Okay with me. What's up?" Sam watched as several pigeons landed at their feet to eat the peanuts Frank tossed on the ground.

"I've been hearing some very distressing things about your present presidential leader at the teamsters." Frank broke another shell open and tossed the nut to a waiting bird.

"Hoffa?"

"Yeah."

"What about him?" Sam turned to face Frank.

"I've just been concerned about a brief conversation I had with Peter a few days ago." Frank hedged his bet. "He wondered if the teamsters were okay with Joe Kennedy."

"Really?" Sam raised an eyebrow. "Well, he hasn't paid out nearly what he claimed he would. I know that from Hoffa."

Now it was Frank's turn to raise an eyebrow. "I find that completely out of character for the old man. He's always paid his debts promptly."

"Maybe he hasn't because he's been sick."

126

"Nah, he would have paid even if he was dying. He's a man of honor. It just doesn't add up."

Sam stood up and wiped the seat of his pants with a massive paw. "Do you want me to do some checking on what's been paid so far?"

"Yeah, I think that's wise. Other rumors indicate that he's been skimming union dues off the top."

"I'll get back to you."

Jackie and Lee sat on the deck outside the villa sipping drinks and watching as the sun set over the ocean.

Lee sighed. "I think your photo shoot went well. We haven't seen nearly as many photographers this last week."

"Yes, but its galling to have to give them a schedule with our daily agenda."

"True, but now I can invite Ari out and no one will be the wiser. This will work very well. Stas won't mind if I engage in a little activity." Lee stretched her arms over her head with a mighty yawn. *There are benefits being married to a prince.* Rising, she turned to her sister. "Yes, that's an excellent idea."

Frank arrived in front of the brownstone house a little before five p.m. He took the steps two at a time and rang the bell.

Rose Kennedy answered the door. "Hello, can I help you?"

"Uhm, is Mr. Kennedy here?" Frank asked struggling to keep his eyes focused on her face.

"No sir, he won't be in for another hour. We're going to the park with our grandchildren so I really must hurry." Rose started to close the door in his face.

"Mrs. Kennedy, you may not remember meeting me, but I'm Frank Sinatra. I just came to ask your husband a few quick questions, but I bet a lovely lady such as yourself could be most helpful to me." Frank smiled at her.

Rose opened the door for him. "Do come in, Mr. Frank. I'd be delighted to help you."

"Thank you, Mrs. Kennedy. What a lovely . . . er . . . um outfit your wearing."

"My daughter sent this to me. She said it would be cool and comfortable in the heat. Do you like the color?" Rose twirled around in front of him, the sheer skirt of her bathing suit minutely danced in her wake, her red Wizard of Oz slippers sparkled with the radiance of the finest rubies on 5th Avenue. She pointed up to the hat on her head; it was a pale blue with large flamingos on it. "She said it's all anyone's wearing in Florida this season."

Frank smiled and gave her a thumbs up. "Absolutely stunning. You'll certainly draw attention anywhere you go."

"Do have a seat. Where are my manners? I've been so caught up in this outing I've lost my head."

Not to mention all sense of fashion. Frank sat down. "How's Mr. Kennedy feeling nowadays?"

"He's better now and able to go to the office in the afternoons. It's such a relief from his yelling and threatening me."

"Oh?"

"Yes, just between you and me he's mighty touchy about money these days. He gets very upset anytime Mr. Hoffa comes to visit, though I think Mrs. Hoffa is delightful. I'd really like her to marry my Teddy, but the girls insist she's married to that dreadful Mr. Hoffa." Rose sat down beside him and offered him a mint from the candy jar.

Frank shook his head. "You've met Mrs. Hoffa?" *Oh, this doesn't look good for you, Hoffa.*

"Oh yes and she's really very nice. It's great that they've come into some money lately and she's able to buy all new things. I bought a new vase at an auction that I was told was priceless so Mrs. Hoffa won't be able to top that. I'm pretty sad about the loss of Georgie though."

Frank was hardly listening to her at this point. *What have you been doing with all the money?* He noticed the silence and her staring at him and ventured a guess. "A pet?"

"No, a teacup. But really you must be going now so I can finish getting ready for our outing. It was so nice of you to drop in, Mr. Frank. Do have a pleasant drive home." Rose ushered him to the door by his elbow and waved to him as he slowly descended the steps.

"Is everyone ready?" Agent Wes Latimer asked the assembled group.

The question received silent thumbs up as the agents finished preparing for the sting.

Agent Stansel nodded his agreement, and then turned to Bobby. "Mr. Kennedy, does your father have a good grasp of the questions he should lead Hoffa through?"

"Yes he does, and he's grateful that you'll have agents in the restaurant all evening to protect him." Bobby sat in a folding chair in the corner of the basement. He removed himself away from all of the equipment sitting on long tables around the perimeter of the room.

"All right then. I guess this is a go. The waiters know what table to seat them at and the plant has been wired. We also have a surveillance camera behind the bar pointed right at them so we can watch any and all movement. That should cover the upstairs." Agent Stansel wrapped up with a motion of his hand and all of the agents took up their positions.

Two hours later, Frank approached the bench in Central Park to find Sam had beaten him there.

"What did ya find out?" Frank asked as he sat down beside Sam.

"Hoffa's received a million dollars from the front company and only given a few thousand to the teamsters." Sam shook his head. "I had thought better of him. I guess we'll have to kill him now."

"Oh yes, he has to go. I saw Mrs. Kennedy and she said Josie Hoffa has been buying nice new things recently. Apparently she's come into some money." Frank relayed his visit with Rose.

"Yep. He's a dead man." Sam ground his teeth together.

Joe Kennedy watched as the maître d' led Jimmy Hoffa to his table. He extended his hand as he sat down.

"Mr. Kennedy, I'm surprised at this location for a meeting. Nothing amiss I hope?" Jimmy looked around him, and finding nothing wrong, he turned back to Joe.

"Mrs. Kennedy is getting upset with your frequent visits Hoffa so we had to meet away from the house. You understand, sometimes the missus can be a real pain." Joe chuckled and returned Hoffa's hand shake.

"Yea, I know. So, what did you want to talk about?" Jimmy asked as he picked up his menu and opened it.

"Let's order first. Would you like some wine?" Joe perused the wine list.

"Nah, I'd rather have a beer." Jimmy laughed. "I'm not refined, Mr. Kennedy."

The waiter took the orders and left the two men.

"So, after I've given you nearly a million dollars I'd say we're done. I've called this meeting to discuss a peaceful end to this 'partnership' as it were." Joe broke a bread stick in half and pushed it into his mouth.

"I don't see it that way, after what you Kennedys have done to me. You'll never be finished." Hoffa took hold of the draft beer and sloshed its contents down his throat. "Your sons have caused me more embarrassment than any one person could live down in two life times. I'm a laughing stock and not respected with anyone but gangsters. They simply appreciate my cunningness in beating my raps in short order." Jimmy paused to think for a moment. "No, Mr. Kennedy. I'm afraid you'll attack me with all your power, and once I'm gone, who'll ever believe that we were partners? It's much better this way."

"My sons and I are not in allegiance.   You should understand that we serve on opposite sides of the fence. They're for justice and the end to organized crime, but that's how I made my fortune.   I'm too old to change that now." Joe sniffed his wine, swirled it and sipped at it. "I'm dying. I won't be a threat to you for long."

"Really, that's not my problem, Mr. Kennedy."

Joe replaced the glass on the table. "My wife has been in competition with your missus for some weeks now.   Josie's been seen around our home in lovely designer clothes not befitting the wife of a union leader.   Rose also informed me that Josie has purchased all new furniture and had a decorator in to do complete remodeling of the place."

"What are you getting at, Kennedy?"

"I wonder how much of the money I'm giving you is actually making it into the coffers of the teamsters union?"

"What can it possibly matter to you?" Hoffa slammed a big hand down on the table. "I'll do whatever I deem right for me and my family. I've earned a little extra dough."

"Considering that you've been known for your corruption and ambition, I think I'll just have the attorney general's office check out your books for the teamsters union."   Joe took an appreciative sip of his wine.

"Your threats fall on the wrong ears. If you value the lives of your sons, you'll refrain from telling anyone what information you have and pay me another hundred thousand to keep me from knocking one of them off. I'd love to live in a world with one less Kennedy."

Before Joe could respond, the couple sitting behind Jimmy grabbed his arms and had him in cuffs before he knew what to do.

"Thanks, Mr. Kennedy. We got everything that we need to put this guy away for a very long time."   An agent nodded toward Hoffa.

Jimmy struggled and cursed, but the female agent stuck her handkerchief in his mouth, effectively cutting off his angry retorts.

"Pardon me, Agent Stansel, could I have a few words with him before you take him away?" Joe leaned over the table towards Hoffa.

"Make it quick." Agent Stansel tapped one foot on the floor.

"Hoffa, do you really think I'm that stupid? I've lived a hell of a lot longer than you and I've learned never to trust anyone. Perhaps while you're sitting in jail being a laughing stock you'll think about that jewel of wisdom." Joe Kennedy stood up and left the table with his head held high.

Bobby was standing just outside the restaurant waiting for his dad. When Joe caught up to him, Bobby took hold of his father's arm and led him to the waiting limo. "Good job, Dad. Are you all right?"

"Yeah. Boy I hate that guy. Now get me home to your mother so I can apologize for being such a beast to her lately."

"Are you actually showing remorse Dad?" Bobby stopped outside the car door to look at his father.

"Maybe just a little; she's been a good wife to me and she hasn't deserved the treatment she's gotten."

Frank answered the phone on his bedside table with sleep filled eyes. "Someone better be dead or dying to be calling me this early."

Frank sat up as he listened to Sam on the other end. "What? He didn't. He isn't. No." Frank was fully awake now and switched on the lamp. "He's not in jail. He can't be."

Frank slammed the phone down on the cradle. "Dammit! Now what the hell are we gonna do?"

Chapter 15

September 2, 1962

Peter walked along the shore until he blocked the sun shining on Marilyn's prone form lying on a beach towel. "Hey, kid. How's it been going?"

"Not too bad for a ghost." Marilyn sat up on her good elbow, moved her legs and waited for Peter to sit down on the end of the towel.

"I'm sorry; I can't even imagine how rough this is for you." Peter patted her foot.

"Rough? Are you kidding? I can't call my friends because I'm dead. I can't go home and I can't leave here. You should've just let me die, Pete. No one should have to live this way." Marilyn fought back the tears by biting her lower lip, but a few spilled down her cheeks anyway.

"Look, hon. You've always had to be the toughest woman I know, but you don't anymore. You can rest and recover until we figure out where to go from here."

"Yea, there is nowhere from here. Damn it don't you get it? No matter where I live I'll always be somebody else, not Marilyn Monroe sex goddess and lover of Jack. Jack..." Her tears fell in rapid succession down her cheeks as she mourned the loss of her love. "I've lost everything I've worked so hard for. I've lost the one person I could've spent the rest of my days being happy with." Marilyn put her forehead on her knees and allowed the sobs to rack her body.

"I know, I know. We'll figure this out somehow." Peter rubbed her foot with awkward motions until she calmed down.

"One thing that has bothered me since 'my death', is why would Sam want me dead?"

"It had to be an order from someone. Sam doesn't do anything without orders from someone else, or money." Peter rolled up the cuffs of his dress slacks, and then pulled off his shoes and socks.

"Frank?"

"Maybe. But I thought you two were friends."

Marilyn watched as the tide drew nearer to the blanket. Peter stuck out one foot and tried to touch the water with the tip of his big toe.

"We were friends until that awful party. He was so mean to me and Jack. I called Maggie, you know, Joe DiMaggio, and he said he would come to Frank's to set him straight. I was so mad I just left without telling anyone and never even saw Joe."

"What happened later that week?" Peter inched his way closer to the water's edge. He continued to push his toes toward the waves without getting off the towel.

"You're such a little boy." Marilyn smiled. "Jack left the party right after I did and we spent the rest of the weekend in a secluded hotel room. I just couldn't let our weekend end with us fighting. It was the last time I ever saw him."

"But what about Frank?" Peter persisted.

"He tried to call me several times during that week. One afternoon when Eunice was out I answered the phone. It was Frank. He apologized for treating me so badly and said it was all Joe Kennedy's fault. Joe wanted us to stop seeing each other because Jackie was having a fit. Frank was instructed to get us to break up no matter how he had to do it."

"Well, couldn't he have been a bit more tactful? He didn't succeed at any rate since you spent the weekend elsewhere." Pete had successfully gotten his big toe into the wave and let out a loud "Whoopee."

"You're such a child," Marilyn teased. "Frank doesn't know how to be gentle. That's why he never keeps a woman. Oh he's got it going for him in the bedroom, but his other manners are lacking."

"I really don't want to hear about your old beaus. So if you left the party, why did Sam try to kill you anyway?"

"Beats me. I did talk to Frank about my fears. He was very nice after I accepted his apology. He would never do anything to hurt me. Even with our differences we respected each other."

"Well, who else did you talk to about Jack?"

"Nobody. I didn't talk to anyone else. I tried to tell you and Bobby, but couldn't get you to understand what I was explaining."

"Had I known then what I know now, I would've had you leave the country for a while. I wasn't a very good confidant."

"Since Greenson tried to convince everyone that I was nuts I don't blame you for not listening." Marilyn wiggled closer to the end of the towel with Peter and poked her toe into the sand. The waves trickled over her foot and slowly melted back into the ocean.

"What did you tell Frank?" Pete stuck his toe in the sand like she had.

"I told him why Jack had decided to remove 1,000 troops from Vietnam before the end of this year. I told him that Jack would never support a full blown war and how upset that made his father."

"Maybe you should give me details. It's probably why someone wanted you dead. It's what you knew that could potentially harm the president or the White House or the US. Wow, this is huge!"

"I told Frank that the scaling back of the troops was to keep the US involvement from growing. Jack is afraid that if Castro throws his weight around, he could get this escalated to a full-fledged world war. The country doesn't need to be involved in helping that effort."

"There are lots of reasons why people in the White House would want to go to war, especially those who would gain from the use of those armaments and munitions. The letter you found could have a lot to do with that and so would the memo."

"What memo?" Marilyn asked, pulling her sunglasses down her nose to look him in the eye.

"The one that states the name of the company responsible for the contract of the guns and ammo. It's rumored to be sent by or to LBJ."

"You don't have it?" Marilyn pushed her sunglasses back to the bridge of her nose.

"No, we don't. Bobby has been working on getting it, but hasn't been successful so far."

"What about Jack? Is he aware of what's going on? He had the White House tapped so he could keep tabs on LBJ and Senator Smith, among other things." Marilyn wiggled her toes in the sand.

"Senator Smith? What's the senator got to do with this?"

"I don't really know, it's just a name I've heard." Marilyn dug her toes in the sand forming heart shapes. "Do you think Jack is aware that he is in real trouble? I mean, he says he knows his number is up and soon, but that's just ridiculous. He's hiding his fear, isn't he?"

"Probably, you know how childish we men can be. I know Bobby talked to him and now he's being very cautious. We're going to get to the bottom of this. Don't you worry."

Bobby hung up the phone and grinned at Ethel. "Well that was an interesting conversation I just had with your brother-in-law."

"How's Peter doing? What's up?"

"He's been with Marilyn and he was asking some great questions. The first being when Frank spoke to Marilyn two nights before her death, why didn't he tell Peter he had done so?"

"That's right. Pete went to Frank and asked about the party and Marilyn. He said he never spoke to her again after the fight at his house. Why would he lie?"

"Ah, that is an excellent question and one we'll have to find out the answer to somehow." Bobby put his arms around his wife.

"What else did Peter have to say?"

Bobby kissed the top of her head before answering. "He said that Marilyn knew about Jack's reasons for pulling out troops in Vietnam, but what she doesn't know is how that will effect Dad."

"What would your father have to do with this?" Ethel tilted her head back to look up into her husband's eyes.

"I think his connection with the teamsters is the key to this whole thing. Once I retrieve the memo from LBJ – someway – I'll be able to give you more details of Dad's involvement. I'm terrified that he's in this up to his neck and sinking fast in this quick sand he's created."

"Oh honey, surely he's not that corrupt." Ethel defended.

"I pray not, but he seems to be in pretty tight with LBJ and he is adamant about Jack and me backing off of organized crime. I hope my instincts are wrong, but I'm gonna be surprised if he's not involved in this." Bobby pulled Ethel closer to him and hugged her.

"You're squishing the breath out of me, honey." Ethel pushed him away with the palms of her hands.

"Sorry, honey. I'm just worried." Bobby let go of her waist and let her step back.

"How's Marilyn handling her predicament? It's nearly been a month since her death."

"She's apparently not happy that she still has that cast on her wrist and the nurse has been released back to the hospital. Susan Strausberg is due home in another week so we need to figure out where to move her. I think she's lonely and getting stir crazy, which is a bad combination." Bobby walked into the kitchen with Ethel following close behind.

"I need a drink. Would you care for something?" Ethel asked.

"Yeah, I want some milk and cookies. Did I smell fresh cookies when I came in earlier?"

"Yes, you're lucky that I stuck some back for you or the children would've devoured them before they hit the plate." Ethel smiled as she pulled a Tupperware dish out of the uppermost cabinet over the stove.

"You're the best, honey." Bobby pulled open the lid and sniffed deeply before pulling out one of Ethel's famous homemade double chocolate chip cookies. "Better than Mama used to make."

"You're welcome." Ethel handed him a tall glass of milk and kissed his cheek.

"So where are you going to move her?" Ethel asked after Bobby had devoured two cookies and half his glass of milk.

"Peter doesn't have any ideas. Maybe rent her a cottage somewhere in the mountains or find a secluded house. No, that would pose a security problem if anyone suspected she was still alive. How did this get so complicated?" Bobby finished off his milk.

"I couldn't tell you, honey. It seemed like such an easy thing, go in rescue the girl and be the hero."

"Yeah, but once we saved her and found out all of this information it's understandable that they wanted to kill her for what she knew. . ."

"She did have access to White House secrets and mob bosses.   That   would   get   her   hurt   under   normal circumstances. Throw in the 'I'm in love with the president' aspect and it spells death." Bobby stood up.

"But back to my question. What are you going to do with her?" Ethel took his hand and led him toward the staircase.

"I wish I knew. Do you have any ideas?"

"Why not our house in Malibu? Nobody's going to use it now that school is getting back in session." Ethel tapped her index finger against her temple. "If she wears a uniform this just might work."

"Oh no, you're not going to suggest she masquerade as the care taker of the property?" Bobby stopped on a step, and holding onto the banister, he turned to look at his wife.

"Why not? She won't really have to do any work, but she'll need to look the part. We could stock the place with essentials and you could arrange for things to be delivered in boxes or bags like regular packages from the post office."

"Now Ethel, I don't think that's a good idea." Bobby placed his arm around her waist and drew her on up the stairs.

"It may not be a good idea, but so far it's the only one that's even plausible."

Chapter 16

September 3, 1962

Bobby entered the White House with a purposeful stride. *I've got to get Jack to help me find that memo. It's become too much of a liability. What if he won't help - then what?*

Bobby smiled as he recognized the secretary of the vice president coming toward him. "Ms. Avery, how are you today?"

"Oh, Mr. Kennedy, I would like to talk to you for a moment if I may." Ms. Avery looked around. "It's important."

"Sure, where do you want to talk? My office?" Bobby took her by the elbow.

"Oh no, sir. We can't talk in here. Can we go to the lawn for a walk?"

"I really need to see the president this morning, Ms. Avery." Bobby sighed, glancing at his watch.

"I assure you that what I need to tell you is urgent." Ms. Avery turned toward the door that led out onto the garden area of the White House lawn.

Bobby had no recourse but to follow her. After a moment he caught up with her, but she kept walking until they were well out on a grassy slope.

"Now what is this all about, Ms. Avery?"

"I just don't know who to turn to, but you should be able to help. You see, Mr. Johnson has been receiving an unusual amount of phone calls from Senator Smith. Generally after these conversations he goes out for an hour or two and when he returns he's in a terrible mood."

"So? Maybe he doesn't like the senator; needs time to regroup his feelings after they talk." Bobby sat down on a cement bench and motioned for the secretary to do the same.

"No, it's more than that. They have correspondence back and forth and much of it is in some sort of coded wording that they understand. But this morning, Mr. Johnson received a call from the senator and he seemed happy for me to put the call through. So, when I forwarded the call, I stayed on the line and listened." Ms. Avery had blushed to the roots of her red hair. "I know that I shouldn't have, but it's all such a mystery. I just had to know what they're doing."

"Well, Ms. Avery, what did you find out? I promise that you're in no danger from me. I'll investigate the situation, but no legal action will be held against you. You may have done your country a huge favor if you suspect some sort of misbehavior." Bobby patted the hand that rested on the cement bench between them.

"Oh thank you, Mr. Kennedy. I was so afraid that I'd lose my job, at the very least, or go to jail if I'd done something wrong. When the line went dead, I replaced the receiver and quickly hid the paper I wrote everything down on." Ms. Avery pulled a folded piece of paper out of her skirt pocket and handed it to Bobby.

"Don't worry about any of that. Just tell me what you heard."

"Okay, here's what was said exactly. I paged him and said, 'Sir, Senator Smith is on the phone for you.' He said, 'Patch'r through.' I heard some rattling and rumbling in his office and then he answered. 'Smith?'

'Yes.'

'I've turned off those damned recorders. Progress?'

'We almost have all the king's men in line, sir.'

'Excellent.'

'Everything will be in place when the time comes.'

'And the governor's aide?'

'All is ready there, sir.'

"That's when the conversation ended. The line just went dead." Ms. Avery smoothed her wind-blown skirt down.

"This is all very interesting, but what does it mean?"

"Really, Mr. Kennedy, I was hoping you would know. Did I do the right thing?" Ms. Avery twisted the edge of her skirt into a knot.

"Good work, Ms. Avery and now I'm going to ask you a couple of questions. Maybe we can make some sense out of this together."

"I'll sure try to help you in any way I can."

"Excellent. I'll see that you get a raise. Now, what sort of correspondence has passed between the senator and the vice president?"

"Mostly brief memos with titles like 'Munitions' or 'Diem' or 'Arms'. I'm afraid that they're plotting to stop the president's Memorandum #263 or worse."

"You're talking about 'NSAM,' the one with orders of the withdrawal of one thousand troops and military personnel by the end of next year?"

"Yes, that one. They're both opposed to retreating and think it should become a full scale war instead of this 'conflict' thing. I've also put a few calls through from Mr. Joe Kennedy."

"My father?"

143

"Yes. I didn't listen to those calls and they were brief. The light on the line never stayed lit up for more than thirty seconds to a minute. I thought it was a bit strange, but they're both trying to forward this conflict into a war."

"Why? Our troops are suffering enough with just the conflict that we're involved in. The Diem political powers call it a war for their purposes so what would Dad and Mr. Johnson have to gain?"

"Money?" Ms. Avery asked.

"It's possible. I'll check into this matter and keep you up on what I find out. You must tell no one about this – it's a matter of national security."

"I realize that Mr. Kennedy. That's why I came to you." Ms. Avery stood up. "I better get back before I'm missed. I'll let you know if I find anything else out."

"Ms. Avery, can you get me copies of those memos that were between the senator and vice president?"

"Yes, Mr. Kennedy. I'll try to get them to your office by late this afternoon."

"Thank you, Ms. Avery. You've been very helpful and your country is most grateful to you." Bobby walked around the lawn for a few minutes after Ms. Avery returned to the White House.

Marilyn walked through the bungalow putting everything back in the exact order it had been in when she'd arrived. Her suitcase sat beside the front door along with the last of the trash from her stay.

Satisfied that Suzie would be none the wiser that there'd been an uninvited visitor, Marilyn closed the drapes in front of the French doors that led to the deck.

She rubbed her wrist. *Well if I ever do get to act again I'll be able to portray a realistic grimace when cutting off my own cast with a hack saw and a pair of kitchen scissors.* Flexing her fingers and wiggling her wrist slowly back and forth, Marilyn smiled at her own strength.

A horn sounded outside indicating the taxi had arrived. Marilyn picked up the trash and shoved the suitcase forward with her foot. She nodded to the case as the cabbie came to the porch.

"Is this all, ma'am?"

"Yes. Let me just set this by the curb and I'll be ready to go."

"Sure lady. It's your dime."

Marilyn climbed into the back seat and pulled the door shut.

"Where to, lady?"

Peter arrived a few hours later with a brown paper sack with soda pop, candy and new magazines riding beside him in the front seat. He pulled into the carport. *Why is the door closed?*

He got out of the car, retrieved the bag and tried the screen door. It opened, but the wooden door wouldn't budge. Panic seized him as he found the key behind the apron still hanging on its hook.

"Marilyn?" he yelled as he came into the kitchen. Setting the bag down on the bar he called out again, "Marilyn, where are you?"

This is all too familiar. Now where is she? Maybe she's on the beach.

He went into the master bedroom. Nope, not in here either. He went through the living area and tried to open the French doors. *Now, why'd you lock the door?*

Realization struck him. *She's gone. Damn it to hell, she's gone. Where would she go?*

Bobby entered his office and tackled a mountain of paperwork. He continued to pull the paper with the mysterious phone conversation out of his suit pocket. After several attempts to figure it out, he picked up the phone.

Scrolling through the rolodex on his desk he found the number and dialed.

"Agent Stansel, this is Robert Kennedy. I've got a cryptic message that I'd like your help with. I'll be there in thirty minutes."

Peter ran out to his car, and dialed Bobby's office. After two rings the secretary answered.

"Is Mr. Kennedy in his office? This is Mr. Lawford – it's urgent."

"I'm sorry, Mr. Lawford. He's stepped out for a while. Can I have him return your call?"

"Yes, on my car phone. He's got the number and please tell him it's most urgent."

"Yes, Mr. Lawford. I'll be certain he gets the message as soon as he gets in."

Peter hung up the phone, locked up the house, hung up the key and raced out of the driveway. "You better not be where I think you are."

Bobby returned to the White House and went straight to his brother's oval office.

"Jack, I know that you're busy running the country and important stuff like that, but I need to talk to you about something I've just found out."

"Give me ten minutes." John covered the receiver with his hand. "I'm on hold with the British Prime Minister."

"All right." Bobby plopped himself down on the couch and took up the bowl of mixed nuts.

After a couple of minutes his brother joined him on the sofa. "What's this all about?" John settled his long frame in a more comfortable position.

"I've just left the FBI and it doesn't look too good. We've uncovered a possible plot on your life."

"Another one? There must be ten a day, which is why I'd nearly given up." John laughed.

"There's no reason to laugh at this one. It's on the inside."

"Okay, you've got my attention."

"What do you know about Senator Smith?" Bobby asked.

"Power mad."

"It's more than that. I need you to unearth a memo entitled, 'Arms and Munitions' dated around August 6 of this year. It may hold the key to the cryptic message I got this morning."

"Come on Bob, you can't just tell me there's another death threat and then ask for a memo."

"John, you know I'd never waste my time on something that isn't of the direst circumstances. Can you just get me the memo?"

"Did you say the FBI is involved in this?"

"Yes, they may be able to crack the code if we can get our hands on that memo. I really need it, John."

"All right. I'll get my aide right on it."

"I'm going to my office. Have it brought to me as soon as you've located it." Bobby got up, and picked up a last handful of nuts. "You may want to read it before you send it to me. I think it may be of some interest to you."

Peter sped down Highway 101. *Please don't be there. What am I gonna do when I get there? Knock on the door and say, 'Hey there is Marilyn with you?'*

The car phone jangled. "Hullo?"

"What's up, Peter?" Bobby crackled over the line.

"Marilyn, she's gone. I went to the bungalow to bring her supplies and discuss where she should be moved, but she's no longer there."

"Keep your shorts on, Pete. Where are you now?"

"I'm heading to Frank's house. My gut says that she's gone to confront him. Oh Lord! I hope I'm wrong."

"Don't go alone, Peter. You'll need someone with you. Besides, I don't think she'd be that stupid to go confront Frank alone."

"Well, where else would she be?"

"You know women. Maybe she went to the hairdresser." Bobby's voice crackled and faded over the line.

"She's not at the beauty salon. I also found plaster on the floor of the carport. She's cut off her cast."

"What?"

"I say she's a woman scorned and on her way to get her revenge."

"Why don't you call Frank and see how he acts?" Bobby suggested through a buzz of static as Peter rounded a curve.

"No one has spoken to Frank since the funeral. He's been banished by your dad. I can't just call him after all these weeks of silence."

"Great. We can't call the police or FBI to help us rescue a dead woman. How can she be so selfish?"

"We are still talking about Marilyn, right?"

"Gotcha. Go home Peter, until we can decide what to do. I've got big things breaking loose on this end, too. Sit tight and I'll get back to you as soon as I get some answers."

The line went dead before Peter could answer.

Chapter 17

September 4, 1962

Marilyn sat in a dark corner of the hotel café reading a magazine. Keeping her head in the shadows, she enjoyed watching the couples come and go in their normal day to day routines.

She had spent the last twenty four hours at a hotel, a mere five minute walk from Frank's place. Finishing her coffee, she waited until only a few customers were left before she paid the check.

Thanks Barbara, for giving me the tip Peter left you. You were right. I do need it more than you do.

Marilyn picked up her suitcase and started walking along the beach path. It was dark now with little foot traffic. Watching as groups formed on the beach around campfires, Marilyn sighed. *I'll never be a normal person again. Always hiding, always afraid, always alone. Knock it off, Marilyn. Being morose won't help!*

She continued along the path until Frank's lights were visible. She nipped into the bath house and put on the dark pants, top and dark ballet slippers.

Listening for any outside sounds, Marilyn slowly opened the door of her makeshift dressing room. Tiptoeing, she made her way to the shrubbery beside the deck.   The light was on over the bar top in the room where she'd had her last martini with Jack. *Jack, I miss you....*

She didn't hear a sound or see anyone so she tried the door, pulling it open with deliberate slowness.   Once it was wide enough to allow her to wiggle through, she closed it behind her with the same care.

Her form was noticeable in the mirror behind the bar. She crouched down and duck walked without a sound to the door that led into the front room. Frank was sitting in the dark at the piano bench with only a candle glowing.

His fingers were poised over the keyboard, but he wasn't moving.   He looked like a wax figure in a museum.   Marilyn crept back to the bar silently, and slowly opened the drawer under the bar top.

"Oh Marilyn, I'm soo...." Frank shifted on the bench, but paused, deep in thought.   Marilyn crept back over to the door frame and stared at him.

Nothing moved; time was frozen for the moment while Frank sat so still his breathing wasn't visible. After a long pause his Adam's apple bobbled when he swallowed.

The spell was broken and Marilyn stood up behind the door frame.   She tossed her shoulders back and made a low moaning sound from deep within her throat. *You bastard you deserve this.*

A loud discordant sounded from the piano where Frank dropped his hands as he heard her moan.   "Who's there?" he called in a whisper.

"Oh-hhh."   Marilyn crooned from her hiding place, relishing his fear.

"Sam?" Frank gripped the piano bench.

"No-ooo-ooo," came the singsong reply. *He's really scared.*

"Who's there?" Frank demanded in a shaking yet stronger voice.

"Why?   Oh-hhh-hhhh why?"   Marilyn's velvety stage whisper drifted to him.

"All right the gag's over. Who's there? Juliet is that you? Damn you, this isn't funny."

"Why?" Marilyn stood on her toes and did a ballet twirl past the doorway and across to the other side. Good. *He didn't see me. Maybe too much risk is making me giddy.*

The piano bench landed on the floor as Frank's abrupt reaction forced it backward.

"M-Marilyn?" he whispered through clenched teeth.

"Why?" she repeated, but remained in the same position behind the door frame.

"I don't know what you're talking about. Go away, you're dead." Frank licked his dry lips and placed his hands on top of the piano's surface for support.

"Why –yyyy?"

"What? Why are you haunting me?" Frank trembled as he tried to light up a cigarette.

"It was you, you, YOU!" Marilyn twirled past the door again, a little further away from it this time.

She bounced into the bar and the sound of glass clinking together broke the illusion. The noise reverberated like the tinkle of Christmas bells on a snowy night.

Frank flipped on the light as he rushed into the room. Marilyn tried to hide behind the bar, but he caught hold of her upper arm and swung her around.

"What trick is this?" Frank grabbed her. Marilyn struggled to get away as he roughly shook her.

Frank jerked her head up toward the light. In her surprise, Marilyn hadn't uttered a sound. He held her arm so tight that the blood stopped circulating and pinpricks began tingling in her fingers.

"Let go of me, Frank." she demanded. Furious now, the color returned to her cheeks.

"I can't. Oh hellfire, you're dead! Why couldn't you stay dead?"

"Why did you want me dead?" Marilyn leveled her gaze on him. "Who did you order to do it? Sam? And who else?"

151

"Oh hell." Frank sucker punched her under the jaw and she dropped to the floor in a heap.

He jerked the cord off the drapes and tied her hands behind her back, stuffed a dirty rag in her mouth and pulled the sheers off the French door wrapping her legs in them. He tied the whole of it together at her feet.

Grabbing up the phone, he dialed with lighting speed. "Sam? Get Greenson over here ASAP!"

Peter waited helplessly by the phone in the den. Pacing the length of the room, he turned, stared at the phone and continued pacing. *Why hasn't Bobby called yet? I'm going to go crazy if we don't find Marilyn soon.*

Pat came into the room with two highballs. "Darling, you're going to wear a hole in the rug if you don't stop that pacing."

"Can't help it." Peter accepted the drink and sipped it.

"Silly man, sit down."

"I'm too nervous."

The ringing of the phone caused Peter to slosh his drink all over his white linen shirt. "Damn."

He rushed to the receiver. "Hullo?"

"Lawford? Greenson here. Where's that letter? I simply must have it."

"I'm trying to find it, doctor. I've looked for it at the studio, but it isn't there. I'm going to try to get access to her vehicles. Maybe she hid it in one of them." Peter stalled.

"I want it tomorrow. No excuses." Dr. Greenson slammed the receiver down on the other end.

"Just what I need - another crisis." Peter slumped down on a chair, pulling off his wet shirt.

As the last bell tolled out the midnight hour, Sam and Tony Pro stood on the back porch of Dr. Greenson's house. Tony picked the lock with practiced ease and opened the door.

Motioning for Sam to follow him, Tony went through the hallway and up the stairs to Dr. Greenson's room. The door stood open and the moonlight filtered in through the slats in the Venetian blinds.

Dr. Greenson lay sleeping on his side facing them. Tony took a gag and stuffed it in the doctor's mouth.

His eyes flew open just before Tony hit him in the temple with a light tap. Dr. Greenson's body relaxed in a dead faint.

Sam and Tony hefted him out of the bed, down the stairs and into the van parked by the back yard.

Frank opened the front door to allow Sam and Tony to carry Dr. Greenson inside. He placed a finger over his lips as they came in and pointed to the sofa.

After the two goons dropped the doctor on the couch, they stepped out of the room with Frank.

"What's so urgent?" Sam asked when they were seated on the bar stools.

"I just need to get the doctor's opinion about something. Did you bring his bag?" Frank crossed his arms and tapped a foot.

"Uh, no." Tony answered looking a bit sheepish. "That wasn't part of the order."

"Never mind. Go on with you. Out." Frank followed them to the front door, locked it behind them and found a large vase with water in it. Taking out the flowers he flung them to the carpet, and dumped the vase over Greenson's prone form.

Sputtering, the doctor sat up. Pulling the gag out of his mouth he turned to look up at Frank. "What the hell do you think you're doing?"

"We've got a problem. No, you've got a problem that you need to fix." Frank handed him a cloth to dry his face.

"Okay, what's up?" Dr. Greenson wiped off his face, neck, and arms. He blotted at his pajama top and pants.

"The letters you've been all fired up to find that you said Marilyn had? Well, the reason that they haven't turned up has arrived here tonight." Frank sat in a chair across from the doctor.

"I'm not following you. Be clear." Dr. Greenson continued to blot his button down pajama top.

"You want clear? Fine. I can do clear. How clear is it to you that Marilyn is at this moment tied up in my bedroom?" Frank lit a match and stoked his cigarette to life.

"Marilyn? Monroe?" Dr. Greenson shook his head to clear it.

"Yes. Marilyn Monroe. She showed up here tonight pretending to be a ghost and tried to scare me into telling her why she was killed."

"But there was a death certificate and a funeral. How can this be?" Dr. Greenson lit a cigarette and blew out a smoke ring.

"I don't know. I freaked out and punched her in the jaw, knocking her out cold. I tied her up and dragged her into the bedroom. What're we gonna do with her?" Frank stood up and fixed himself a drink.

He lifted the snifter toward Dr. Greenson. The doctor nodded his head in the affirmative and joined Frank at the bar.

"This is bad, very bad. Whoever saved her and went to the trouble to cover up her death knows all about us." The doctor downed his drink in a quick swig and held out his glass for another.

"That's about the way I see it. So I panicked and had you brought here. I knew you'd never believe me if I called you so...."

"Right. Under the circumstances, who can blame you? Now Peter and Bobby were both there that night when I arrived. I took a cursory glance, but she was decidedly dead."

154

Dr. Greenson frowned as Frank poured a miniscule amount of liquor into his glass. "Stingy, aren't you?"

"We need to be sober to sort this all out." Frank replaced the stopper on the bottle and then put it back on the shelf. "Well, if you're right and the body on the bed was dead, then it wasn't Marilyn."

"How can anyone, even Robert Kennedy, get a corpse that fast? Or do you think Sam messed up?"

"No, I'm sure it's not Sam who made the mistake." Frank glared at Greenson. "You told me you'd done a great job of convincing everyone that she was suicidal. How did she manage to convince those two that she was being doped? And when?"

"I don't know." Dr. Greenson tapped the ash from his cigarette into the tray at his elbow. "Eunice Murray was careful to keep close count on the drugs I'd prescribed. Marilyn was taking them faithfully according to Eunice."

"Well, she convinced them one way or the other and now she's very much alive right here in my house. This isn't good." Frank began pacing around behind the bar.

"Shit." Dr. Greenson downed his drink.

"If we do anything to her now Bobby and Peter will know it was us. This is all your fault. I never wanted any part of this. Besides, they're probably on to where she's gone by now and forming a plan to rescue her." Frank came out from behind the bar and joined the doctor on a stool.

"Is she still out?" Dr. Greenson blew another smoke ring followed by a swirl of smoke at the end of his breath.

"She was right before you got here. I've tied her up in the sheers from the French doors so tight that even if she comes to she won't be able to escape the tangle I've made."

"We have to find those letters and get her to tell us what she knows. It's not going to be easy especially if she knows I'm here. She doesn't trust me."

"I can't blame her for that. I don't trust you either."

155

"That last session we had on Friday afternoon is when she told me that she wouldn't be coming to see me anymore. She was no longer in need of my services. We argued about it, but she left without changing her mind. She insisted that I was trying to hurt her." Dr. Greenson shrugged and put out his cigarette in the tray.

"So she knew then that her life was in danger?"

"Yes. It's because of what she knew that led to the order to kill her. I didn't want to do it. I liked her well enough, but the higher powers decided it was time for her to go."

"Which powers gave you that order?" Frank demanded. "She thinks I'm the one that ordered the hit. She accused me of planning to break up her and Jack the week before she died."

"Didn't you? Weren't you acting on orders?"

"I thought it was Joe who wanted her out of the picture and Jackie. So who are you talking about?"

Chapter 18

Sitting on the edge of the chair, Peter answered the phone before the first full ring. "Hullo?"

"Peter, Bobby here. I want you to listen to me and don't get panicky. I've been thinking this over about Marilyn. Now she either went to a safe secluded place or she went to confront Frank. No matter where she went we can't do anything about it until she contacts us."

"But if she went to Frank's he's bound to kill her." Peter wrapped the phone cord around his finger.

"That's possible, but we don't know for sure where she's at. Try to remain calm and just wait until we see what she needs us to do. She's either put herself in a position that we can't help her with, or she's safe and will contact us in a day or two."

"But Bobby," Peter whined.

"No buts. Just wait it out. I'll call you tomorrow."

The phone went dead while Peter still held the receiver in his hand. After some time he noticed that his finger was blue and throbbing so he un-wrapped the cord.

"Pat!"

She came running into the den. "What's happened?"

"Bobby told me not to do anything about Marilyn, but I think I'll call Frank and feel him out."

157

"You better do what you're told, Peter. Now you're messing with something that's way over your head. Frank may hurt you if he thinks that you're fishing for information. Don't do it."

"I can't just sit around and do nothing. I need to find her." Peter began his pacing again.

Pat stepped in front of him, placed her arms around his waist hugging him close. "Pete, if you don't listen to what Bobby advises you could get us both in real trouble with the family. If Bobby thinks you need to sit tight, then he has a good reason to have you do so."

"Aren't you worried about her?" Peter leaned his forehead against his wife's skull.

"Yes, of course, but she's a big girl. I'm betting she can take care of herself."

"I certainly hope that you Kennedys are right. I'd feel awful if anything happened to her now."

Marilyn sat on Frank's bed and she wriggled her jaw. *That's the ditziest blonde thing I've pulled since grade school. What now?*

She managed to work her legs free of the sheers and was now trying to free her hands from the corded rope securing them.

Footsteps approached the door. She shoved her legs under the sheers in an effort to appear helpless.

Frank opened the door. He came in and flipped on the light. "So you're awake."

"Yea, no thanks to you. Why'd you slug me?"

"Shock," Frank shrugged. "Just a reaction. Hell, I don't know."

"Well I certainly didn't deserve to be socked unconscious. Don't you think I've had a rough enough time?"

Frank sank down on the mattress beside her. "I'm sorry I slugged ya." He traced his finger along the bruise welling up along her jaw line. "This kinda reminds me of old times.

You used to sit on my bed and wait for me to finish my act at the club, remember?"

Marilyn raised an eyebrow. "Why are you making nice all of a sudden?"

"You're pretty smart, I've gotta give you that. You managed to make an entire world think that you were dead, yet here you sit on my bed."

"So?" Marilyn prompted.

"Hell, if you can do that I'd like to know your secret." Frank gave her a lopsided grin.

"Don't try to be cute with me, Frank Sinatra. It won't work. I'm not telling you anything. I am a smart girl and you won't get nothing from me."

"Are you sure that's what you want?"

"I've gathered that you'll kill me once you get the information you need. And you can get away with it too, since I'm already legally dead." Marilyn faced him without emotion.

"You're a tough bitch. I'll give ya that. How bout we share some secrets, you and I?"

"You go first. I want you to tell me what you had to do with my death."

"Nothing. Absolutely nada."

"Right, and I'm a virgin." Marilyn held up her hands for him to untie.

"Not yet, not until we get some things sorted out. For instance why are you so certain that I had something to do with your, um.... accident?"

"Easy. Sam is one of the goons that was in my house the night I was attacked. I also think that Tony guy was there with him. They usually like to pair up on a job."

"True they were there, but not at my request. I believe that someone else has them in their pocket and I can't figure out who. We're both being taken for a ride here. Now if we can decide who is playing both sides of the fence, we can straighten this mess out." Frank shifted on the bed in an effort to get more comfortable.

"If what you're saying is fact, then we do have a problem." Marilyn watched him take off his shoes dropping them on the floor. "What are you going to do with me? You can't keep me here. Your maid will see me."

"Well, it seems that we have an abundance of problems. First off, I don't trust you to tell me the truth about what happened that night at your house. Secondly, you don't trust me at all. Third and most pressing, what do I do about you?" Frank ran his finger lightly over her bottom lip, pulling it down enough to view the row of perfect white teeth. "I could make love to you and then kill you, but that wouldn't serve any purpose." He moved his fingers to caress her cheek and neck.

Sitting stiff Marilyn allowed him to touch her for a moment. "That's enough, Frank. That part of our relationship is over."

"Aw come on, Kitten. You used to love it when I nibbled your neck and ears. Why not? One last time as a remembrance?" He leaned forward to kiss her nape, but she moved away.

"Stop it. If you're going to have me killed at least have the good grace to say so."

"Feisty, but then you always have been. No one gets the better of you, do they Marilyn?"

"Damn right. So what's it going to be?"

"Not death, at least, not right now. I need to talk to you first."

"You may as well get it over with because I won't answer your questions." Marilyn slumped down against the headboard.

"Okay, let's view this like a crap game. You get one shot at asking me a question and I have to give an honest answer. Then it's my turn to ask you and you have to be a straight shooter with me. Deal?"

"Deal. What is your involvement with the conflict in Vietnam?" Marilyn watched his face for any signs of deceit.

Geez, I never have thought you'd ask that. But here's your answer. My involvement is money. I want to help provide a commodity to all parties that will enhance the advancement of the conflict and my wallet."

"Right." Marilyn smiled. "You certainly know how to chase a skirt around a room without catching anything, don't you?"

"Yeah. Now it's my turn. What information did you have that caused you to be on the hit list?"

"Don't you think my relationship with the president was enough? Jackie made it clear that she wanted me out of the way no matter how that was accomplished. It wasn't a secret that Jack was going to ask her for a divorce."

"Yeah, right. That's true, but you've avoided the real answer."

"I gave tit for tat, Frank."

"That you did. Well, it was a crap game. I'll let you sleep for now." Frank pulled himself up from the bed. "I've got all the security cameras and alarms set. If you so much as move from this room, it'll light up brighter than the Vegas casinos at night."

"Where would I go?"

Bobby sat at his desk early the next morning, working through the maze of phone conversations and memos now stacked on his desk from Ms. Avery. She'd found the memo in question as well as several other key pieces.

"King's men. King's men." Bobby traced the outline of the words over and over with a pencil. "What king?"

His intercom buzzed. "Mr. Kennedy?"

"Yes."

"There's a Rex Stansel on the line from the FBI."

161

"Excellent. I'll take the call." Bobby let go of the intercom button, and waited for the light to blink on his phone indicating what line to answer.

"Robert Kennedy speaking."

"Mr. Kennedy, can I meet you somewhere today for a few minutes?" Agent Stansel asked.

Bobby stood on the sidewalk in front of sixteen hundred Pennsylvania Avenue waiting for Rex Stansel. *Should I tell John about this new evidence?*

"Mr. Kennedy?" Stansel stared at him, waiting.

"Okay, Stansel. Whatcha got for me?"

"'All the 'king's men' in a line refers to assassins."

"Well, I thought as much.   What else do you have?" Bobby motioned for Stansel to walk beside him.

" 'Governor's aide' could be a code word for a state."

"Really?   Good work.   I've been reviewing the president's schedule for the next several months.   He's going to be abroad until his scheduled appearance in Dallas."

"As cryptic as the message is, Mr. Kennedy, it does appear that the hit is meant to take place here at home. You want me to get Latimer on it? He's the best decoding agent on the force."   Agent Stansel stepped over a large crack in the sidewalk.

"Of course.   This is the president's life we're talking about." Bobby turned around and started back to the White House. He looked at the man beside him. "Go on, Stansel. Don't follow me back."

Peter slumped in his chair, eyes closed, head listing forward. The jangling of the phone jerked him awake.   "Hullo?"

"Greenson here. Where the hell are those letters?"

"I'll get right on it. I haven't had any luck getting into her vehicles, but perhaps today I'll get lucky."

"You better." Dr. Greenson snapped.

Bobby stood in front of John's desk in the oval office waiting while his brother skimmed it.

"Well Bob, this is no good. I'd never sign anything that would further the conflict in Vietnam. Why would I want to procure firepower to both the North and the South?"

"You wouldn't. Who drafted this?"

"It certainly wasn't me." John skimmed the page. "It's apparent that there are communist forces at work here in the White House. This paper calls for the escalation into a full blown war. This document could cause a war to continue for years."

"Do you know the name of the company that gets the contract?" Bobby asked.

"It says here *FACILITIES MANAGEMENT CORPORATION* FOR THE ESTIMATED AMOUNT OF $6,185,599.32. That's for the first year alone. It's a three year contract to be increased by 15% each year with multiple one year options after that. My God!"

"That's got to be a front company. Now, who's the front?" Bobby sat down in the leather chair across from John's desk.

"No doubt about it," the president agreed. "I can't believe it's Johnson. We're in opposition on the Vietnam conflict, but he's not shrewd enough on his own."

"That's true. He's not the brightest bulb in the box. I'll dig into it. In the meantime you just act normal."

"I'll keep it under wraps, Bob. Don't you worry about me."

Bobby sat on his front porch that evening with his head leaning against the wooden post. Ethel was beside him rubbing the back of his neck. They sat in silence for a long moment before Bobby turned to look at her.

"Honey, what's wrong?" Ethel lightly scratched his back.

"I can't put all the pieces together. There's Marilyn's disappearance, and the memo's front company. Who's behind that? Not Johnson or even Frank. It's got to be someone smarter than either of those two dupes." Bobby shook his head.

"Perhaps it's Sam," Ethel said. "He's smart. Isn't he the one that gave Frank his start in show business? He has a reputation to uphold, so he could be involved."

"Yes on both counts hon, but even he's not that smart. It has to be someone who is a money-hungry, power-mad cog in this conspiracy. I'll just have to call in some favors on this one."

"You're intelligent enough to outsmart whoever is behind this, Bobby. I know you'll save your brother and Marilyn." Ethel turned his face to hers and kissed him.

"What a wife." Bobby encircled her holding her tight.

Chapter 19

September 7, 1962

Marilyn sat on the sofa listening to Dr. Greenson and Frank quarrelling in the next room. Frank had untied her earlier in the day, allowed her to dress in the clothes she had left hidden in the bath house and then retied her to the wooden leg of the couch.

"Fine. We'll do it your way. But it better not fail." Dr. Greenson stomped into the room and sat down across from Marilyn.

After a minute Frank came in with a tray of drinks and some fruit. "Here, Kitten. You should keep your strength up."

She hesitated for a brief moment, and then took a handful of grapes. He sat the tray within her reach and went back into the bar room.

Finishing the grapes she reached for an apple. Staring at Dr. Greenson, she took a large bite and crunched it as loud as her sore jaw would allow.

He glared back.

She smiled as she took another crackling bite, tearing the skin slowly away from the meat.

Dr. Greenson let out a choked laugh.

Frank returned carrying her suitcase. He placed it by the door before sitting down on the coffee table.

"Now, what do you know about the Facilities Management Corporation?"

"What?" she asked between bites.

"Come on, Kitten. Play nice or Dr. Greenson will shoot you with a truth serum and you'll tell me everything. But that's the hard way, so tell me what you know." Frank picked the tray up and moved it just out of her reach.

Marilyn pushed out her bottom lip in a pout. "I don't know anything about any manager corp or whatever."

Dr. Greenson picked up the black bag sitting at his feet and opened it. He withdrew a needle and a little vial.

Marilyn shook her head. "I swear I don't know. Who would have told me about it?"

"Any number of your powerful friends. Now be a good girl and make this easy."

Marilyn gritted her teeth and said once again, "I don't know."

The doctor got up from his chair and walked to the couch; he injected the needle into the vial and held it up. Squirting out the air, he then leaned closer to her. His smiled evilly as he attempted to inject the shot into her arm.

As he got to her flesh, she jerked sideways and the needle plunged into the cushion behind her.

Dr. Greenson sneered at her as he withdrew the now empty needle from the sofa. He turned to Sinatra, waving the shot at him. "Hold her next time, you dolt. Can't you see she's going to fight?"

Marilyn laughed. "Even if you give me that shot you won't find out what you're looking for. I told you I don't know and I don't."

"Get her ready to go. It's almost time," Sinatra told Greenson as he stood up, "and don't ever make the mistake of calling me a dolt again or I'll have you fitted for cement shoes."

Dr. Greenson lowered his head as he dug in his bag. "Sorry." he muttered.

Sinatra left the room without acknowledging the apology.

"Now, this is to help you calm down, Marilyn. You're awful nervous aren't you?"

"I'm not taking anything you give me. Who are you working for? Frank? What's he want me dead for?"

"Marilyn, you're overwrought and don't know what you're saying. Here let me help you calm down."

"NO!" Marilyn jerked until the rope cut into her ankle and calf.

"I'm going to need help subduing her." Dr. Greenson yelled into the room where Frank had disappeared.

Agent Latimer met with Bobby in a coffee shop just off of Pennsylvania Avenue. "Here's what I've got for you, Mr. Kennedy." He slid a piece of paper across the table.

"You see, 'king's men' refers to the assassin or assassins, but the 'king' is the problem. We've searched all of our codes and found that 'king' in this instance must mean the mafia head."

"I suspected as much when Stansel told me about the assassin. When do you think they're plotting to make the hit?" Bobby asked as he sipped hot coffee.

"It would appear that Stansel's guess is accurate. The president is not well liked in Texas, and that being his first stop after returning to the states, is the most likely time."

"I agree with that." Bobby looked at the paper again.

"We also did some digging and found several thwarted attempts on the president and his family. We're going to go over those cases thoroughly again and see if we missed any mob connections. With the president being on the outs with the teamsters, it would appear that all of this is connected." Latimer finished his coffee and stood up. "I'll be in touch."

Sinatra and Greenson succeeded in getting the straight jacket on the unconscious woman. They pushed her into the back seat of the car and sped away.

Marilyn awoke as the car slowed to a stop. *Where are they taking me? Am I going to die now? Oh Jack. I wish you could save me. How could I be so stupid? Can anyone save me?*

After a couple of minutes the back door opened and Dr. Greenson pulled her out of the car. "Come on dearie, everything will be all right in no time at all.

The doctor smiled at her confusion. "That's right, just walk in front of me now."

Two huge shadows lurked behind the car, adding to Marilyn's trepidation. "Where are we?"

"Why we're taking you for a rest. Don't you remember? We talked about it all the way here." Dr. Greenson continued to push her forward into the darkness.

Glancing around she noticed that Frank was still in the car. *That's not a good sign. Greenson's going to kill me.* Her legs trembled as she put one foot blindly in front of the other. No moon shone tonight, no stars to guide her steps, and no light to help her stumble across the grassy expanse they were leading her through.

The two goons followed behind Greenson, almost stepping on his heels as they walked. Marilyn tripped over a rock, but Greenson jerked her up hard by the elbow. "None of your tricks. We'll be there in just a moment and then you can rest."

Oh God, I'm going to die. Please let me have at least saved Jack. Let him live.

Marilyn continued to stumble her way across the uneven ground until her foot hit the edge of something concrete.

As she stepped up, a bright light flooded the area. She blinked in rapid succession to refocus. When her vision cleared, she could see that she was standing on a narrow porch. The outer door was opened with a key by one of the white uniformed men.

Terrified, Marilyn realized what was going on. *I've read about places like this. I'm at an insane asylum. Why don't they just kill me? Surely someone will recognize me and blow their plan – whatever that is.*

Dr. Greenson pushed her into the foyer and led her to the front desk. A woman in a nurse's uniform looked up from her paper work.

"I'd like to check this woman in. I'm her doctor. She's a little bit confused about who she is. It seems she was a big fan of Marilyn Monroe's and now she believes that she's Miss Monroe."

The nurse turned a kind gaze to Marilyn and smiled in a way that showed pity for the woman. "Come right this way, doctor. We'll get her settled in a room and you can tell me all the particulars after that."

"Excellent idea." Dr. Greenson propelled Marilyn down the hallway and into the room indicated by the nurse.

Marilyn looked around. The walls were padded, no windows, no sheets on the bed and no bits of comfort. Marilyn started to shake even more as Dr. Greenson roughly pushed her into the room and the nurse slammed the door.

"Let me out of here." she screamed through the padding on the door. There wasn't a handle on the inside, nor was there a window to look out into the hall. "Let me out!"

Dr. Greenson walked out of the sanitarium with a smirk on his face. As he got in the car, he turned to Frank, who sat behind the wheel shaking.

"Who else knows that she's alive?" Greenson demanded as he slammed the car door shut.

"Just us." Frank placed his forehead on the steering wheel.

"Don't forget Lawford and Kennedy." Greenson smacked a beefy hand on the dashboard. "Tell anyone and we're both dead. Do you understand? If the boss gets wind of this we won't finish out the hour."

"I swear I'll keep it to myself." Frank lifted his head turning the ignition switch.

"Good! Get us back to town and see what you can find out from those two. They aren't telling so they must know something." Greenson leaned his head back against the seat and cursed until they were well onto the highway.

Frank looked at his watch for the tenth time in ten minutes. "Where are they?" he asked Sam.

"They said they'd be here. Why the Los Angeles Zoo?"

"It's very public," Frank scowled.

Peter and Bobby rounded the cage that held the monkeys. They spotted Frank.

"Well here you are." Frank extended a hand to Bobby, who ignored it.

"Okay. What did you want to see us about? If my father finds out we've been talking to you we're all taking a hit." Bobby moved on down the sidewalk until he found a picnic table.

Frank and Sam sat on one side while Peter and Bobby faced them.

"I just wanted us to be friends again. Pete, we've been friends a long time. You're one of the Rat Pack and I miss you."

"Well Frank, it's just too much with the teamsters mess. Everything's so political now." Peter ran a hand through his hair.

"Yeah, but it doesn't have to be with us."

"Oh, but it does." Bobby interjected. "I'm sure you've not failed to notice that John and I are against organized crime, and as we have political power, we're in a position to disperse it."

"Everyone knows that. We also know that you were behind Hoffa's nabbing. What does that have to do with Peter?"

"Gee Frank," Bobby tapped his fingers on the table, "you can't play both sides. You're either a good guy or a bad boy. You can't change who you are any more than we can."

Peter found the paper beside his morning cup and poured himself some coffee. He picked up the paper, shook it out and glanced at the headlines.

Spewing coffee all over the table cloth, Peter choked as he stared at the picture glaring back at him. It was the one he'd bought back, negatives and all from that rag.

The caption read, "Jackie Kennedy admitted to Asylum; she now believes she's Marilyn."

The article continued with a full account of the woman thinking she was Marilyn Monroe and was now being treated for her condition.

"I paid you for those pictures. You can't do this I'll sue." Peter screamed into the phone at the managing editor a few minutes later. He slammed down the receiver.

Pat walked into the room, rubbing at her eyes. "What's all the screaming? Did someone die?"

"LOOK! Just look at this." Pat sat down, poured herself some coffee and read the article with a calmness that surprised Peter.

Pat looked at him after she'd finished reading. "Well, at least now you know where she is. What are you going to do about it?"

Marilyn sat in front of her new doctor. "I'm not crazy. I am Marilyn Monroe. Don't you recognize me?"

"Miss. . ." the doctor consulted her chart, "Davison, I realize that sometimes it's hard when one of our idols passes on in such a tragic way. However, you are Cheryl Davison not Marilyn Monroe."

"I am too Marilyn. Just ask me anything about myself and I'll tell you."

"All of Miss Monroe's records were made public so you'd know any amount of details as would most Americans. Now Miss Davison, let's try an exercise. You repeat after me. My name is Cheryl Davison."

"But I'm not Cheryl Davison, I'm Marilyn Monroe. Why won't anyone believe me?"

The doctor consulted her chart again. "It's a good thing that Dr. Greenson paid for six weeks in advance because at this rate you'll be here a long, long time. You do want to go home don't you, Miss Davison?"

"I don't have a home to go to. I'm legally dead so everything has been locked up in trust. I have nothing left."

"Now Miss Davison, you certainly do have a home. Dr. Greenson lists it in Beverly Hills."

"Good ole Dr. Greenson. A girl can always count on him."

"Nurse Hadley?" Peter asked into the receiver.

"Yes?"

"This is Peter Lawford. I was wondering if you could do me a favor."

"What is it, Mr. Lawford?"

"I need you to attend to Norma Jean again. You see it's a delicate situation and she needs a caring friend to help her out."

Chapter 20

September 8, 1962

John stood watching his wife as she slept on the couch in their private chambers at the White House. She still looked pale and sickly after the ordeal of the birthday party, even though that was a month ago now. *I've failed you, Jackie. I could've been more discreet and saved you the embarrassment. I'll try to do better.*

He stroked back a lock of hair from her temple and covered her with the blanket. Even the trip to Italy hadn't done as much for her spirits as they both hoped. She stirred. Though she wasn't crying all the time anymore, she was still avoiding him, her duties and the public.

I know you're grieving for our marriage and hate Washington, but I'm grieving too, Jackie. Life has to go on when you're the commander–in–chief of a nation. You're the First Lady and I need you beside me. What are we going to do? John sighed as he stepped out of the room.

Frank sat on the park bench watching the ocean. He threw bread crumbs to the seagulls as he waited for Greenson to show up.

After the crumbs were gone, he balled up the sack and tossed it into a nearby trash can.   As he sat back down he saw the doctor walking on the sand toward him.

Louse! Look at the mess you've caused. We can't get out of this thing alive no matter what important news you've got. Frank scowled as the man approached.

"I'll make this brief. We've got to decide what's to be done about this 'situation'. "

"You're the doc.   I thought you had all the answers." Frank shaded his eyes with his hand as Greenson settled himself on the bench.

"Funny.   You're definitely the comedian."   Greenson looked out at the current before continuing. "The trouble is she won't talk to me. We're going to have to plant someone in the asylum to ask hard questions."

"How can you do that?"   Frank turned away from him, instead watching the sea gulls dip and sway over the waves.

"I've got a few favors owed to me so I'll call one in. I think Dr. Graves would be the perfect candidate. He knows how to do shock therapy and other treatments to get her to talk."

"Well doctor, what if she won't give us the answers we need? How will we handle that?" Frank smiled as a seagull poked its head under the water in a quick motion, snaring a small fish as it came swooping back into the sky.

"She'll answer. She won't have any choice if she ever hopes to see the light of day again. Try to trust me on this."

"Trust you?   You couldn't even identify the corpse correctly. How can I trust you?" Frank asked as he turned his full attention back to the doctor.

"A mistake; granted and possibly a deadly one if we don't get those letters. It's my hope that she'll tell Dr. Graves where they can be located. Once we have the letters we'll be free."

"Aren't you forgetting another little tiny detail?"   Frank crossed his ankles in front of him.

"What?"

174

"Shouldn't we find out who all knows that she's not dead?"

Greenson turned to Frank. "Good point. Damn this has rattled me more than I'd thought. Yes, we'll need to have Graves drill her on who helped her and anyone else who knows she's alive."

"Thanks for conceding the point. You've got two strikes and if you get a third, we could be dead."

"I'm sorry, Frank. I know that I've screwed up and if the boss ever gets wind of this, we'll both be a memory."

"You've never told me who 'the boss' is."

"It's far safer if you don't know, Frank. You've little reason to trust me, but on this one, the less you know the better." Greenson stood up. "I'll let you know how things progress with Dr. Graves and our 'patient'."

Nurse Barbara Hadley arrived at the asylum two days after Marilyn was admitted. *I hope the papers were right and it was Dr. Greenson that checked her in, otherwise I'll have a hell of a time finding her.*

She approached the front desk. "Where is the head nurse?" *Mr. Lawford this is going to cost you plenty. I'm about to throw up I'm so nervous.*

"She's in with one of the doctors right now. Can I help you with anything?" the young lady asked with a smile.

Oh great, prolong this agony.

"I'm Nurse Hadley. I've been sent here by Dr. Greenson to attend to his patient." Barbara handed her a prescription with Dr. Greenson's signature.

"Oh, I'm sorry, but no one is attending that patient just now. She's still in the padded cell. We haven't been able to calm her."

"I do understand and that's why I was sent. I've helped with her before and she listens to me. Dr. Greenson thought it might be helpful if I came." *Please don't let the lie show on my face.*

"Let me just call the doctor to be certain that it's all right if you work with her." The young receptionist picked up the phone.

"Of course it's what he wants. Why do you think he sent me? He knows she's going to be difficult and she needs a firm touch. Now snap to and show me her chart and her room." Nurse Hadley ordered in her best Army voice.

"Yes, ma'am. Right away." The woman dropped the receiver back on its hook and scurried off.

She returned after a few seconds. "Here is the key to her room and the chart is on the door outside her room."

"Fine. Just point the way and I'm sure I'll find it." Nurse Hadley snatched up the key. "Once I've checked on her I'll set up a station outside her door."

"Yes, ma'am. Just go down this hall a few doors on the right." The girl turned back to her desk.

Jackie sat on the bed, staring at the wall paper. *John, did I lose you because I wanted you for myself? Was it because I ordered your father to help me out? Oh God, does Jack know how I despised that woman and wanted her gone for good? Is that why he's been so distant? Am I ultimately to blame for her death? Oh, get it together! All this morose thinking isn't helping.*

Jackie rose from the bed and straightened her skirt. Looking in the mirror, she firmly set her jaw and placed a smile on her pale lips. "All right, enough is enough. Time to meet up with John and do my duty and vote for Teddy."

Nurse Hadley unlocked the door and slipped into the room, gently closing the door behind her.

Marilyn looked up as the shadow crossed the room. She listlessly stared at the nurse, who was half concealed, as she came closer to her.

"Norma?" Barbara asked as she squatted on the floor beside her.

"Barbara?" Marilyn sat up a little straighter. "Is it really you? How did you get here?"

"I think the better question is how did you get here?" Barbara turned Marilyn around and unlaced the straight jacket.

"Thanks ever so. I can't tell you how numb my arms are from being tied like that for two days." Marilyn flung her arms out to her sides then criss-crossed them over her chest stretching them out as far as she could.

"What happened to you? The papers said that Dr. Greenson checked you in here because you thought you were Marilyn Monroe. Only the caption said you were Jackie Kennedy. They never get anything right and if it wasn't for Mr. Lawford, we never would have waded through it to find you." Barbara helped Marilyn to her feet.

"What about Jackie?" Marilyn shook first one foot then the other bringing the blood rushing back into her veins.

"Apparently she's been very depressed and she isn't making public appearances right now. One paper had a picture with her, Pat, and Peter Lawford at some funeral. The paper claimed it was the funeral of Marilyn Monroe, but that's not true. I don't know where or when the picture was taken and you can't see her face, just her lowered head with a veiled hat."

Marilyn stared at the nurse and then began to laugh hysterically.

"Shush. They'll come in here with a sedative if you don't calm yourself. What's so funny?"

"It's an inside joke." Marilyn put a hand over her mouth and took several deep breaths. "In the last forty eight hours I've been terrified that I'd never get out of here. When you showed up I guess that it was such a relief that I temporarily lost my mind."

"Well, just don't make a habit of it especially in here." Barbara went to the door and looked down the hall. "All clear. No one was alerted to your hysterics. Now here's what you have to do to get out of here."

"You mean you're not just going to walk me out? I have to stay here?" Marilyn stomped her bare foot on the padded floor.

"Yes, that's right. We have to follow some rules or they won't let you out. I have to abide by them or I'll lose my nursing certificate. Sorry Norma, but you're stuck here for a while."

"What do I have to do then?"

"First you have to let them believe that you're settling down. Then you have to pretend to be . . ."

"Cheryl Davison." Marilyn supplied.

"Yes, Cheryl Davison. I realize that you'll have a difficult time remembering the name of someone you're not, but it's the only way to get you moved to a normal room." Barbara peeked down the hall once more.

"What are you looking for?"

"The orderly will probably bring me a cot and desk to set outside your door before long and I didn't want him to overhear our conversation."

"Oh. Once I get a normal room, then what?"

"Then we play the waiting game until the doctor releases you."

"When will that be? I can't stay in here much longer or I really will go crazy." Marilyn paced the room to get the circulation going in her legs.

"I'd say that if you play the game, you should be moved into a ward within a few days. I hope you're a good actress."

"Me too. What does it say in my chart that's wrong with me? Dr. Greenson said I thought I was Marilyn Monroe when he put me here. Is that what it says?"

Barbara flipped open the folder and read through the notes. "Yep, you're suffering from delusions, identity crisis and hysterics."

"That sounds like it could take years to cure let alone convince someone that I'm plain ole Norma Jean."

"Honey, you're not Norma Jean. To them you're Cheryl Davison, and you better start rehearsing that name until you believe that's who you are."

"Repeat after me," Marilyn mimicked the doctor, "I'm Cheryl Davison. I'm Cheryl Davison."

Chapter 21

September 30, 1962

Bobby walked toward the café at a fast clip. *This had better be worth my time. I've got so much work with the mob ring coming to a head. I don't have the energy to waste on nothing.*

He entered the café and saw two men seated at a corner booth. "Stansel, Latimer." He nodded to each man as he slid into the booth next to Stansel.

"We've got some information that you may be interested to learn." Stansel smiled as the waitress placed a glass of iced tea in front of him. "The Facilities Management Corporation is American owned by shareholders. The interesting part of this would be that the origination point is overseas. We haven't been able to trace the exact source as yet, but we're working on it."

"So you're saying this is a legitimate American company that's owned by someone who doesn't live in this country?" Bobby shook his head. "What possible reason is there for that?"

"I'd say that someone has a great deal to gain if they are awarded this contract."

Bobby picked up the sugar jar and flipped the little metal lid up and down with his thumb. "Since you must be an American company to win government contracts, it makes sense to have it divided by stock holders. But who is the main shareholder?"

"We know who the man is, but he's not the owner. He's just a pawn that a favor was owed to and his name fell onto the shareholder vouchers. He doesn't know who paid for them or when. We've reached a dead end in that regard." Stansel stirred his iced tea and looked pointedly at Bobby.

Shoving the sugar jar toward the agent, Bobby asked, "So what about the message that we received from Vice President Johnson's office. Any more decoding there?"

"Well," Agent Latimer began, "I've deciphered that the assassination attempt will take place in Dallas when he returns from his tour. He goes straight to Texas from overseas; so the hit will take place there."

"Anything else?"

"Not at this time, Mr. Kennedy." Stansel stood up.

Bobby pulled himself from the table and shook hands with the agents. "Thanks, boys. Keep up the good work. I want full details on the hit in Dallas before the president gets back from his tour. You've got a few months to figure it out."

"Yes, sir." Agent Latimer stood up, threw a few bills on the table and they all left without another word.

"Miss Davison, it's been three and a half weeks since you've joined us. You've made good progress." Dr. Graves smiled at her from across his desk.

"Thank you." Marilyn answered with a meekness only an actress could muster.

"I see that you had a little set back with hysterics in the cafeteria last week." The doctor was looking at her chart.

"That wasn't my fault. They served me gray meat and I refused to eat it. The worker then asked me if it wasn't good enough for a sex symbol and I told him no, it wasn't. He sneered at me and I threw the tray on the floor." Marilyn lifted her chin and sat up straighter.

"Don't get you're hackles up, Miss Davison. Sometimes the workers aren't exactly tactful. I see he signed his name to this report. I'll check into it."

"Why bother? Everyone here knows that never does any good. You always believe the staff over the patients. After all we're nuts; they're sane. Why believe that the staff might take advantage of that to taunt us?" She crossed her arms and leaned back in the chair.

"I'll make a note of your complaint." Dr. Graves turned a page in her chart. "You're making out fine in the semi-private room you've been assigned. No problems there."

"Dorene is all right. But I really want a private room. When can I have a one?" Marilyn glanced over at Barbara.

"Let's just see how today continues, all right?" Dr. Graves made more notes in the chart.

"I'd really appreciate a room of my own. I feel sort of strange sharing a room when I have a private nurse and Dorene only has whoever is working that shift."

"Let me make a quick note of that." He scribbled on her chart.

"Do you ever get writer's cramp?"

"Patient in humorous mood," he wrote and looking up, he grinned at her.

"You didn't answer the question, doctor. Are you trying to be evasive?"

"Not at all. I'm just doing my job." Dr. Graves put his pen down and folded his fingers together on the desk. "Now today we're going to have a different session. I'm going to do some hypnosis therapy on you. Would you be willing to do that, Miss Davison?"

"What like make me quack like a duck or walk like a chicken?" Marilyn sat with a straight face.

"No, Miss Davison. I want to try to bring to the surface why you feel compelled to act like you're Marilyn Monroe. I'll ask you leading questions and then tell you why you're not the dead actress."

"I guess that'll be all right as long as Nurse Hadley is with me. You won't object to her staying in the room will you?" Marilyn leaned forward and propped her elbows on the desk and then her chin in her hands.

"Of course I have no objections. Shall we begin?"

"Here? Don't you want me to lie down or something?"

"Miss Davison, I don't expect that you'll need to be under that long. I'm only going to ask you a few questions this time and bring you back out." Dr. Graves took out a silver pocket watch on a chain.

"Listen to the sound of my voice and keep your eyes on the center of the watch. All right?"

"Yes, doctor." Marilyn leaned back in her chair and relaxed. *I'll let you think you put me under.*

"You're going to listen to me count to ten slowly and then you'll be asleep. Now watch and listen. Ten, you're getting sleepy, nine, your eyes are getting heavy, eight, heavier, seven, sleepy, six, your eyes won't stay open, five, sleepy, four, sleepy, three, you must breathe slowly, evenly, sleepily, two you're sleeping, one you're deeply sleeping."

He waved his hand in front of her face. She didn't flinch. "Open your eyes and talk with me, Miss Davison."

"Yes, I will." Marilyn opened her eyes wide.

"No, open them like normal."

"Okay, I will." Marilyn blinked and opened her eyes correctly. *He believes he's done it, the arrogant bastard.*

"Will you answer some questions, Miss Davison?"

"Who are you talking to? I'm Marilyn Monroe." *I wonder if I'll ever get back on stage. This is an Oscar worthy performance.*

"You're Miss Davison, not Miss Monroe. Why do you think you're Marilyn?" Dr. Graves asked.

"Because I am."

"But she died last month. Do you think she lived?"

"I know she lived because I'm Marilyn and sitting right here." *I hope I don't laugh out loud and blow this.*

"How did she . . . um you live? There was a funeral for Marilyn."

"I just kept breathing. Doesn't everybody?"

"No. Let me ask again. Who was there?" Dr. Graves took more notes.

"Pete and Bob helped."

"Pete who?"

"I don't know." *This is too much fun.*

"Bob Kennedy?"

"Who is that?" *So you want to play mind games? Well I've lived most of my life telling people what I think they should know.*

"Robert Kennedy is the attorney general for the United States and happens to be the brother of the president. Do you know who the president is?"

"Of course. Jack. He's my lover." *Let's see what you do with that.*

"Your lover? When was he your lover, Miss Davison?"

"I haven't seen him since my death, but we were having a great time up until then."

"Miss Davison, you've not had an affair with John Kennedy. He's married to Jacqueline. You must know that you can't have me believe you." Dr. Graves scribbled some notes, frowned at the nurse and shook his head. "I'm going to bring you back around now, Miss Davison. On the count of three I want you to be fully awake and remember nothing of this conversation. Do you understand?"

"Yes, doctor."

"I will count to three and snap my fingers. When you wake, you will be relaxed and rested. Do you understand?"

"Yes, doctor."

"One, two, three." He snapped his fingers and she sat up rubbing at her eyes.

"How do you feel Miss Davison?"

"Great. I feel wonderful."

"Good." The doctor took a few notes and closed her chart.

"Did I answer all right? When can I find out what you asked me?" She leaned closer to the chart.

He placed his hand over the closed folder and shook his head. "You're not allowed to see things that we chart and you know that, Miss Davison. Please return to your room now."

"What did you ask me? Did I do all right?"

"You did just fine. Now please go to your room and I'll see you again in a few days." Dr. Graves stood up, crossed the room and opened the door for her. "Nurse Hadley, please escort her back to the unit."

"Certainly, doctor." Nurse Hadley took Marilyn's elbow and gently led her charge out of the room.

Chapter 22

<u>*October 5, 1962*</u>

Dr. Greenson answered his office phone. "Yes Graves?"

"I've got a report for you on our patient."

"I'm listening."

"Our patient is a little vixen. She tried to convince me that she was under hypnosis, but was evasive when answering my questions. I allowed her to think I was playing along with her little charade."

"You'll have to be crafty about it. Next time you'll need to medicate her first and then put her out." Dr. Greenson drummed his fingers on the receiver.

"Well I doubt that she'll take anything I prescribe. I'll have to get one of the orderlies to slip it into her applesauce at lunch. Her appointment needs to be right after that if we want to learn anything. I'll keep you posted."

"Good job, Graves."

Peter looked over his shoulder for the fifth time that morning. *Is Pat's dad having me followed again? If so, how long has this been going on?*

Picking up his car phone, Peter dialed Bobby's office. "Hullo, Bobby?"

"Now what?" Bobby sighed.

"I'm being tailed again."

"Okay, but I'm busy. Can't you handle this?"

Peter checked the rearview mirror. "Do you think your dad knows about Marilyn? I'm worried that he's been watching me for a while."

"What makes you think you're being followed?"

"I've been driving all over town running errands today and I've noticed the same car behind me at least five times. I don't think even coincidence would allow for that frequency."

"I'll call Dad and see what's up. You know he does this if he thinks you're fooling around on Patty."

"I know, but I'm not. When have I had the time?" Peter stopped in front of the dry cleaners. "I just pulled into a parking space and that car passed me. I'm going to wait a few minutes before I leave to see if I can lose him."

"All right, Pete. I'll get back to you after I visit with Dad. Surely he doesn't know about Marilyn or we would've heard about it by now."

"Yeah, sure. I'm just being paranoid. Maybe that's why I took the diary into the dressing room with me instead of leaving it in the car. Maybe I sensed that I was being followed again. I often get the feeling that my stuff has been moved around."

"Keep your guard up." Bobby hung up his end.

Replacing the receiver, Peter left the lot. After a few minutes he smiled. *I've lost them. Yahoo!*

The phone rang, startling Peter into the next lane. Fortunately, there was no oncoming traffic.

"Hullo?"

"Where are the documents, Lawford?" Greenson asked.

"I'm still working on getting them. There's no telling where she hid them." Peter turned on his blinker.

"Find them. You're running out of time."

"Really?   And what happens if they're not found, Greenson?"

"Do you have to ask?"

McGeorge Bundy shifted nervously as he was escorted up to the president's private residence. He kept shifting the folder in his hands with the damning evidence.

As he stepped off the elevator, John Kennedy met him in the foyer. Kennedy was straightening his tie as Bundy held out the folder.

"Mr. President, this is a matter of national security."

Kennedy took the folder and flipped through the photos of various military bases in Cuba showing nuclear missiles on launch pads.

"What type of range do these have, Bundy?" John studied the photos closer while he was briefed.

"Intermediate range missiles, sir."

"Where did Castro get them?"

"Khrushchev."

"I knew that bastard was lying about only having defense weapons. What does this do to our coast along Florida?"

"It brings the Cold War within eighty miles of our borders, sir."

"How did they get to Cuba?" Jack slapped the photo of the missiles.

"They arrived on Soviet ships."

"Call an emergency meeting with the pentagon."

"His house is clean. No sign of any papers from the White House." Sam sat beside Frank on a bench in Central Park.

"What about his vehicles or dressing room?"

"Clean."

"You're sure?" Frank tossed bird seed on the pavement.

"Absolutely. Tony disguised himself as part of the cleaning crew. He was able to check everything out. He came up with nothing."

"Are you still following him?"

"Yea, but there doesn't seem to be much point. He only goes to the studio and home."

"All right. Keep watching him for now. He may be waiting until he thinks we're not tailing him anymore."

"Hi, Dad." Bobby held the receiver closer to his ear.

"I'm busy, Robert. What do you want?"

"Are you having Peter followed again?"

"Not since late August. He was seen on the beach with a dark haired woman with a broken arm and a week or so before that he was seen taking a blonde to a bungalow in Malibu. I stopped having him tailed when he didn't stay more than a few minutes on either occasion."

"I see. He knows that you watch him, but he swears he's faithful to Pat."

"Look Bobby, must we talk about little family disagreements right now? I've got to get back to Johnson."

"The vice president?"

"Yes. Goodbye."

"I've traced the source back to a Swiss bank account. It went from the US to Canada and the trail ends in Switzerland. I'll keep trying to trace the exact source, but it usually takes a while to unearth," Agent Latimer reported.

Bobby sat across from him at a picnic table near the White House. "Great work. Have you determined if there are other smaller companies involved with the Facilities Management Corporation?"

"Yes, we've traced three; one in Cuba, one in Canada and one apparently began in Wisconsin. I've sent Agent Stansel to Milwaukee to see what he can uncover. I'll keep you posted."

"Did you have a nice lunch, Miss Davison?" Dr. Graves ushered her into his office.

"My applesauce tasted a bit sour." Marilyn raked her tongue across her top teeth for emphasis.

"I'm sorry that it didn't meet with your approval. Shall we get started with today's session?" Dr. Graves led her over to his couch.

Marilyn sat down and crossed her legs.

"Miss Davison, I need for you to lay down flat and relax completely. I'm going to dim the lights for a few minutes and hopefully when I return you'll be ready for the session."

"Mr. Lawford? Something happened today." Nurse Hadley whispered into the phone.

"I can't talk to you on this phone. I'll call right back."

She answered the phone on the first ring.

Peter gripped the receiver so hard his knuckles turned white. "What's going on?"

"The doctor drugged her applesauce and he put her under. She told him that Joe Kennedy was trying to work with LBJ to get the conflict blown into war. When John refused, Joe bribed LBJ to get involved with a contract to provide weapons on both sides."

"Great job, Barbara. How's our patient doing?"

"She's all right. She got moved into a private room today. It has a little balcony and her meals will be brought to her by an orderly."

Peter hung up and dialed again. "We need to talk."

Bobby was waiting at a booth when Peter came in. He sat down, ordered a drink, and then repeated his earlier conversation.

"Do you think this has anything to do with the Pro-Castro faction?" Bobby asked more to himself than to Peter.

"I don't know. Aren't they the same group that tried to kidnap Caroline last year?"

"Yes. Thank God we were able to foil that. Who can blame John for being so protective of his family?"

"What do we do with this information?" Peter swirled the olive around in his glass before sipping the martini.

"The better question is what is Greenson going to do with this information?" Peter shrugged.

"We've been lucky that they've kept this under wraps because whoever is the head of this mess, would kill them if they found out that Marilyn is alive. Frank is much smarter than we gave him credit for; but we're running out of time to find out who the mastermind is."

"So you don't think it's Sinatra?" Peter moved the silverware around on the table.

"No. There's someone much more powerful at the top. Greenson is scared shitless of him. That's why there's so much pressure for you to deliver the letter and memo that was in LBJ's office."

"You don't think it's your dad either, do you?"

"No. It's bigger than he can pull off. I have forged documents in this envelope that one of the staff found. Don't ask how or where. Trust me. Give these to Greenson as though they were the ones he was after. You're an actor. It shouldn't be difficult for you to trick him. Marilyn's life depends on you."

October 22, 1962

John stood back as the helicopter landed and his children tumbled out of the cab. He swept Caroline and John John up into his arms. Jackie waited for the rotors to come to a complete stop before carefully exiting the copter with Hill's help.

"What's this all about, John?"

Hoover met with Bobby over a quiet cup of coffee at three that afternoon.

"I'll cut right to the chase, Kennedy. I have evidence that your clan of brothers enjoy the favors of, shall we say, women outside of their marriage vows?   Now how do you think the public would feel about these 'indiscretions'? "

As the press set up their cameras and got settled, John Kennedy seated himself behind the desk in the Oval Office and readied himself to address the nation.

"My fellow citizens, let no one doubt that this is a difficult and dangerous effort on which we have set out...but the greatest danger of all would be to do nothing. The path we have chosen for the present is full of hazards, as all paths are - but it is the one most consistent with our character and courage as a nation and our commitments around the world. The cost of freedom is always high - and Americans have always paid it. And one path we shall never choose, and that is the path of surrender or submission. Our goal is not the victory of might, but the vindication of right - not peace at the expense of freedom, but both peace and freedom, here in this hemisphere, and, we hope, around the world. God willing, that goal will be achieved. Thank you and good night."

Having finished his speech, the cameras were turned off. Kennedy sighed audibly and leaned back in his chair. Secretary of Defense Robert McNamara came into the room.

"I've initiated DEFCON 3 as requested."

Kennedy nodded, turned to the credenza and grabbed the bottle of scotch. He poured out a generous helping and held the bottle out to McNamara.

Robert took the bottle, splashed a glass full and took a healthy swig. "We are staring down the gun barrel of nuclear war."

Chapter 23

October 26, 1962

"Oh Clint, thank God you've come!" Jackie hugged the secret service man in an uncharacteristic moment of pure joy. "Khrushchev is going to keep his ships out of the quarantine zone for 48 hours so he can talk to Jack!"

"Why Mrs. Kennedy, I didn't know you were so interested in politics." Clint laughed at her child like happiness.

"Of course I am, but this means the children and I get to go back to Virginia. Now we need to find a new place to live because Mrs. Tartiere isn't renewing the lease on the Glen Ora Ranch." Jackie pouted for a moment and then her frown cleared. "Oh! Now I can have a place of my own. Of course, it will have to be fitted with a pool and stables. And perhaps a tennis court?" Jackie smiled as the plans developed in her very fertile mind.

Clint sighed. *My wife is going to be so mad. I'm not going to be home for dinner or weekends until this 'ranch' is found.*

October 27, 1962

Peter stood outside his home watching the shrubbery move in suspicious rhythmic ripples. The hair on the back of his neck sent chilling tickles down his spine as he watched a dark figure emerge from the bushes.

Jumping back into the car he sped away, *Thank God Pat isn't home tonight.* He made it to the stop sign at the end of the block before he stopped shaking enough to pick up his car telephone and dial the police.

Joe would never send anyone to the house. Who the hell did? Is it just an obsessed fan or something more?

Peter stayed in his car in a well-lit parking lot until he saw the police cruiser turn onto his block. He followed them back to his home and watched as they searched the grounds.

"Mr. Lawford, there's nothing here. Do you want us to check inside?"

"I'd like to be certain. My wife is due home tomorrow and I don't want any surprises for her." Peter walked behind the officer up the steps to the front door.

"Is there any reason why she would be surprised?" the policeman asked as Peter opened the door with his key.

"No. Probably just a prowler," Peter shrugged, "but you know how paranoid women are."

"That's true."

Peter flipped on the lights. He poured himself a drink and waited for them to finish the sweep.

"All clear, Mr. Lawford. Everything seems to be in place."

Peter got up and showed the officer to the front door. "Thanks."

Joe Kennedy sat at his massive desk watching his irate daughter storm back and forth across his office. She turned on her heels and marched back up to him.

"Now Dad, you know that Peter isn't being unfaithful. Why did you have him followed?"

"I've had some disturbing information that is not your business young lady, but with his ties and connections in Vegas, he could be dangerous."

196

"MY Peter?" Pat laughed. "He's so wrapped around my finger that he doesn't go anywhere but the studio and right home."

"That may be what you think honey, but we both know that hasn't always been the case." Joe leaned back in his chair watching her face.

"That's true," she conceded.

"I'm just looking out for your safety, honey. I don't want you to get hurt." Joe got up, came around the desk and put his arm around her shoulders.

"Why would you think that?"

"He's always been a playboy. He's got a reputation with the women."

"He's a good looking man and an actor with a British accent. Of course he'll have women falling at his feet. You shouldn't worry so much." Pat walked away from him, arms crossed with her chin up. "My marriage is my business. Stop upsetting him. He's got enough to worry about."

"What should he worry about?"

"Oh, well, he's not having much interaction with the Rat Pack and he's working on a movie right now. So he's preoccupied." Pat drew back her shoulders and purposely kept her nerves in check, hoping she hadn't just let the cat out of the bag.

Her father studied her for a long moment, noticing her stiffening. "I've a feeling it's much deeper than that."

Dr. Greenson strolled into the Brown Derby Diner like he owned the place. Peter watched as the doctor made his way past numerous people who nodded at him.

As the doctor approached the table, Peter pushed the manila envelope to the edge. Greenson walked past, snatched the packet and walked on without slowing down.

Bobby stood in his office scratching his head. The meeting with the CIA had not gone well. *Maybe I'm just reading too much into this. Surely they want to keep the organized crime rings down as much as I do.*

He walked down the hall to John's office. Opening the door, he walked in without knocking. "Busy?"

"Yes. This missile crisis is going to be the death of me yet. I can't seem to get the Cuban's to understand our position."

"That and Hoffa. Are you aware that he's out of jail and causing problems on the docks?"

"Let the weasel alone for now. I've bigger things to contend with. Surely the CIA can help you." John glanced up from the stack of papers covering his desk.

"That's the problem; they don't seem to want to help. Maybe it's me, but they're taking a passive aggressive approach to this situation that has me puzzled." Bobby straightened his tie. "I thought we'd gotten past the whole McCarthy ordeal."

"The CIA is still recovering from the clean sweep. You know that's going to make your job more difficult."

"Yes, McCarthy was pure in his commitment to rid us of the crime rings and communists, but he sure left a bad taste. How am I going to get them to protect us?"

"You can handle it, Bob. You always get your way."

Lee watched as Ari put his robe back on. He came to her outstretched arms and held her close. "It's so good to be with you again, my darling."

"I've missed you, Ari."

Their lips met in a long caress. "I must be going. We can't let anyone catch me here at this hour."

Lee pouted. "But I'll be so lonely." She pulled him into her embrace, kissing him long and lingering.

"Don't worry. Nothing will keep me from returning to your arms." Ari kissed her hand and left through the French doors.

"Frank? Greenson."

"What do you want?"

"Lawford said he found the letters. But once I had them, they don't seem to be what we're looking for. Are you sure Marilyn had hard evidence?"

"How would I know? I was just following orders to get her and Jack broken up. The rest of this is your mess." Frank slammed down the receiver.

"Pat, darling, I've wonderful news." Peter twirled her around in his arms as she came into the house.

Laughing, Pat looked up to meet his eyes. "What is it?"

"I'm going to do a week with the Rat Pack in Vegas. They've invited me to join them at the Sands."

"That is wonderful; I know you've missed your old pals. What about Frank?"

"Everything's fine." Peter let go of her, but held her hand as he led her to the couch.

"You two have been on the outs since Marilyn's 'death'." Peter sat down and pulled her onto his lap.

"I know honey, but he called and wants me to come."

Pat gave him a questioning look.

"It was Frank who begged that I join them next month. He said it'll be a scream." Peter grinned and kissed her cheek.

"I'm really glad he called."

"Me too."

"Of course you'll be careful. We know that Marilyn pulled that stupid stunt at Frank's house that landed her in the asylum. Perhaps you should talk to Bobby to make sure you don't give anything away." Pat sat up, gently pulling away.

"Well, we're going to see them this weekend; I'll tear him away from Ethel for a while."

"Yes, there's bound to be lots of things you will need to be on the lookout for. Frank isn't just inviting you to Vegas for the show. My guess is he still wants to be in the middle of the political world."

"Pat, don't. You know how much it means to me." Peter reached out his hand to her, but she stood up and walked over to the side board for a drink.

"I saw Daddy. He's so paranoid that you're having an affair. He's doing his best to make a unified family showing since Marilyn caused so much trouble with my brothers. I heard him telling Bobby to do his duty with Ethel and get her in the family way. Maybe they'll have an announcement to make."

Agent Rex Stansel stood facing Bobby around the corner from the White House. "I've found out a few interesting facts, Mr. Kennedy."

"About the codes or the company?"

"It's about the company. We've traced it to a small bank in Milwaukee, but the funds don't originate there. They are sent directly from Las Vegas. Seems that the monies from casinos are deposited in Wisconsin, filtered to Canada and finally in a Swiss Bank Account with only the name 'Hughes' on it."

"Is that a first or last name?" Bobby leaned against the lamp pole with his arms crossed.

"We can't tell. We won't have any more information for you until we can determine which casinos the money is coming from in Vegas, but that will take time. It's all cash."

"Keep me posted on that. Have you deciphered any more of the message?" Bobby pushed himself upright.

"I'll have Agent Latimer get with you when he gets more determined. I think that's pretty much a dead end. Latimer said there's not enough information to get an exact read on it."

Chapter 24

November 2, 1962

Bobby embraced his mother as she entered the house with Joe. "Hello, Mother. How have you been? Dad?"

Rose smiled up at him. "Fine Robert, and how's Nellie?"

Joe nodded and walked away into the den. Bobby frowned before he answered.

"Ethel and the children are fine, too. How's Dad?"

"I don't really know. He keeps talking about Johnson and some conflict in his sleep. It's driving me crazy."

At that moment, John and Jackie came into the house, interrupting Bobby's chance to ask more questions.

"Jacqueline, you're looking lovely and refreshed." Rose leaned in for a tepid hug from her daughter-in-law. "Did you meet any nice men while you were away?"

John pulled his mother into his arms and hugged her mouth close to his chest. "Mother, it's so nice to see you. We're here to have a good time so why don't we go take your coat to the other room?"

Jackie silently handed her wrap to her husband as he turned toward the hall.

Rose went along for a moment and then dug in her heals. "Why won't you let me visit with Jacqueline? She's got such an interesting trip to talk about."

"Mother, you weren't being nice and it might embarrass her." John tugged on her arm.

"I don't mean to dear, but it would be nice if she'd find a way to stop pining for you when you were so smitten with that nice actress. I loved the way she sang 'Happy Birthday' to you. That was a woman in love."

"No Mother; that was a woman who's an actress. You can't continue to bring up someone who is dead. It's not polite and we don't want to hurt Jackie, now do we?"

"Do you really think that you matter to her? Your father just paid the woman to stay with you when she got back to town. He's had to bribe her from the beginning and you're not making much of an effort to hide your affairs."

John hung his head.

Rose continued. "I know your father wasn't faithful to me, but he never let me know who the whore was." Rose stopped in front of the bed as she tossed her coat on it.

"You knew?" John asked placing his wife's coat next to his mother's before he took off his own.

"Of course. Men like your dad don't feel worth anything if they can't have an occasional conquest." Rose turned back toward the hall. "Just hide it better, son. Don't publicly humiliate her anymore. It'll make everyone happier." She reached up and patted his cheek.

"Yes, Mother. I'll do my best."

"You'd better. She needs to get happy and add to your family to help cover up this scandal of that woman actor's death." Rose went back to the living room to join the family.

John stood for a few moments before he went toward them. As he entered the main room Peter and Pat came in. For a couple of minutes there were warm greetings.

Jackie was seated on the couch. John sat on the arm next to her. Rose watched and nodded her approval from a straight backed chair.

Once the initial conversation died down, Bobby stood up pulling Ethel up with him. "We have an announcement to make." Bobby smiled.

Rose lifted her hand. "Nellie's got that 'glow'. When are you due?"

"July." Ethel just smiled in return.

Joe stood up. "To Robert and Ethel, many congratulations."

"Thanks, Dad."

Agents Stansel and Latimer sat in the office.

"Did you decode the rest of the message yet with the senator and the vice president?" Stansel asked biting into his hamburger.

"I think so. The last part of the message 'and the governor's aide' is an old reference to a past CIA operation ran by 'Howard'."

"Howard who?" Stansel dropped his hamburger onto his plate.

"We don't know yet."

After dinner, Peter met Bobby in the den. "I hear you're going to go to Las Vegas and be with the Rat Pack this month."

"Yeah, I'm real excited about it, but Pat's afraid that I'll mess something up." Peter tapped his cigarette onto the table, struck a match and lit up.

"I don't blame her for that. This is a touchy situation. Frank knows our secret. I'm sure he's going to try to trick you into divulging information." Bobby sat down on the leather couch and crossed his ankles.

"When he called he just wanted me to come be with the Pack again. He said it'd be like old times. That we needed a little fun again." Peter blew out a smoke ring.

"Yes, but he is also trying to lure you into giving him ammunition. What are you going to say if he asks you why you saved Marilyn?"

"I won't be alone with him at any time, so he won't have the chance." Peter stood up straight.

"Right. What if he wants to know where the real papers are from the White House? I'm certain that Greenson has contacted him by now with the truth." Bobby raised an eyebrow.

"Maybe I shouldn't go. I don't know if I can handle that kind of pressure." Peter slumped into the armchair beside Bobby.

"No, you have to go and you have to pull off a few sneaky questions of your own. I've learned that our Facilities Management Corporation actually gets its funds from casinos in Vegas."

"Great. Now I have to watch out for whoever that evil force is."

"On the contrary, I want you to find out who they are and report back to me. This is a huge operation. I'm going to send in some 'others' to help you, but you won't know who they are until you get to Vegas."

"You mean some of the sympathizers of McCarthy who are on the CIA payroll?" Peter flicked ash into the tray.

"Well, look who learned something during the presidential campaign. I'm impressed, Peter. I really thought you were only chasing the cute college girls who volunteered at the various offices."

"That too, but you must learn something when you spend all that time with a political family."

"Okay, so I'll send you the information when you're in Vegas as to whom you're looking out for and where you might find them. I haven't got many details just now other than the name, 'Hughes'." Bobby raised himself up to a standing position. "Just be careful in Vegas, Peter. We're all counting on you."

Closing the door for the evening, Bobby turned to Ethel. She came willingly into his arms. "I think that went well."

"Yes, but you missed the conversation between your dad and John." Ethel pulled out of his embrace and picked up a glass.

Bobby followed her with a plate of half eaten cake and some ashtrays. "Ethel, you can't drop that kind of news and not tell me details."

She looked back over her shoulder at him. "Oh, yes I can." Giggling she picked up the pace.

"What have you discovered from the money trail?" Latimer sipped his coke.

"You know we've traced it to Las Vegas. You'll never guess whose casino it originates from." Stansel picked up a fry and stuffed it in his mouth.

"Who?"

"Hughes' place."

"Howard Hughes?" Latimer choked.

Bobby placed the last plate on the dish rack and turned Ethel to face him. "Okay, I did my end of the bargain. Now you tell me what happened."

Ethel wiped down the side of the sink with the dripping dish towel. "Be a sweetie and get us some milk. I'll sit here in the kitchen and tell you when I'm settled."

"You expectant mothers are so exasperating."Bobby grumbled as he went to do her biding.

Handing her the glass, he kissed the top of her head. "Now tell me please, darling."

"Well, Joe jumped on Jack with the Vietnam conflict issue. He asked why John was being so difficult when it was clearly agreed to before he entered the office that he would escalate this into a full blown war.

"John told him that the political affairs were his business and Joe needed to stay out of it. By this time both men were on their feet and shouting at each other." Ethel took a sip of her milk and then pulled a chair out to sit in.

"Was that it?" Bobby asked tapping his finger on the table.

"Of course not. You know your family better than that." Ethel put her cup down.

"Right. So what did Dad have to say about that?"

"He yelled at John that he'd talked with Johnson and they were both upset that John was being so difficult.

"John got right back in your dad's face and asked what he was doing talking to the vice president behind his back."

"Oh, I bet Dad couldn't believe he would be questioned about anything." Bobby sat up straighter.

"Well, judging by the red face I suppose you're right. Joe informed John that he would rescind his orders and declare war.

"John told him he was full of shit and that would never happen while he was in office." Ethel put her bare foot in Bobby's lap

"Sounds like Dad. Did Jack back down?" Bobby began massaging her ankle.

"Thanks, honey," Ethel smiled. "No, he didn't. In fact John told him that he would fry in hell before he'd declare war and there was nothing Joe could do about it."

"I guess that's why Jack and Jackie left before we came out of the den."

"There's no guessing. That's exactly why. But before they left, Joe got in the last word." Ethel moaned as Bobby hit a sore spot and rubbed it with tenderness.

"So what do I need to do to get the final shot?" Bobby caressed her calf.

"Hum? Oh, rub my back when we go to bed."

"Deal. So?" Bobby helped her up from the chair.

"Joe asked John where Jackie spent the money he'd paid her to stay with his sorry excuse for a son."

Chapter 25

November 3, 1962

Peter stood at the registration desk at the Sands hotel. He signed his name in the register and signaled to the bell hop.

As he started to walk to the elevator, the doors opened spewing out Spyros Skouras, owner of the studio Lawford was under contract with.

"Lawford. What are you doing here?"

"Mr. Skouras, I'm here with the Rat Pack for a week."

"It's odd that you would be here and not at Fox where you belong."

"As you've been on vacation, Mr. Skouras, you wouldn't have heard that the picture is finished and is now in edits."

"Congratulations, Lawford. At least you can complete a few tasks that are asked of you properly."

"If you're still sore that I whisked Marilyn away to sing to the president, you can be assured that I still believe you could've paid her more."

"I gave her everything. She was a dahlin', but not a princess."

Agent Stansel sat facing Bobby at the little café across the street from the White House.

"Mr. Kennedy, we believe that we have an idea about the assassination attempt. There are a couple of theories that might fit with this. The Governor of Texas has that right hand man, code name 'Howard' that could possibly be the one orchestrating the attempt. We aren't certain at this time, but we're getting closer to finding out his true background."

"What about Hughes? Anything further with that?" Bobby shifted in his seat.

"Yes, he definitely is running Las Vegas and is possibly the sole reason it's become so popular. Agent Latimer and I are flying out this afternoon to help keep an eye on Peter and just look around."

"Excellent. I'm so busy with the Hoffa trials and hearings that I'm in court more than in my office. I want him to go to prison for a very long time." Kennedy stood up and Stansel followed.

"We'll keep you informed."

Peter walked into his suite behind the bellman. After he tipped the boy, he surveyed the room. On the table was a huge basket of fruit, a large bottle of champagne and a bouquet of flowers.

He walked over to the table and picked up the card. "To Peter. Welcome back to the Pack! Frank."

Two hours later they were standing on stage together with Dean Martin and Sammy Davis Jr. Frank put his arm around Peter and announced to the audience.

"Ladies and Gentlemen, we're so glad to have our dearest pal, Peter Lawford, here with us this week. He's just finished in Hollywood and deserves a vacation. Somebody fix this man a vodka and tonic."

As the audience applauded, Frank turned to Peter and gave him a full bear hug. The normal routine began.

This is great. I'm back, here on this stage, here smelling the arid smell of matches burning and candle flames flickering.

I've missed these guys. If only I could get Marilyn out here the Pack would be complete.

After the show Frank shook Peter's hand. "Come on up to my room with the gang. We've got to catch up, don't we pal?"

Marilyn stood on her little balcony with her arms crossed over her chest. "Really, Barbara. I'm sick of this place. I need out."

"But Mr. Lawford thinks it's better for you to be here for now."

"I don't care what Peter thinks. He's not the one stuck in this two bit dump. I've paid for my mistake with Frank. I need to move on." Marilyn stomped her foot.

"I'll get in touch with Mr. Lawford and see what can be arranged. He'll need to find you somewhere else to go." The nurse tilted her head up to see her charge better.

"Don't you understand, Barbara? I want to help Jack, need to help him, must help him. I haven't done very much to make his life safe. I need to get back to my house. I've hidden some tapes there that are valuable to saving him." Marilyn plopped down in the chair opposite Barbara.

What? Does Mr. Lawford know about this?"

"Peter, it's so great to have you here." Dean placed a drink in Peter's hand and then he sloshed more into his own glass.

"Thanks for having me back, guys." Peter sat down near Sammy.

"So Frank tells us you've just finished a picture, '*Advise and Consent*'?" Dean held out his pinky finger exposing the large ring on it, while he raised his snifter to his lips.

"Yes. It's a great movie about a Washington politician."

"That shouldn't be hard for you to manage. You've got lots of experience with Washington politicians." Frank blew a cloud of smoke out from his cigarette as he exhaled, then he chuckled.

211

"Yeah," Sammy put in, "how's it going in the White House these days?"

"I wouldn't really know. I've been so busy making this film that I've only been to one family get together in the last month. We don't really talk politics when we're together."

"Sure, Pete, and they're not Catholic either." Dean poured himself more brandy.

"We just catch up on the happenings in the family. John and Jackie are building a house in Virginia, Bobby and Ethel are expecting, and the kids are all doing well." Peter took a sip and leaned back in his chair.

"Well, it all sounds very cozy." Frank held up the decanter with a raised eyebrow.

Peter shook his head in the negative. "They're just trying to have normal relationships."

"Right, that's why Jackie was in Italy for a month and John's been tucked into the White House with the Cuban missile crisis. I saw in the tabloid where Aristotle Onassis was on the beach with them." Dean poured himself another snifter.

"Yes, he was there to visit with Jackie's sister, Lee. She's keen for him."

"I bet her husband doesn't mind too much since he has a reputation for inviting high-paid hookers to stay with him." Frank laughed.

"Well, none of us are saints. I mean are any of you fellow's faithful to your wives or girlfriends?" Peter defended.

"I'm faithful to Juliet." Frank wiggled a finger at Peter. "But after the wedding, that may be a different story."

"Isn't it always?" Sammy raised his glass in a manly salute.

"So, back to your picture; how close to your family does the screen play run?" Dean wondered as he leaned his head back against the cushion of the chair and closed his eyes.

"I guess there are some parallels." Peter frowned.

"Right, like does the secretary of state resemble anyone you know? It's about the sec-right?" Dean opened his eyes and took another swig.

"Yes Deano, that's what it's about. I just played my part and went home to Pat every night."

"So Daddy's been having you tailed again?" Sammy teased.

"Yeah, or someone." Peter sent a look to Frank.

"Well, I've been busy here in Vegas and staying away from the teamsters as much as possible. You know, Sam and Hoffa have been in lots of trouble and I don't need to be associated with that kind of thing." Frank took a drag of his cigarette.

"Really? I didn't know." Peter sipped his drink and crossed his legs.

Frank snuffed out his cigarette. "Yea, your brother-in-law is giving them hell. He could benefit from my advice in this one situation."

Johnson walked into the oval office as the aide closed the door behind him. "You wanted to speak with me, Mr. President."

"Have a seat." John motioned toward the chair in front of his desk.

Johnson sat down and waited for his commander-in-chief to speak.

"I've asked you here because I want to know why you're having conversations with my father."

"Well, Mr. President, Mr. Kennedy called me and wanted me to see if I could convince you to escalate the Vietnam conflict into a war. I agree that we need to get this over with and war should be declared. So I've offered to try to help him get you on the same page with us."

"You really must decide where your loyalties lay, Mr. Johnson. You're either with me or against me. I need to

213

know which." John placed his hands on the desk and waited.

"Against."

Nurse Hadley watched Marilyn finish her lunch. She was just about to speak to her patient when a knock sounded on the door.

"Miss Davison? The new administrator wants to see you right now." An orderly stood by the door until Marilyn rose from her chair and followed with a slight shrug to Barbara.

Returning an hour later, Marilyn seemed a bit dazed.

"What?" Nurse Hadley turned with a pillow in her hand, poised half way over the bed. "Norma?"

"You'll never believe it."

"What?"

"I've been released." Marilyn leaned against the closed door.

"What?" Barbara stood motionless.

"The new administrator is evaluating all of the patients. He said there are numerous budget cuts; he's low on staff and needs to release any patient who isn't an immediate threat or danger to someone else." Marilyn plopped down on the bed, shaking her head.

"Well, there you are. You get to go without having to escape." Nurse Hadley straightened up with the pillow still hanging from her fingers.

"Yes. We're to gather our things and be ready to leave within the hour."

"Wow! That's quick."

"I told him I didn't know if you'd be leaving as well, but he said you'd have to go. He's not big on allowing private pay nurses into his hospital." Marilyn giggled. "He says they could be spies."

Nurse Hadley dropped the pillow onto the bed. "He's right to be paranoid. You never can tell what someone will do who isn't paid staff."

Marilyn rolled over on the bed. She closed her eyes for a moment and sighed. "Freedom. What does that really mean for me?"

"Right now it means you're not protected from Dr. Greenson. He'll know you're out and will be on the hunt to get you." Barbara sat down on the bed.

"Will you take me with you?" Marilyn asked.

"Where do you want to go? Anywhere you're likely to go they'll find you, catch up with you and kill you this time."

"Let's just get out of here and I'll call Peter."

"That's the most sensible thing you've said all day." Barbara nodded.

"Maybe he or Bobby will have an idea. I must get those tapes into Bobby's hands; he'll know what to do with them."

"Let me pack the few things we've got and we'll figure out a plan from there. We need to be far away before Dr. Graves figures out that you've been released." Barbara picked the suitcase up, threw it on the bed and began to toss things in it.

Marilyn changed into the dress she'd arrived in and brushed down her hair. After a moment, Barbara snapped the latch closed on the suitcase.

"Do you have the release papers? We'll have to show those at the reception desk to get out." Barbara stood near the bed balancing the suitcase on the mattress.

"Yes, they're right here." Marilyn picked the documents up off of the small dresser and opened the door.

Chapter 26

November 4, 1962

Pat took the receiver from the maid. "Where are you?"

"I've been released from the asylum. Where's Peter?"

"He's in Las Vegas with the Rat Pack." Pat sat on the edge of a chair, twisting the cord around in the air.

"I can't believe you'd let him go there. Frank and Greenson are the ones that had me put in the nut house."

"He's trying to find out some information from Frank. There's also some speculation that 'Hughes' is in on this scheme to kill John."

"Well, that may be true, but I need a place to hide so Greenson doesn't find me. He won't let me off so easily next time – he'll kill me for sure."

"Let me call Bobby and see what I can do. Where are you?" Pat pulled the drawer of the end table open for a pen and paper.

"No soap. I'll call you back in an hour. Don't let me down, Pat. My life and probably John's depend on them not finding me."

Peter jumped when he heard the knock on his door getting louder. He sat up rubbing his eyes. "Just a minute."

He got out of bed, pulled on his robe and went to the door. "Who's there?"

"Frank. I've brought breakfast, old pal."

Opening the door, Peter moved out of Frank's path as he pushed a cart loaded down with waffles, orange juice, sausage, toast, bacon and scrambled eggs.

"That's a real feast." Peter snatched a piece of bacon off the platter as Frank pushed the cart in front of the couch.

"Nothing but the best for you, buddy."

"Well, I appreciate the thought, but I'm a little confused as to what brings you here so early. You're not a morning person, Frank."

"We just haven't had a chance to talk and I wanted to play catch up." Frank loaded a plate for Peter and passed it to him.

"Thanks. Is there syrup?"

"Sure." Frank pulled a silver lid off a large container and handed the bottle to Peter.

"Umm, this looks wonderful." Peter tucked his fork under the eggs and scooped up a bite.

Frank fixed himself a smaller portion and sat down on the chair next to the sofa.

"It's sure good to be back with the Pack. I'm glad you asked me to come." Peter grinned through a mouthful of pancakes.

"It's good to have you back." Frank poured them both a glass of juice and drank his down in one gulp. "You know that I've long admired your connection with the Kennedys."

Peter stopped eating and looked at Frank with a frown etching his eyes. "And?"

"Well, I was hoping you'd have more pull with John than I'm seeing lately. He's not really been talking to you very much has he?"

"He is busy running the country. The Cubans have been causing him trouble since early October, not to mention the

Cold War in Russia, and this conflict that never seems to end in Vietnam."

"All of what you say is true, but he could end the Nam thing if he would blow it into a war. Maybe you could help me see him. I'd like a chance to persuade him that it would save America a lot of time and trouble if he'd just get on with it."

"I can try, but he's getting ready to leave the country for a tour. I doubt if he'd see you or anybody that's not a diplomatic leader right now." Peter took a bite of sausage.

"That's too bad. I could definitely save him later grief if he'd just listen to me for ten minutes." Frank shook his head.

"Sorry, Frank. I'll see what I can do, but it's really out of my hands. He hasn't been seeing much of anyone of late, not even family." Peter was trying desperately to get Frank to drop the subject. He had no intention of carrying out this request.

"That's odd. Wouldn't he do anything for family?"

"Ethel?" Pat asked rather too loud into the receiver.

"Pat, what's the matter?"

"Thank God, Ethel. I've tried to get Bobby, but he's in hearings with Giancana and Hoffa. Marilyn called me."

"Oh dear, is she all right?" Ethel sat down.

"They've released her and she's afraid Greenson is after her. What can we do?"

Pat sat down with a thump on the stool at the kitchen bar.

"Where is she?"

"She wouldn't tell me, Ethel. She's going to call back in a few minutes and we need a plan to keep her safe."

"All right. Here's what we'll do for the moment. We'll put her in the house in Malibu. That'll give us time to formulate another plan. I'm catching the next flight to Hollywood. Get her to my house. I'll be there in a few hours."

"Yes, that sounds good." Pat sighed and hung up.

Ms. Avery sat at her desk typing up contracts as the phone rang. "Vice President Johnson's office."

The secretary clicked on the tape recorder that Bobby had instructed her to use anytime a caller might have information. "This is Senator Smith. May I speak to Mr. Johnson?"

"I'll put you through. Just one moment." Ms. Avery punched the hold button on the keyboard and paged her boss.

Once he had picked up the call, she held the receiver to the microphone.

"Senator Smith. How nice to hear from you." Johnson's voice boomed over the receiver.

"Yes, are you ready to back me as a candidate for president in the '64 election? I can promise you that I despise the Kennedy defense policies as much as you do, if not more."

"My dear Senator, I plan to run against any candidates. Perhaps you'd like to be my vice president? We'd make a wonderful team."

"Don't patronize me, Johnson. You and I both know I'm a better man for the job than you are."

Ethel arrived at her home in Malibu to find Marilyn, Barbara, and Pat all sprawled on the living room floor eating takeout pizza and drinking bottled beer.

"Want some?" Pat held up a slice.

"Sure." Ethel dropped her purse and jacket on a nearby chair and perched on the end of a footstool. "But don't expect me to sit with you on the floor."

"Congratulations." Marilyn held up her beer. "I guess you'd rather have a cola or water in your condition."

"Yeah, I'd better." Ethel agreed.

Nurse Hadley was already on her feet. "I'll get it while you girls chat."

Ethel smiled up at her. "Thank you so much."

"You're welcome, Mrs. Kennedy."

"She's certainly turned out to be a great help." Pat laughed.

"Yes, and she's a good friend too. Now what are we going to do to keep me safe?" Marilyn swallowed another bite of pizza.

"I hope you have a plan Ethel. All I could do was get her here." Pat leaned back against the sofa.

Ethel kicked off her high heels and leaned against the arm of the chair. "I think we should have you pose as an employee and just live here. Who looks at anyone serving you?"

Marilyn sat up straighter. "I don't mind losing my identity, but I don't want to be a common maid or cook."

"Well, let's think for a minute about what else there is." Ethel sat tapping her forefinger against the chin.

"She could come live with me and Pete. No one would ever think to look there." Pat crossed her legs Indian style while snatching another piece of pizza.

"Bobby said that Peter's been followed so you'd be too easily found out. No, that won't do at all, but. . .."

Greenson picked up the phone in the den. "Hello?"

"Do you have the letters yet?"

"No, sir. Lawford brought me some, but they can't be the real thing."

"Oh? So now you're me and you can determine if they're what we're looking for or not?"

"Of course not, boss." Greenson shook.

"Get me those documents unless you want to end up like your patient, Miss Monroe."

"Yes sir, right away. I'll be right there. Where do you want to meet?"

"You're disgusting, Greenson. A sniveling dupe in this magnificent scheme. You know where to meet. One hour. I'll send someone."

"Yes, boss."

"Oh and Greenson, one other thing. If these aren't the right papers, if they are fake, it won't matter very much whether you were right or wrong. No, it won't matter at all."

Chapter 27

November 8, 1962

"Dr. Greenson's office, how can I help you?" The secretary filed her nails as she waited for the response on the other end of the receiver.

"I need to talk to the doctor." Graves barked out.

"You and every other patient he has. He's been out of the office for days." The scraping of her file could be heard on the other end.

"Where is he? This is urgent."

"Look, whoever you are, the doctor's practice has been closed. I'm just here until the end of the month to finish up the books. If you need an appointment I can recommend someone for you."

"What do you mean he's closed his practice? What is this?" Grave's voice rose to a yell.

"Sir, there is no need to be so loud. I've got my orders and that's what I know. You'll have to find someone else to treat you. Do you need the name of another doctor?"

"No you idiot. I am a doctor!" Graves slammed down the receiver.

"Okay Marilyn, where are the tapes hidden?" Pat asked as they sat outside the dark house that she'd purchased right before her 'death'.

"I hid them in the bricks in the patio. There's a hedge row made out of concrete, but some of the mortar was loose. It should be easy enough to get them." Marilyn stared out of the car's tinted window.

"Good. Is it safe to go up the drive with the car or should I walk?" Pat sat with her hand on the steering wheel.

We can drive. Once you round the corner you won't be able to see the car from the street. If we pull up to the garage, we're only a few feet from where they're hidden." Marilyn picked up the flashlight and waited until the car pulled to a stop under the awning.

Ethel opened the back door and picked up the flashlight. "I feel like we're on a treasure hunt like in Girl Scouts."

"Yeah, but this one could save the life of the president." Marilyn got out of the car, flicked on her flashlight and led the way to the patio.

Kneeling down she ran her fingers under the brick. "I found it. Now let's hope the tapes are still here."

Pulling the bricks away, she felt into the hollow spot for the tapes. After a few seconds of absolute silence she stood up with a small box.

All three of the women leaned forward; Ethel held the flashlight up while Marilyn tugged off the lid. They peered into the open box.

"They're still here. Now we need to get them to Bobby."

"Not so fast, ladies." A male voice halted them in their tracks.

Peter stood on stage with the rest of the Pack for his last night. Frank was singing and Dean was drinking while Sammy flirted with a girl in the audience. *Just like old times. This week has flown by. I hope Frank leaves me alone tonight. He's been hinting all week that we need a heart to heart.*

Frank finished his song and Dean began "Amore" while the women went crazy with applause and screams.

Peter stood slightly to the side to let the spotlight hit only Deano. Frank walked up behind him. "Hey pal, let's go back stage for a minute."

Nodding, Peter followed him.

"I just wanted to let you know that we're glad you've been here this week." Frank shook his hand.

"I've been happy to be back." Peter leaned against the wall wondering what the real point of this conversation was.

"If you want to continue to be a part of the Pack you need to help me out." Frank took a drink from a small table beside the curtain.

"Help you out?" Peter frowned at the question.

"I need you to get me in to see John; I'm tired of this run around."

"I've told you that I don't have that kind of pull with John. He's leaving on a world tour next month." Peter folded his arms across his chest.

"Well, if you want him to continue to live a healthy life you better see that he talks to me." Frank sipped his drink.

"What do you mean?"

"I mean that I know of a plot to kill him and since we both are aware that Marilyn is still alive you better pull some strings if you want her to stay that way."

Peter stared at Frank stunned. "I'll see what I can do. What else do you know Frank?"

"I know that someone is watching you, following you and I know they might be persuaded to kill you if you don't give up access to the president real soon." Frank winked one of his blue eyes and walked back on the stage.

Agents Latimer and Stansel sat outside the Palms casino waiting for their contact to come give a report. A minute later a couple walked past. The man dropped a matchbook; Latimer picked it up and handed it back to him. The man nodded and kept walking.

Five minutes later the agents went into the casino, walked up to the bar and asked for two beers. When the barkeep handed them the drinks, the men sat on two stools at the end of the bar.

Latimer leaned down to adjust his stool and pulled out a small folded paper. He tucked it into his pants pocket while they drank their beer. Stansel leaned down to tie his shoe and picked another matchbook up off the floor, which lay under his stool.

Once they finished the drinks, they left the casino and went into a small restaurant inside the hotel. They found a secluded booth in a corner and ordered coffee.

Latimer pulled out the note. "Hum. . . 'Hughes' can't be gotten close to. 'Guarded closely. Never alone'."

"That's not surprising." Stansel opened the matchbook. "11 pm, Sands, Pack."

"Well I guess we know where the mysterious man will be this evening. Let's get some sleep."

"Meet you at 10:30 in the lobby." Stansel threw some money on the table and they left without drinking a drop.

Marilyn nearly dropped the box. The man came around to face the ladies.

"Really officer, I can explain." Ethel took a deep breath.

"You're intruding on private property, stealing and destroying said property."

"Sergeant Clemson?" Ethel asked.

"You know who I am?"

"Not personally, but my husband is Robert Kennedy. He would be able to clear this all up. You see, he asked me to come here with my sister-in-law, Patricia Kennedy Lawford, to get a box that Marilyn had told us about."

"Why didn't you come during the day?"

"Well, we didn't want anyone to recognize us. It's kind of a touchy situation, if you remember." Ethel coughed.

"Oh yes, isn't it a shame? Well, I'll let you ladies go this time, but you have your husband call me tomorrow to clear this up."

While Ethel talked with the officer, Marilyn had silently taken the tapes out of the box and put them in her shirt. She replaced the lid

"I'll just take that box and you can be on your way. If Mr. Kennedy wants it he can request it from the chief."

Marilyn handed the officer the box.

"What's your name, miss?"

"Cheryl Davison."

"All right ladies, go on home."

"Thank you, Sergeant Clemson. I'll have Bobby submit that request." Ethel pushed Marilyn toward the car where Pat had already fled behind the wheel.

Climbing in, no one said a word until they had driven out of the driveway and onto the road.

"Lord, that was close." Pat sighed.

"Yes, but he got the tapes." Ethel leaned toward the front seat.

Marilyn pulled the reels out of her shirt and laid them on the armrest.

They all burst out laughing.

"Now ladies, on to plan B." Ethel said clapping her hands together.

Peter continued to lean against the wall, not sure if he was leaning or it was holding him up. After several minutes his knees returned to normal so he stood up, walked off the stage and into the dressing room. He picked up a decanter of vodka and poured himself a stiff drink.

Agent Latimer stood outside the open door. "Peter Lawford?"

"Yes?"

"Wes Latimer. I need to talk to you." The agent held out his badge and Peter came forward to check it.

"What can I do for you?"

"We need you to get some information from Sinatra."

"I can't. He just threatened to kill me if I didn't get him in to see the president." Peter poured himself another drink and gulped it down.

"I understand your concern, but we need to find out who 'Hughes' is and you could get that information from him for us. Tell him anything to appease him for now. We'll provide all the protection you'll need."

"Oh, Frank won't be the one to come after me."

"Look Lawford, time's getting shorter to save the president and if you don't cooperate you could be held as an accessory to murder." Latimer stood where he was until Peter finally nodded in agreement.

Marilyn's face was veiled with no make-up as she boarded the airplane with Ethel. They took their seats in first class, but no one noticed the two ladies.

"I'm glad that's over." Marilyn sighed, taking her seat.

"Try to relax and enjoy the ride. We'll be in DC in a few hours." Ethel pulled a miniature blanket over her legs and positioned the pillow behind her head.

"Do you really think this will work?" Marilyn fidgeted with her seatbelt.

"It's the safest plan I can come up with. It better work."

"What if somebody recognizes me?" Marilyn reached over head and adjusted the air control.

"Look, if you don't stop worrying about it someone will. Now once we get you settled there won't be anything else to concern yourself with." Ethel snuggled into the pillow.

"Ethel?"

"Yes?" she turned her head to look at Marilyn.

"Thank you so much. I don't know what I would've done without your help."

"You're welcome. May I please go to sleep now?"

Agent Stansel waited for Latimer in the casino. He was playing blackjack when his partner returned. Stansel raised an eyebrow and folded his hand.

"Well is he in?"

"Not willingly. He's been pressured by Sinatra and doesn't want to play anymore." Latimer shook his head. "He's such a pansy."

"Does he know anything about 'Hughes'?" Stansel dropped a coin into a slot machine as they passed by and pulled the lever.

"I don't think so. I told him to try and get more information. 'Hughes' is better protected than the Pope."

"He wasn't at the show as far as I could tell." Stansel dropped in another coin.

"Yes, he was. Hughes was in the balcony behind a sheer curtain. Tricky fellow that one." Latimer dropped a coin in the slot and the bell on top started beeping and blinking. "Great, that's all we need."

"It's never me." Stansel lamented.

"Let's find someone else to take this and get out of here. I don't want any undo notice." Latimer grabbed a young man by the arm and firmly stood him in front of the slot machine. "You dropped the coin in and the machine went crazy. Got it?"

The young man's wife stepped up eagerly. "Yes, we won!" She jumped up and down. "James, we won, we won."

As the security guard approached, Latimer and Stansel melted into the gathering crowd.

Lyndon B. Johnson sat on a bench in front of the White House with Senator Margaret Smith.

"So you want to be president?"

"Yes, I've proven myself in more ways than any man has ever done. I was responsible for helping women gain a

229

permanent place in the military. I sat on the House Naval Affairs Committee and I've scrutinized the Secretary of Defense exposing holes in his policies. Hell, yes. I think I'm an excellent candidate for the presidential race."

"Wouldn't it be better if you just stayed in the senate and stirred up trouble there?"

"What? And miss all the power? No way, Johnson. I want to be numero uno."

"Senator, while you've been a great help to me, I don't think you know what you're doing." Johnson shifted on the bench.

"I want to have the power to get rid of all the ninny-hammers in the military. This thing needs to go to war. We need to help the Vietnamese out of this jam."

"We both want to accomplish the same goals, but I'm next in line to be president. War is not the only thing that needs to be declared."

"We're both opposed to Kennedy's namby pamby ways." The senator agreed.

"Look Margaret, I know how you feel, but I don't think we're ready for a woman president."

Peter met up with Agent Latimer in a small hotel coffee shop at two in the morning. As he approached the booth where the agent sat, Peter ran a hand through his hair.

"Well?" Latimer asked stirring his coffee.

"Frank was evasive, but I managed to get the name from Sammy. He was very drunk." Peter signaled to the waitress and pointed to the agent's coffee mug.

"Good. Is it Howard Hughes?"

After a moment the waitress brought a fresh cup, turned it upright on its saucer and filled it to the rim.

"Thanks." Peter dumped in some cream and sugar, stirred and took a sip.

Latimer sat strumming his fingers on the table. "Is it Howard Hughes?"

"Look, I've had a long night. My life has been threatened, I've been forced to spy, and I'm leaving for home in four hours." Peter took another sip of his coffee, taking his time before giving an answer to Latimer.

"I'm sure it's a rough life for a famous actor such as yourself. So save me the sob story. Just tell me who the guy is and I'll leave you in peace."

"Rector." Peter took another pull on his coffee as the agent left the booth.

Latimer stopped before he left and dropped a couple of dollars on the table. "Thanks, Lawford. We've been trying to track this down for weeks. I appreciate how difficult this must of have been for you."

"Yea, I just hope you guys are better at protecting than you are at spying."

Chapter 28

December 20, 1962

Marilyn hung over the railing and watched as John and Jackie came into the house. She caught her breath in her throat as he pulled off his wife's mink stole.

"It's so good to see you." Ethel came forward and gave John a hug, turned to Jackie and gave her a quick peck on the cheek and then greeted the children. "We're so glad you could join us for this family gathering. Your mom and dad are in the dining room. You two and Caroline and John John join them and I'll go see if my children are ready to come down for a moment."

"Thanks, Ethel. We'll make ourselves at home." John took his wife's elbow and led her and the children to the other room.

"Really, Marilyn," Ethel scolded as she topped the last stair. "You could get caught standing in plain view like that."

"Yes, but as you've pointed out, nobody notices the servants." Marilyn sighed as she followed Ethel back into the nursery.

"I'm surprised at what a wonderful job you've done with the children. I didn't expect you to enjoy it." Ethel straightened a hair ribbon and tied a shoe.

"I love them. I'm so content here. They seem to need me." Marilyn scooped up the youngest and gave him a big kiss. He laughed and hugged her tight.

"All right, I'll bring them back in an hour. Take some time to rest because they'll be on a sugar rush when they come back." Ethel gathered her half dozen plus one babies and marched them like little soldiers down to meet the family.

Frank sat in his house drinking scotch and tonic, tinkering with the keys on his piano. He stared at the doorway where he'd captured Marilyn and clanged his glass on the shiny ebony piano top.

"You bitch!" he yelled to the empty room. He crashed several chords down on the keys and threw his glass against the wall.

Sam Giancana came into the room at the commotion. "What's going on in here?"

Frank ran his hand through his thinning hair and lit a cigarette. Gathering the smoke into his lungs he blew out a long puff. "Greenson. Have you no idea where the man is?"

"No trace. He's just gone." Sam picked up the largest piece of the glass and held it up as he raised an eyebrow at Frank.

"I just need to know where the son of a bitch is. We have unfinished business and you know how I hate that." Frank stood up, walked over to the bar, found another glass and poured himself a drink.

"All trails led nowhere. We've had all our men on it and he's vanished without a trace." Sam grabbed a trash can and placed the shards in it.

"Look harder. He's one man. How far can he run or how long can he hide before he turns up? I want to see him. Find him." Frank glared at Sam.

"You know I'd do anything for you, but some things are out of my control. If he could be found, we'd have had him by now." Sam stood up dropping the last shard loudly into the metal can.

Frank downed his drink. "I'm sorry. My nerves you know."

"Yes, we all know. You're famous for these fits." Sam patted him on the shoulder and left the room.

"Bitch. Bitch. Bitch. Where are you?" Frank began humming and stabbing at the piano keys. He sat back down on the bench and hung his head. After a moment he stopped humming and frowned. *Now why was I humming that? 'Fools Rush In'. Boy, that's too close to home.*

Rose sat at the dining room table with Joe sitting next to her. She smiled at him and he leaned in to kiss her cheek. "It must be the holidays."

"Yes, Rosie. It's the holidays." Joe handed her a chocolate candy from a crystal bowl.

"I always know when it's Christmas because you're nicer to me." Rose accepted the candy and popped it into her mouth.

While she chewed, Rose watched her family. Bobby was refilling glasses and laughing with Pat and Peter. Ethel was busy chatting with John and Jackie while keeping an eye on the children running around bothering the adults. Teddy and the rest of the clan sat around playing cards and drinking.

Rose smiled at her family. They knew how to play nice when it mattered and tonight it mattered.

Bobby came around with the teapot and refilled his mother's cup. "How's it going?"

"Great." Rose smiled and took Joe's hand. "It's so nice when it's Christmas time and I get to have my family all together for a few days."

"We love being together with you. Ethel and I are so delighted that you came to our home this year." Bobby patted her hand and kissed his mother's cheek.

"Yes, dear. Nellie is looking a bit peaked. Why don't you have her go lie down?" Rose picked up her teacup with a tear in her eye.

"What's wrong?" Bobby wiped at the tear.

"I was just thinking of poor Georgie. I hope he's having a lovely time in heaven." Rose took out her handkerchief and dabbed at another tear.

"Georgie?" Bobby looked puzzled. "I don't remember anyone by that name, Mother."

"My teacup, dear. Don't you remember the monkey tea set?"

"No, but I'm sorry for your loss. I'm sure your teacup is being well used by Mary in Heaven." Bobby patted her arm.

"I certainly hope so dear. Georgie was such a lovely little monkey." Rose accepted another chocolate candy from Joe, who simply shrugged at Bobby's questioning look.

Ethel gathered the children and started with them up the stairs. John came to her side with Caroline and John Jr. "Can I put them to bed in the nursery?"

"Um sure. Come on. We'll have to pull out the trundle for Caroline and there's a crib in the corner for John-John.

Bobby watched Ethel and John ascend the stairs for a split second before he ran to catch up to his wife. "Honey, let me take care of the children. Why don't you go help Ms. Davison with the preparations while we get them into their pajamas?"

"Thank you, dear." Ethel hurried on up the stairs after handing the baby over to him.

Ethel came into the room visibly winded. "Ms. Davison, you must help me prepare a place for the children. The president wants to put them down."

Marilyn jumped nearly two feet when she heard Ethel's warning. She stood rooted to the spot. "Oh, dear."

"I never thought he'd come up here. He never has in the past. Why now?"

"What shall I do?" Marilyn placed a hand to her mouth.

"Pull out the trundle for one and get some sheets for it. The men are dressing the kids and we only have a few minutes before they'll be ready. Bobby heard John and came to the rescue."

Marilyn opened the closet and pulled out sheets, blankets and pillows. She tugged the bed out from under its mate. Throwing the sheets into place, she had it made in record time. "Where should I go?"

"Just stay in your own room until John has left. I'll come get you." Ethel pushed Marilyn through the connecting door and closed it just as the men came in.

"Where's the new nanny? I wanted to meet her." John asked as he laid Caroline on the trundle.

"She's finishing up a few things before she officially takes over for the night. You can meet her some other time." Ethel took the baby from Bobby and sat down in the rocking chair.

"I'll stay with you until she's ready." John insisted. "I want to make certain the kids are well taken of."

"Really Jack, don't you think we take excellent care of our brood? Come on downstairs and have a drink. You look like you could use it." Bobby urged him out of the room after he put John Jr. in the crib.

"A drink would be nice. I'll come back and check on the kids in an hour or so." Jack followed his brother out of the room.

Ethel sighed in relief. The door opened slowly and Marilyn peeked around the corner.

"Come on in. John's restless and I need to rock him, but I can't while this one is awake." Ethel handed her the toddler and went to pat John Jr.'s back.

"Why does he want to come back in here?" Marilyn asked in a sing-song voice to help soothe the children.

"Maybe he wants to see if the new nanny is beautiful and sexy. You know how he likes to play. Um I mean – oh hell, you know what I mean." Ethel patted the baby's back a little too hard and he squirmed under her hand.

"Yes, I do know what he's like. I doubt he'd ever be faithful to one woman. He likes variety too much. I love him, but I don't know if we could've ever been true to each other."

"I'm glad that you can see him that way. John's such a ladies' man." Ethel kept her hand on the baby's back, but didn't stand up.

Marilyn laughed a little. "This is the longest I've ever gone without sex since I became old enough to have it. I just could never turn down a man who thought I was sexy. I didn't want to hurt his feelings or insult him in any way. For the longest time, I thought my only worth was in sex."

"Oh honey, you should have more faith in yourself as a person. Look at what you've accomplished in your life. You've climbed the ladder to become a successful actress. I'm impressed with all your accomplishments."

"Yes, but that's all gone now. I'm nobody again." Marilyn placed the toddler on the bed and covered him up.

"It is. But now that you've accomplished stardom, you've proven that you are special. You'll find a life that makes you happy, Marilyn. Don't worry so much. Your life has a plan; we just don't know what that is yet."

"Oh Ethel, you're so good to me. I don't know what I'd do without your friendship." Marilyn's eyes misted over.

"Okay we need a plan." Ethel changed the subject, "When the president comes back you should be dressed with your hair covered in a turban, your face with cold cream and in your robe. That should trick him. Just nod, don't speak and act like you're a matronly woman not a sex symbol."

While the women sat around the table with Rose, the men adjourned to the den to smoke and drink their port.

"That was certainly a nice dinner you served, Nellie. I'm so glad that Bob dropped that dreary Ethel for you. You're such a dear." Rose popped another piece of cake into her mouth.

"Thank you for the nice compliment. I'm glad that you're enjoying your stay." Ethel smiled and poured her mother-in-law more tea.

Pat pushed her tea cup toward Ethel. Nodding, Ethel filled her cup. "Thanks Ethel. You throw a fine party. Doesn't she, Jackie?"

"Oh yes, fine."

"How are things going at the White House?" Pat asked.

"Hectic. I've been trying to redecorate some of the rooms and it's just not going as well as I'd hoped." Jackie sat with her hands folded in her lap.

"I'm sure that it'll come together like you want it to." Pat sipped her tea. "So how's Lee doing? I understand she's off with Aristotle Onassis and Maria Callas on his yacht again."

"Yes, Stas is going to join them next week for the New Year."

"I think that's fun. I bet the fireworks off of a yacht would be gorgeous when viewed from the water."

"Yes, she's having a grand time. I don't know what she sees in him." Jackie shook her head without moving a hair on her head.

"So Bobby, how's it going with Hoffa?" Teddy asked as he smoked a Cuban cigar.

"I think he's done for now. He got off lighter than I thought, but he's making a lot of noise on the docks. Something's going on with the shipping industry that I'll need to look into after the break. I'd really rather not talk shop tonight." Bobby lit his own cigar then moved to the sofa and sank into the soft leather.

"Well John, how's Jackie spending Daddy's money?" Teddy asked. "You two aren't exactly looking chummy and she's positively unhappy."

"She's come across some difficulty with her schedule and the redecorating. Just women stuff." John blew a smoke ring and tried to ignore the jab.

Joe leaned against the mantel of the fireplace. "You need to get her with child. I'm surprised you haven't made an announcement yet. It's vital to the family that we show you are devoted to your wife and this country. You know it won't be long before you'll have to run the country and against a running mate."

"I know, Dad. I'm willing, but she doesn't want to."

"Nonsense. You're her husband; she'll do what she's told." Joe blew out his breath. "I'll talk with her."

"Speaking of talking to people," Bobby began, "I think we need to do something about Lee traipsing all over the world with Onassis. It looks pretty bad that he's flaunting his affair with Maria and Lee at the same time. What are we going to do to control the damage she's creating to your image?"

"I've spoken to Lee, but she's not ready to do anything yet. She doesn't feel that she's causing any undo stir and for once, she's in the limelight not Jackie. I almost feel sorry for her." John stubbed out his cigar in the ash tray.

"Yeah, but if she wasn't running around with that Greek we wouldn't be having this conversation." Bobby drank down his brandy. "He's been charged with violating the citizenship provision and he's had to pay the US millions in fines. He thumbs his nose at us and treats us like we're his government to run. Wake up, Jack. She's got trouble by the balls and we need her to cut them off."

Chapter 29

March 12, 1963

Agent Stansel hung up the phone and turned back to Bobby. "Mr. Kennedy, this is what we've discovered so far. The tapes you gave us are definitely the late Ms. Monroe and another as yet unidentified male. Some of the voices you might recognize. They're somewhat embarrassing in spots, but we've got good political information from them as well."

Stansel turned in his swivel chair and moved the tape recorder onto his desk. He plugged it in the outlet and turned the recorder to 'play'.

The sultry voice of a sleepy Marilyn came on. "Why'd you want me to marry the Prince of Monaco?"

"Well babe, you know that I don't want you to be just a movie star your whole life. You deserve to be a princess."

Stansel stopped the recording. "We don't know who this is for certain, but you can tell that he's foreign."

"I know who that bastard is. Play the rest." Bobby sat with his hands gripping the arms of the chair until his knuckles turned white.

"But the prince married Grace Kelly." Marilyn sounded pouty.

"Yes, but I don't have to pay hefty French taxes in Monte Carlo. You Americans have such a fondness for royalty and it makes the world happy to see you smile, babe."

The agent turned off the recorder and placed another reel on the spool.

"What else did you find?" Bobby leaned forward as Stansel started to turn on the recorder.

"The female voice is always Marilyn. She had a lot of men friends. Here's another one that will interest you."

The voice came through loud and strong. "Marilyn, I need you to stop going to Frank's house. It's been discovered that we meet there and take a cabin outside of the lodge. If Jackie finds out about us, it'll be a divorce for sure."

"Don't be angry with me, lover. You know that we can't keep this a secret. I love you." Marilyn answered.

"I'm not angry with you. But if Dad finds out we're still seeing each other, he'll do something awful to your career. He has enough power to do it too. You know he practically still runs the place."

"No matter what it costs I want to be with you."

"Listen, Marilyn. This has to stop at least until the election is over in '64. I care about you too, but I won't risk my presidency for you."

There was silence for a moment, the clicking of the line going dead, followed by the half ring. "Hello?"

"Marilyn, this is Dr. Greenson."

"Hi, doc."

"There's been a lot of gossip that you're not showing up on the set of 'Something's Gotta Give'. Are you all right?"

"Yes, I'm just a bit depressed over my love life."

"You have to get it together; I've a lot riding on your movie."

"What do you mean?"

"Look Marilyn, just get your act together." A click and a buzzing sound.

Agent Stansel clicked off the machine. "We're not sure what the dates are for any of these tapes. We can't tell if they're days or weeks apart."

"I understand. Is that all you got?"

"No, sir. Here's one last tape that you may be interested in hearing."

Jack gave a low whistle as he stood in the vice president's office. "He's really out done himself."

"Yes, Mr. President."

"Tell Mr. Johnson to stop redecorating and get on with the business of running the country." Jack moved slowly around the room taking in the elegance of the draperies and the new furnishings.

"Yes, Mr. President."

"Such opulence rivals the First Lady and she won't like it one little bit if she's one upped."

"No, Mr. President." The secretary lowered her head to hide her snicker.

Ms. Avery came around the desk and shut the door. "Mr. President, while the vice president is out of the office I need to tell you something."

"What is it?" John leaned against the door.

"I've noticed that there are gaps in the recordings for your bugging device. I think that the vice president has figured out how to turn it off when he is talking to Senator Smith and some others."

"How do you know that?" He stood up listening.

"The attorney general asked me to transcribe them since they're top secret. There were several calls that I know Mr. Johnson took and they aren't on the tapes." Ms. Avery picked up a large notebook filled with typed conversations.

She opened it and showed him a log. "Here, Mr. President, is a space that is empty. But I have it personally jotted down as a call from Senator Smith, yet it's missing from this log."

243

"Ari darling, can I take a few minutes to call Jackie? We've not been in port for a while and I need to check up on her." Lee kissed her lover.

"Of course. I'll go get us our table." Ari squeezed her hand and left her in a phone booth.

Lee waited until the operator placed the person to person call. Finally Jackie's voice came on the line. "Lee, is that you?"

"Yes, Jacks. We're in some port in Greece. I couldn't go another minute until I spoke to you." She tapped her toe against the metal surrounding the glass door of the phone booth.

"I'm glad you called. Have you heard the news?"

"No. What's going on?" Lee leaned against the glass.

"I'm pregnant. I've had my schedule cleared beginning next month and I'm going to Squaw Island in May to get some rest."

"Oh, Jacks! That's wonderful news. When are you due?"

"August."

"Have you told anyone else?"

"Just the family knows for certain. I've wanted to tell you, but you've been jet setting in Greece."

"We're just having a great time and Ari has told me, privately of course, that he wants to marry me. He wants to have the Kennedys as in-laws."

Bobby leaned forward in anticipation of this last tape.

The menacing, foreign voice began talking, almost as if reciting a well-rehearsed scene in a play. "So here's the ultimate goal, Marilyn. I would have all the recognition I deserve from your country. I know there are ways to accomplish my goals, to run the government without their knowing I'm 'in charge' and to place the mafia in every position of power."

"Whatever do you mean by that?" Marilyn's sultry voice sounded astonished.

244

"I mean that I have key players in positions just like back in 1957 when the Guatemalan's had their president assassinated by Rosselli. That sap Sanchez died for a noble cause, but he wasn't aware that he was the dupe.

"Poor President Armas never knew that his death was primarily a test to see if a communist could be blamed successfully in a conspiracy theory."

Peter sat across from Agent Latimer at the Brown Derby in Hollywood. "I have to tell you that I've found solid proof Howard Hughes has not been outside of his estate in years."

"What proof?" Latimer raked a fry through the ketchup before popping it in his mouth.

"Rector has become so adept at portraying Hughes that no one even questions him anymore. But he was on the set the other day and I happened to yell out to him. He turned to look for who had called him before he realized I'd called his real name, not Hughes'." Peter took a bite of his chicken salad.

"Clever, Lawford. What else?"

"I've done some snooping around and found that Hughes has become so anal in his obsession with cleanliness that he won't even let anyone in his room without them using eight Kleenex, and opening the door only twelve inches to ensure no flies come into the room." Peter sipped his cola.

"Wow! That certainly doesn't sound like the man we know as Hughes." Latimer nodded his approval.

"Not only that, but it's rumored that Maheu had the real Hughes kidnapped in the late fifties so that Rector could run his fortune. They are both under the scrutiny of a much bigger power." Lawford grinned in triumph.

"Maheu? Robert Maheu? Isn't he a detective or an agent?" Latimer placed a twenty dollar bill on the table, shook Peter's hand and walked away.

President Kennedy sat at his desk staring at his vice president. "Really Johnson, you don't have to agree to my withdrawal of the troops, but a thousand of them are already shipping out."

"I believe that is the wrong way to handle this conflict. You managed to pull out the Cuban missile crisis, but this is bigger. Let me take care of the Vietnam dealings and it'll soon be over." Johnson leaned forward in his chair, coming eye to eye with his commander-in-chief.

"That's not for you to decide. I'm in charge, I've got excellent military advice and I believe what I'm doing is right." Kennedy stood up, gaining the upper hand.

"Well, you're wrong and you'll regret this decision just like you'll regret taking the authority of the Federal Reserve and giving it back to the US Treasury to print our bank notes. You're leading this country to disaster. Why can't you see that?" Johnson stood as well and shook his fist at his president.

"The problem with you, Johnson, is that no matter how much I try to include you in the affairs of this office, you refuse to play nice. You wanted to be the leader and ended up in second place. What you fail to realize is that second place in this government is better than first place in many other countries. The only mistake I've made was appointing you as my vice president. Now get out of my office." John pointed his finger toward the door as the vice president left.

Bobby, Ethel, and Marilyn sat out on the back porch in the cool evening air enjoying the silence of sleeping children.

Bobby was gently massaging Ethel's foot as she rested against the arm of the porch swing with her legs across his lap. The gentle creaking of the swing lulled them into a short silence.

"Okay, Marilyn. Tell us about your adventures with Khrushchev." Ethel sipped at her lemonade.

"Isn't a woman allowed her little secrets?" Marilyn grinned and sipped on her beer.

"Not when it could affect Jack's life you aren't." Bobby frowned at her in the dim light from the porch.

"You have a right to fear him. The 'Red Bear' is fierce, but he's willing to be loyal to the United States for now. As long as he gets his nukes, he'll be happy."

Agents Latimer and Stansel sat hunched around the papers spread across the desk at the agency. Latimer flipped a few pages and sat down.

"How does all this tie in to a plot to kill the president?" Stansel asked, looking through the pile of notes and data for the tenth time.

"Rosselli? Is there a newspaper report of that and the aftermath here somewhere?" Latimer asked.

Stansel opened a file cabinet and pulled out several clippings. Latimer studied them for a moment. "Look at this, Stansel. Isn't that the same Guy Bannister that is now with our agency?"

Agent Stansel took the paper. "Guy Bannister, chief of police in New Orleans?" He looked over at Latimer. "Yes, this is the same picture, same man. What was he doing in the middle of a communist plot to assassinate a foreign president several years ago and now he's one of the inside men who guard our very own president?"

Bobby threw down the latest release from the associated press then stormed out of the den to find his wife. "Ethel!"

"What is it, Bobby? You're going to upset the whole household." Ethel rounded a corner.

"That Greek has told the Washington Post and I quote: 'Onassis's romance with opera star Maria Callas is reported on the rocks and his ambition is to be a brother-in-law of President Kennedy. . .' ."

"Now dear, calm yourself." Ethel patted him. "It'll never happen. Lee is still married to Prince Radizwill. He's just trying to upset you."

Bobby allowed her to stroke his back while she held him closer. He put his arms around her expanded waist and sighed into her hair. "You know how I despise that man. How can he even joke about a thing like that?"

"Honey, because you're his enemy he wants to do whatever he can to politically hurt you and Jack." Ethel smoothed the lock back from his temple.

"I hate him and his stupid superiority. I hate what he stands for and I hate that he's captured the attention of Jackie's sister of all things." Bobby pulled back from Ethel, took her hand and led her to the sofa.

Sitting beside him, Ethel continued to comfort him. "You're smarter than he is, Bobby. Think of a way to get them apart. I know that if anyone can do it, you can."

"Dad?" Bobby asked into the receiver.

"Robert, what can I do for you?"

"I need a favor."

"Well, that's different. You and I don't usually play on the same side of the fence now, do we?" Joe laughed.

"No, Dad. We don't." Bobby agreed.

"Well, what is it Robert? I don't have all day."

"I need you to use your connections and find out who is really behind the Facilities Management Corporation with funds filtering in and out of Las Vegas casinos under the name of 'Hughes'."

Chapter 30

June 4, 1963

Latimer and Stansel sat in a car parked outside of a suburban neighborhood in New Orleans. They had been surveying the area for a couple of weeks without any success.

"Are you sure this is the right place?" Latimer asked.

"Yes. Our sources are reliable."

"When was this supposed to take place?"

"Anytime. Keep your shirt on, Latimer."

As the two men bickered, Guy Bannister drove up the street in an ordinary sedan and parked in front of the house they'd been watching.

Bannister got out of the car, walked up the steps and rang the bell. A lanky young man with an Army haircut and thick glasses answered the door.

"Oswald?" Latimer whispered.

Ms. Avery met Bobby as he approached the elevator to his office. He nodded and turned toward the formal grounds outside. She followed a few minutes later.

"Mr. Kennedy, I've been trying to catch you for a couple of weeks. I wanted to tell you that there was a meeting in Mr. Johnson's office with Senator Smith and Guy Bannister."

"Do you know what they said?" Bobby leaned toward her.

"Yes, sir. I had the bug turned on in his office when I went in to straighten up before they met."

"Good work. Get me the transcripts."

"Yes, Mr. Kennedy. I'll have them to you this afternoon."

Rose, Ethel and Pat sat around the pool outside of Ethel's house watching the children and the nanny swim.

Ethel rested her feet in the chair opposite her and sipped lemonade while the other women drank mint juleps.

"How are you doing, Nellie dear?" Rose held her pinkie out as she sipped her drink. The mint floated into her mouth and tickled her nose, which caused a tremendous sneeze.

"Bless you." Pat handed her a Kleenex.

"I'm fine, Rose." Ethel answered trying her best not be annoyed. "It'll be over next month and I can hardly wait to see what we have this time."

"Well, it'll either be a baby or a baby. What else could it be?" Rose shook her head.

Pat snorted. "You're right, Mother. I personally am rooting for a baby."

"Speaking of babies, how is Jackie doing on Squaw Island with the kids?" Ethel looked over toward the pool at the children.

"She's doing pretty well. I think she's lonely without Jack, but he'll be home from the European tour to see the baby born," Pat answered as she popped a peanut into her mouth.

"Well, Jack isn't faring so well either because he needs a beautiful lady at his side. Bobby has come up with an answer to a couple of problems." Ethel returned her attention to her sister-in-law.

250

"You mean he's figured out a way to keep Lee's affair with Ari from embarrassing us anymore?"

"Something like that. Apparently Ari has been flaunting his double affair with Lee and Callas in the papers. Bobby had a big to do with her husband, Stas, and told him to get Lee away from Ari. Unfortunately Stas said that as long as she is helping him make money, he doesn't care who she's with."

Rose opened her mouth in astonishment. "You mean he doesn't care who she has relations with?"

"Not so long as he's gaining millions, Mom." Pat handed her a bowl of chocolates.

"My word. This world has certainly changed since I was a girl." Rose lamented. "Men cared where their women were even if they weren't faithful. Men bought women nice things to keep them happy after they learned about the affairs. Just look at what Aristotle Onassis did. He bought an entire island in Skouras to help keep his woman happy."

"Who would that be, Mother?" Pat raised her eyebrow.

"Why Jackie of course, dear. Who did you think?"

"But it's Lee he's dating right now."

"Well Pat, honey, don't you know that he really is just letting Lee in the limelight, a place she's always wanted, to be so that he can get closer to Jackie? Any crazy can see that." Rose put a handful of chocolates into her mouth and chewed with purposeful chomps.

Ethel and Pat giggled. Pat got her laughter under control and answered, "Yes, Mother. You may be right at that."

Marilyn walked by with a baby in her arms. "Mrs. Kennedy, I'm going to go put the baby down for his nap. Would you feel like watching the rest or should I bring them in?"

"They'll be fine. I'll send them up when I'm tired."

"Yes, ma'am."

Ethel and Pat exchanged glances as Rose stood up and blocked Marilyn's departure.

251

"Young lady, just who are you?"

"Ms. Davison, ma'am. I'm the nanny."

"Really? You have a striking resemblance to that actress who died last year. If you were blonde I could swear you were her."

Marilyn smiled and winked. "Why thank you, ma'am. That's the nicest compliment I've gotten in my entire life. I'll treasure it always."

Rose sat down, shaking her head.

"So would you like another drink?" Ethel poured her glass to the top.

"Mother, what's Dad been up to lately?" Pat asked, changing the subject.

"He's been talking to Bobby and they've been rather chummy. I can't understand it. They're usually at each other's throats. I wanted to make some lasagna for him, but Bobby has been too busy with security for Jack's tour that he hasn't come to the house."

"He'll be home in a little while and you'll be able to see him then."

Rose wandered over to the pool and stuck her stockinged feet into it, kicking and splashing with the children.

The women watched for a moment before Pat turned to Ethel. "What's Bobby going to do about Lee?"

"Why, it's brilliant. He's going to have her join Jack in Germany."

June 26, 1963

Standing at the Berlin Wall, Lee listened to her president deliver a speech entitled, 'Ich Bin ein Berliner' to the crowd: a speech that would make top magazines and she would be on the cover with him for this triumphant moment.

As the hands were being shaken, President Kennedy turned to Lee. "I need to talk to you about something urgent when we are finished here."

Smiling with the happiness of the moment, Lee squeezed his arm. "Of course, dear Jack. Anything for you."

They were sitting in the limo on the way to the airport when he finally spoke. "I need you to do me a small favor, Lee."

"I'd do anything you want."

"Good. I need you to renew your vows with Stas in a Catholic church right away. My campaign may depend on it."

"What?" Lee sat ringing her hands together.

"Yes. You know that we went to bat for you and managed to bribe the Vatican; by the grace of God and the gall of Bobby, in order to have your marriage annulled with Canfield."

"So, this is duty. Not a request, not a matter of love, not a matter of trust, but an order that must be obeyed." Lee had clenched her jaw so tight, her head was beginning to hurt.

"If you will."

"Why?"

"Because, simply put, I've given you several wonderful weeks away from your lover and you haven't suffered because of it. Now, I would hope you would be willing to do me and my presidency a favor by renewing your vows to keep our family honorable." John took her hand and kissed it.

"I'll talk to Stas, but we're over. I doubt he'll be willing any more than I am. You know I'm hoping that Ari will marry me."

"Yes, that's exactly the problem right at this moment. You have to wait until the November elections next year to get your way."

"I see."

"I'll make sure that you're monetarily rewarded." John stroked her cheek.

"Well, there's no question. If there's money to be had, then Stas is in."

Marilyn sat on the city transit bus with her hair covered by a headscarf and dark sunglasses over her eyes. The bus slowed to a stop in front of the Capitol Building allowing several people to exit.

Kenny O'Donnell stepped onto the bus and looked for her. He smiled in recognition and moved to take the seat next to her.

"Good to see you again, Norma. How's it going?" Kenny placed his briefcase in his lap and opened it up. He took some folders out of the case and handed them to her.

"It's pretty boring. I could really use a night on the town." Marilyn opened the first folder and glanced at the title, Hoover V R.F. Kennedy. "What is this for?"

"Apparently Hoover has been keeping close tabs on the Kennedy clan for many years. Do you have any additional information that you could add to help the case?"

Marilyn scanned the pages as the bus moved on. "I could tell you that Hoover was trying to blackmail me as well. He wanted me to give up information regarding my affair with Jack. I never told him anything he wanted, but the man was ruthless."

Kenny frowned. "Really? God, what did he think he'd get from you?"

She pushed the sunglasses on top of her headscarf and wrinkled her brow. "He wanted me to tell him if we were really intimate and if Jack gave away state secrets to me. He also asked me about Jack's friendship with Sinatra and if I thought Frank was a commie."

"Frank? He's a blue blooded American if ever there was one. Hoover is really grasping." Kenny took the folder back from Marilyn as she looked at the next one. "Here's one about him. It's funny you should tell me about that conversation with Hoover."

Marilyn read over the pages and laughed out loud. "Where did he come up with this crap?"

"He just makes it up off the cuff, but since he's the head of the FBI, no one can question his right to interrogate, even spy on Sinatra."

"But Frank has known Sam Giancana since they were in Hoboken."

"Yes, but if he can prove Frank is a commie, he'll be held up as an example. He's after Charlie Chaplin as well."

"That man is power mad." Marilyn watched as the people started to get up in anticipation of the next stop. "I've got to go. I hope this helps you."

Marilyn got in line behind a large woman and screaming child, waved at Kenny and disappeared as the bus door opened.

August 20, 1963

Jackie lay sleeping on the hospital bed surrounded by dozens of bouquets of flowers from well wishers for the birth of their third child, a son. It had been a sad day for the entire family. Patrick, who was born premature, had died of weak lungs the previous day. Less than three days of life had been allowed for their poor boy.

John stayed by his wife's side throughout the horrible ordeal, but Jackie remained distant, cold and numb. He ran his hand over her hair, leaned down and kissed her temple, and then covered her with another blanket.

Lee stepped into the room. "I'll stay with her for a while. Go get some rest."

John nodded and left.

Jackie opened her eyes at the sound of the door shutting behind her husband. She focused on her sister.

"Jacks, do you need anything?" Lee rushed to her side, falling on her knees in front of the bed.

"Just Patrick."

"Oh, Jacks. I'm so sorry." Lee hugged her through the blanket and kissed her cheek.

Jackie's tears dripped on the pillow. "I'm so hollow."

"I know. I'm here for you for a little while longer."

"You're leaving?" Jackie took the box of Kleenex her sister handed her and wiped her eyes and nose.

"Not till tomorrow night, but then I have to catch the late flight back to Greece."

"Oh."

"You've got the whole family to take care of you. John's here and he won't leave you. He's grieving, too. You'll be a great comfort to each other." Lee took the soiled Kleenex and threw it in the waste can.

Jackie's eyes were closed again. "It doesn't matter; just go back to your yacht and your lover."

"Don't be mad, Jacks. I love him, and I'm not sure how much more time I will get to spend with him." Lee tucked the blanket closer around her sister and sat back in the chair next to her bed.

Latimer and Stansel had returned to the office. They sat looking over new reports and data sheets.

"So we've identified Guy Bannister as the man behind the Rosselli plot and now he's associated with this Lee Harvey Oswald. Oswald has a communist wife and he's an ex-Marine. He's got weapons training and is said to be a sharp shooter." Latimer handed the data sheet over to Stansel.

"Okay, so Oswald is our man. What I don't understand is why his files are classified as 'need to know basis'." Stansel looked over the sheet and sat it back on the desk.

"Yes, we need to figure that out. I was talking with one of the CIA men and he said that he'd heard Oswald was involved in a communist plot against the president and the code name the CIA is using is 'Howard'."

September 12, 1963

Frank sat at the bar of the lodge with a large drink in hand; his eyes were fixed on the doorframe where he'd last seen Greenson.

Sam Giancana stood behind the bar nursing his own drink. "I'm worried about you, man. You're not looking so good."

"I'm still hoping that Greenson will show up." Frank took a long swig and slapped the glass down.

"Well, I don't think we'll ever see him again. Word on the street is that he's swimming with the fishes in custom made concrete shoes."

"Really?" Frank looked up, fully alert.

"Yea, hadn't you heard?"

"No, Sam. When would I've heard anything like that?" Frank's hand shook as he lifted the snifter back to his lips.

"That's not all I've been told lately. I guess you know about Hoffa and the docks." Sam sipped his drink and watched the chairman tremble.

"What?" Frank looked at Sam, his blue eyes twitching in the corners.

Sam watched him for a moment, took a drink, and then launched into his story. "Well, it seems that Onassis wanted to purchase a fleet of ships from the US, primarily those that Hoffa works with. This would have put many men out of work. For some reason at the last minute, Onassis invites Hoffa to lunch. He pulls out of the deal and leaves Hoffa's men to their work."

"Oh my God!" Frank jumped up. "I need to see Hoffa. Get Jimmy here and do it NOW!"

Chapter 31

September 30, 1963

Jackie stood in the doorway to the Oval Office. "I'm going John and that's all there is to it."

"Look, Jackie. You shouldn't be cruising around on a yacht with Onassis. It's bad enough that Lee's doing it, but you should know better."

"John, I've made up my mind and I'm going. I need this to help me get over Patrick's death. I just feel run down, tired of everything and I need some time."

"There are other ways to get away, Jackie. Go to Europe, take a cruise, anything else."

"I'll be back in a month. What could happen?"

"I'm putting ship to shore phones on that yacht whether he likes it or not. I need to protect you even when you're on the water."

"Whatever you need to do, but Lee and Stas will be there, and so will Mr. Hill. It'll be all right." Jackie stepped out of the door way and out of sight.

Agent Latimer sat on the usual bench outside the White House listening to Bobby tell him about the meeting with Johnson, Senator Smith and Guy Bannister. "So what you're saying is that the vice president has agreed to assassinate the president to gain control over the Vietnam conflict."

"Yes. Now how do we stop them?" Bobby fidgeted with his tie.

"We've already got a communist ex-Marine in custody. His name is Oswald and Bannister visited his home in New Orleans. Apparently he was the sharp shooter hired in the hit."

"So we've got it covered?" Bobby watched the agent.

"We think so. There may be a backup plan that we've yet to uncover. We're still working on it."

"I'm going to go have a talk with the vice president and see if I can gain anything from him."

"I don't have to tell you, Mr. Kennedy, to be diplomatic."

"Mr. Johnson, your secretary put me through. I've heard that you have an agenda against the president."

"Frank, it's always nice to hear from you, too. How's the Rat Pack?" The vice president punched the button under his desk that stopped the recordings from the bugging device.

"Are you avoiding my question, Lyndon?"

"Not at all. I just wanted a chance to think about my answer first. I don't agree with Kennedy on most of his policies and I have a lot invested in the private reserve. You can just say we don't see eye to eye."

"Well, let's hope you don't disagree enough to want him to come to any harm. What are you planning?"

"How about you go back to show biz and I'll go back to politics?"

Bobby picked up the ringing phone. "Hello?"

"Robert."

"Hi, Dad."

"I've got the answer to your question."

"So, you know who's behind 'Hughes'?"

"Yes. Are you sitting down?"

October 15, 1963

Marilyn sat in front of her mirror adjusting the long black wig she wore when she went out. She pulled the bangs into place and added the hair pins that would secure it throughout the night.

Ethel called to her from downstairs. "Norma! Your date is here!"

"Be right there." Marilyn slipped her feet into her flats and smiled at the 'beatnik' transformation. Her tight black pants were accented with a huge, gold bangle belt and tight fitting black turtleneck sweater. She grinned at her reflection, grabbed her silk wrap and purse, and left the room.

"Thanks Ethel!" Marilyn twirled in front of Ethel. "Do I pass?"

"Amazing! You look marvelous."

"Thank you so much." Marilyn hugged her friend. "I really do need this night out."

Frank sat across from Hoffa outside the Plaza Hotel in New York. "What's going on with the shipping industry?"

Hoffa spit a wad of gum on the sidewalk. "Onassis pulled out of a big shipping deal with a fleet of container ships. He's concerned that the attorney general will follow through with a threat he'd made to Onassis a few weeks earlier."

"What did he say?" Frank tossed peanut shells onto the ground and popped the nuts into his mouth.

"Robert Kennedy threatened Onassis when he called to keep Jackie from going on the yacht. Kennedy promised that the president would endorse his relationship with Lee if he'd just keep Jackie from coming onto the ship."

"Shit, I bet that went over well with Bobby. Toadying up to Onassis like that."

"Not hardly." Hoffa shifted on the bench. "They got into an argument that ended with Mr. Kennedy yelling, 'I will destroy you. You don't frighten me. What's in the past, you Greek son of a bitch, will be nothing compared to what's in store'."

"Damn. So what's happened?"

"So Onassis came to me, and called off the deal to nip any leverage the attorney general might have in the shipping industry off. He said it had something to do with sending ships into Vietnam with the vice president's blessing."

"We have to tell Bobby this information." Frank stood up and headed inside the Plaza Hotel.

As Norma and her date, Randy, entered the coffee house where the beatniks were going to be reading their poetry, she glanced around to see if she recognized anyone.

Is that Jack? She squinted in the semi-darkened room hoping for a better look in the dim candle light. *It is him! Who is that woman he's with?*

Marilyn watched as the couple headed up the staircase in the rear of the coffee house. They had come in the side door where they were less likely to be noticed by the crowd.

Randy escorted her to some pillows on the floor and helped her to sit down. Marilyn smiled at him and plopped onto the soft seating. *Who was she? I know I've seen her before.*

The reading of a depressing poem began as she continued to frown and puzzle the identity of the woman. *I'm not jealous. He's moved on.* Marilyn wiped a single tear from her eye.

Randy patted her on the shoulder and smiled at her seeming intense attention to the poem. Marilyn gave him a token smile and pulled a hanky out of her small purse. Randy stroked the back of her neck for a moment and then returned his full attention to the poet.

I know who she is! Marilyn sat up straighter. *That's Mary Meyer. Oh, I better check this out with Ethel when I get home. I bet Jackie knows about this and is fit to be tied!* It was one thing for him to be with me, but someone from her own social circle? Noticing that Randy was staring intently at her, she turned and smiled at him. He smiled back and took her hand in his.

"The Facilities Management Corporation is run by Aristotle Onassis under the guise of Howard Hughes' casinos in Las Vegas," Joe chortled.

"Holy shit." Bobby let out a loud whistle. "What else do you know, Dad? I can tell that's not all."

"No, that's not all. My sources have confirmed that in nineteen fifty seven, Howard Hughes was kidnapped, his double put in place, and his fortune taken over by Robert Maheu."

"What?"

"Yes. Maheu is working directly for Onassis who's believed to be the kidnapper. He's had the Mormon Mafia watching over the confined Hughes for years." Joe explained.

"Why would Onassis possibly want to hurt Hughes?"

"Same reason he wants to hurt us. MONEY. Doesn't everything boil down to cold hard cash? Really Robert, you're such a dimwit sometimes."

"Okay, so Onassis is Hughes and Maheu is his front man with Rector portraying Hughes. Where does it lead? What's the reason?" Bobby tapped his fingers on the desk in front of him.

"I did my part, Robert. The rest is up to you. Onassis is a terrible enemy to have, so take the son-of-a-bitch down before he takes us down."

"Jackie, I know you're on the high seas," John continued, "and I don't care how it looks, you have to get off that yacht. I'm sending a chopper. Do you hear?"

The phone went dead without a response from his wife. John shook his head at Bobby. "I don't know if she'll listen and get off or not. We both know she'll do what she damn well pleases."

"That's just great. Onassis is bad news. I think he's got something to do with the shipping industry again. I don't like it. Has he spoken to Johnson?" Bobby leaned across the presidential desk.

"No, I don't think so." John scratched his head.

"I'm going to go talk with him." Bobby stood up. "Watch yourself, John. I've a bad feeling about this."

"Ms. Avery, I need to see Johnson right away." Bobby announced coming into the office.

"I'm sorry, but he's out just now. His appointment shouldn't last much longer. Do you want to wait in his office?"

"Yes. It'll be a nice surprise for him."

"Hello Ethel. Peter calling."

"How are you?" Ethel asked.

"Good. How's the new little one?"

"He's growing. Do you want Bobby?"

"Well, yes if he's home."

"He isn't. Can I give him a message?" Ethel shifted the infant and rubbed his back while she cradled the phone on her shoulder.

"It's about Onassis. I overheard him a few days before Jackie sailed. He was with Robert Allen. I had no idea he was even in town. I thought he stayed mostly in Greece, but there he was sitting calm as you please lunching with Marilyn's old publicist."

"Go on. I can tell Bobby."

"It was a weird conversation and at first I didn't think anything was wrong, but the more I think on it, the more I think Bobby should at least know."

"Peter, I'm sure I'll agree, but the baby needs to be fed so what is it?"

"Righto. Onassis asked Allen if he thought Marilyn really killed herself. Allen said 'No'. Onassis then asked him if he knew about a bugging operation against Kennedy and Monroe in her home in Brentwood a few weeks before she died. Allen again said 'No'."

"Tapes? Oh my."

"Onassis said that he was sure that these tapes existed. He just needed to find them. He told Allan, 'All you need is one golden apple – a single apple that somebody else wants – and you have control'. Allan said, 'Ari, that's blackmail'. Onassis replied, 'No, that's business'."

"Oh my." Ethel repeated and dropped the phone.

"Mr. Kennedy, what do I owe the pleasure?" Johnson entered his office through the side door.

"Well, for one I need to know what you're up to. I've linked the memo that we found a few months back to you and a shipping agreement with Aristotle Onassis."

"It's just standard. No need to get upset." Johnson mopped his forehead with his handkerchief.

"Right. Why do you have my brother going to Dallas when he returns from that European tour at the end of next month? Why is he going straight there?" Bobby pointed to the calendar.

"I just thought it would help bring unity to the office. The President and I have been at odds for a while, and Governor John Connelly thought this tour through Texas would seal the deal for us to win the election in 1964. Besides, Thanksgiving at my ranch is beautiful."

"Does John know about this?"

Hoffa and Frank sat in Bobby's waiting room for over an hour before they were finally allowed to see the attorney general. Hoffa was nervous and his hands shook.

"Mr. Kennedy, I know I'm the last person you'd want to see, but I have some information that may be of great value to you." Hoffa stood in front of Bobby's desk.

"What do you want?"

"I want to cut a deal. You drop the charges of attempted murder against me for threatening Joe Kennedy and I'll tell you something that will assist the president in the Vietnam conflict."

"Let me hear what you have to say first, Hoffa, and then we'll decide if the value is that high."

Hoffa shifted from foot to foot. "Okay, but I'll need your word of at least a reduced charge."

Bobby stood up and glared at Hoffa. "I don't have time to bargain either. Tell me or get the hell out of my office."

Frank finally spoke up. "Bobby, you want to hear this and you'll want to bargain too."

Bobby turned his stare on Frank. "Fine. What is it, Hoffa?"

"Shipping. Onassis just pulled out of a deal that would have had tanking ships heading to aid the war effort in Vietnam. He pulled out to take away any leverage you might have found against him for helping provide Johnson with arms to aid both sides of the conflict."

"Oh my God. . ."

November 22, 1963

As the plane lifted into the air, Jackie and John had their first real conversation since she returned from Greece. She was still reeling from the public's negative reaction to her taking the trip. She hated campaigning, but agreed to come with him anyway in the hopes of doing some serious damage control.

Looking at her husband, she couldn't help but notice that something was different about him. *Oh, well, it's probably his back again.*

"I'm glad we're able to fly to Dallas together." Jackie smiled at her husband.

"Me too. It was a long flight from Heathrow. I'll be happy to see this damned motorcade Johnson's got me in finished so we can rest for a few days."

"Why'd he invite us?"

"He wants to get the Texans liking us. They're all Republicans, so he thought a little face time would make our numbers higher for the reelection run."

"John, why would he care? He's not backed you on any policy you've presented and he wants to be president. He's ambitious and hates both you and Bobby."

"He's trying to make amends."

"Are you seriously that naïve, John?"

"No. Let's give him the benefit of the doubt."

"You're a strange man."

"Can we start over? I'll forgive you the trip to Greece if you'll forgive me for being such a jerk."

He held out his hand. Jackie took it and leaned over and kissed his cheek. "Oh, I have a feeling that by the end of this trip, all will be forgiven."

Agent Latimer rushed toward Bobby standing on a downtown street in Dallas, TX awaiting the motorcade of the president.

"Mr. Kennedy. We've got both Oswald and Bannister in custody. Security is beefed up and we're trying to persuade the limo driver to put the top up."

"Good work, Latimer. I think we should be safe enough now. If we can get through this next hour, we'll be in the clear. . . well until next time." Bobby shifted his feet nervously.

"We won't fail you, Mr. Kennedy. Stansel and I will both be walking alongside the motorcade."

"Thanks, Latimer."

Bobby paced the walk waiting for John to make his appearance. *Onassis, you Greek bastard, I'm onto you.*

John helped Jackie into the limo. He patted her hand and climbed in beside her.   Just as the car began to roll he spotted someone on the sidewalk.   *No, it can't be.*

He did a double take as the car rounded the first corner and he could see the face clearly in the sunlight. *It's not... it can't be. Marilyn?*

Just as the car moved out of view, she lifted her hand to her lips and blew her famous kiss his way.

We had a lot of fun creating this alternate history of Marilyn Monroe and hope you enjoyed reading it.

Darkest Night - Book Two in the What She Knew series is now available for purchase and book three in the series is nearly complete.

We would love to hear from you! To post a review simple go to our Amazon book page. If you would like to stay in touch with us you can go to the following link and sign up for our newsletter.

http://whatsheknew.wix.com/kandtproductions

Authors Page

K. R. Hughes is a native of Amarillo, TX. She has a degree in English, helps with literacy programs and tutors college students. Hughes has two children, Justin and Kayti. Hughes also has two regency, historical novels, "Treasured Love" and "Lord Tristan's True Love," under her pen name Kymber Lee.

T. L. Burns is the foremost researcher and historical guru for the What She Knew Trilogy. Burns and husband Ken have two grown children, Kenny and Deven. Burns is a native of California. She has spent the majority of her adult life working with at-risk kids and adults.

Both authors currently reside in Atlanta, GA where they write and encourage budding authors to follow their dreams. You can connect with them at any of the following social media groups:

www.facebook.com/WhatSheKnewHughesBurns

www.twitter.com/whatsheknewbook

http://whatsheknew.wix.com/kandtproductions

Cast of Historical Characters

Marilyn Monroe – sex goddess and movie star in the 1950's and 1960's.

John F Kennedy – president of the United States, nickname Jack. Married to Jacqueline Bouvier Kennedy.

Robert F Kennedy – brother to John F Kennedy and Attorney General for the United States, nickname Bobby. Married to Ethel.

Peter Lawford – movie star, one of the Rat Pack and married to Patricia Kennedy, sister to John and Bobby.

Joe Kennedy - father of John, Bobby, and Patricia; married to Rose.

Lee Radizwill - Jacqueline Kennedy's sister; married to Prince Stasnislaw Radizwill (aka Stas).

Teddy Kennedy - younger brother of John and Bobby.

Frank Sinatra – crooner, movie star and Rat Pack leader, political ally to John F. Kennedy.

Sam Giancana – mobster wanted to further his career with anyone who paid well, also associated with Frank Sinatra and Jimmy Hoffa.

Aristotle Onassis – Greek business tycoon. Bobby Kennedy was his arch enemy. He provided major business deals in the US through his shipping business – illegally.

Jimmy Hoffa – president of the Teamsters Union, in trouble with the Attorney General for organized crime.

Eunice Murray - housekeeper/nurse maid to Marilyn. Also, a spy for Dr. Greenson.

Lady Adele Beatty - On again/off again lover of Frank.

Joe DiMaggio - Ex-husband of Marilyn; he was devoted to her till the day he died.

Susan Strasberg - Longtime friend of Marilyn.

Lyndon B. Johnson - Vice President to John F. Kennedy; married to Lady Bird.

J. Edgar Hoover - the first Director of the Federal Bureau of Investigation (FBI) of the United States. Appointed director of the Bureau of Investigation—predecessor to the FBI in 1924.

Howard Hughes - an American business magnate, aviator, aerospace engineer, film maker and philanthropist. He was one of the wealthiest people in the world, and very eccentric.

Senator Margaret Chase Smith – A member of the Republican Party, she served as a U.S Representative (1940-1949) and a U.S. Senator (1949-1973) from Maine. A moderate Republican, she is perhaps best remembered for her 1950 speech, "Declaration of Conscience," in which she criticized the tactics of McCarthyism.

Smith was an unsuccessful candidate for the Republican nomination in the 1964 presidential election, but was the first woman to be placed in nomination for the presidency at a major party's convention.

Historical Notes for Reference:

When were slot machines invented? Multiple coin slot machines arrived in the 1960's. Mechanical penny and nickel slot machines evolved into computerized dollar slot machines. Today you can find machines that accept $500 chips. Payouts grew from a few hundred dollars to today's several million dollar progressive jackpots.

When was the car phone invented? This service originated with the Bell System, and was first used in St. Louis on June 17, 1946. The original equipment weighed 80 pounds, and there were initially only 3 channels for all the users in the metropolitan area, later more licenses were added bringing the total to 32 channels across 3 bands. Expansion was slow and expensive, but those privileged few who needed the ability to communicate on the road were able to in the early 1960's.

Why is John F Kennedy sometimes called Jack? John Fitzgerald Kennedy was named in honor of Rose's father, John Francis Fitzgerald, the Boston Mayor popularly known as Honey Fitz. Before long, family and friends called this small blue-eyed baby, Jack and those who were closest to him called him that his entire life.

When did the phrase "Smiling like a Cheshire cat" start? The phrase appears in print in John Wolcot's pseudonymous Peter Pindar's Pair of Lyric Epistles in 1792: "Lo, like a Cheshire cat our court will grin." The phrase really took off in the 1951 Disney animated film, Alice in Wonderland. The Cheshire Cat is depicted as an intelligent yet mischievous, villainous character that sometimes helps Alice and sometimes gets her into trouble.

Fact: Marilyn Monroe had her own house bugged, along with others: CIA, Mafia, and even the FBI. All were found in her Brentwood, CA home after her death. It is reported that the Kennedy's took control of her private tapes right after her death.

McCarthyism is the practice of making accusations of disloyalty, subversion, or treason without proper regard for evidence. It also means "the practice of making unfair allegations or using unfair investigative techniques, especially in order to restrict dissent or political criticism." The term has its origins in the period in the United States known as the Second Red Scare, lasting roughly from 1950 to 1956 and characterized by heightened fears of communist influence on American institutions and espionage by Soviet agents. Originally coined to criticize the anti-communist pursuits of Republican U.S. Senator Joseph McCarthy of Wisconsin, "McCarthyism" soon took on a broader meaning, describing the excesses of similar efforts.

Guatemalan President Carlos Castillo Armas implemented a new constitution in 1956 and had himself declared president for four years. He was shot dead in the presidential palace by a palace guard, Romeo Vásquez Sanchez, on July 26, 1957. It is still uncertain whether the killer was paid to assassinate President Armas, or had other motives. Sanchez was found dead a short while later in what some believed to be a very questionable suicide.

We had a lot of fun creating this alternate history of Marilyn Monroe and hope you enjoyed reading it.

Darkest Night - Book Two in the What She Knew series is now available for purchase and book three in the series is nearly complete.

We would love to hear from you! To post a review simple go to our Amazon book page. If you would like to stay in touch with us you can go to the following link and sign up for our newsletter.

www.whatsheknew.wix.com/kandtproductions

www.ingramcontent.com/pod-product-compliance
Lightning Source LLC
Chambersburg PA
CBHW070322260626
47160CB00003B/926